Ian Ingleby is retired after a varied career in perception management in Australasia.

For nearly two decades, he was attached to a US-Australian public relations group, servicing foreign governments and strategic commercial interests of the governments of the US, the UK, USA and Indonesia, as well as non-strategic commercial interests of these and others, including Australia, New Zealand, Malaysia, Denmark, the Netherlands and Finland.

He was a resident in Hong Kong during the British administration and in Singapore before being seconded to the Suharto administration in Indonesia in the 1980s. In Jakarta, he was senior government adviser and speechwriter for several Indonesian Cabinet Ministers and others. While in Australia, he undertook several assignments throughout Indonesia. In subsequent years, he introduced government and private sector people to Indonesian military and corporate entities for business purposes.

Earlier, he was with the Commonwealth in Papua New Guinea, prior to self-government, for two years. He was responsible for press news and information, acted as press secretary to two Australian administrators, reported on House of Assembly sessions and other significant events of the time, and assisted in monitoring local political developments. Prior to this, he was with a Sydney metropolitan newspaper as a journalist.

Honorary positions held included chairman of the Australian Institute of Export, foundation fellow of the Institute of Company Directors NSW, governor of the American Business Council in Singapore and executive member of the Australia-Indonesia Business Cooperation Committee. Names of some of these organisations have changed over the years. His only current membership (as an ordinary member) is with the Royal United Services Institute for Defence and Security Studies NSW Inc. to which he was introduced in 1990 after assisting the then president and friend in writing profiles of Indonesian political and military leaders.

He is married, with three daughters, the youngest born in Hong Kong in the 1960s (at the then Matilda hospital on the Peak run by an Australian matron). He has eight grandchildren and two great-grandchildren. His schooling was at St Ignatius' College, Riverview, Sydney. His largely unfulfilled hobby is coastal fishing.

Ian Ingleby

UNLIKELY DESTINIES

AUSTIN MACAULEY PUBLISHERS™

LONDON • CAMBRIDGE • NEW YORK • SHARJAH

A CIP catalogue record for this title is available from the British Library.

ISBN 9781035829200 (Paperback)
ISBN 9781035829217 (ePub e-book)

www.austinmacauley.com

First Published 2023
Austin Macauley Publishers Ltd®
1 Canada Square
Canary Wharf
London
E14 5AA

Assistance in gathering material on some security matters by Kara, one of my granddaughters, lawyer and cyber security expert, is acknowledged with thanks.

Construct

The story is of the lives of three sisters. It is presented in three *Parts*.

One may be forgiven for viewing several tasks in *Part 3* as reality today, particularly those about submarines in the Indo-Pacific, foreign coercive interest in Australia, foreign attempts to recruit Western spies and terrorist actions in certain South-east Asian nations.

The *Parts* are:

- Childhood *(Part 1)*
- Scholarship *(Part 2)*
- Tasks *(Part 3)*

Parts 1 and *2* cover the extraordinary backgrounds of the sisters. *Part 3* comprises several secret tasks in which the sisters are involved.

Tasks are preceded by explanations of hostile national and terrorist strategies. A few comparative military capabilities from credible sources are listed. They involve missiles, submarines, drones, viruses that infect weapons and more. Real data is credited. None is classified. Several real East and West intelligence and defence organisations are described. Hostile strategies and tactics are explained and counter-actions outlined, mostly based on the author's imagination.

The story is about three sisters and not intended to be an informed commentary on the risk of international conflict.

The story is fiction.

Preview

Existing in a remote area of Australia—without a care in the world beyond managing their meagre resources, three young girls knew nothing of their future as first female team of counter-insurgent fighters. Delivered fortuitously, their later education revealed extraordinary adaptability to study. They achieved high levels of linguistic, legal, and technical communication skills that equipped them well to operate unexpectedly in high-risk Indo-Pacific environments.

Part One

The sisters regularly witnessed the pastel beginnings of dawn transform silently to hues of blue before changing quickly to the clot of blood that was the death of day, all the while unaware this daily tri-chromatic phenomenon in central Australia was a metaphor of the three phases of their lives, the latter part in far-away places.

Chapter 1: Genesis

Angelina, Theodora, and Lucinda were born and lived for a while in Perth, Western Australia.

At four, three and two years of age respectively, their indigent parents, Fredrich and Lilly Folvig, decided to relocate well away from the big city to a remote area selected largely by a blindfold-pin-on-the-map method.

The pin landed on an area some 600 kilometres north-west of Perth and 200 kilometres inland from the coastal town of Geraldton.

The nearest settlement was Boogardie, a tiny community within walking distance on a cool day from the well-established town of Mount Magnet. Boogardie was more than a century behind Perth and other Australian cities economically, developmentally, technologically, and in just about all other ways.

Time and place seemed to make Boogardie more suitable for this family than anywhere else. It surely was quiet. Living costs were low. It was central to interesting old gold mining areas and its name rolled off the girls' tongues easily.

Their lives would begin afresh here.

There was nothing in Perth that Fredrich and Lilly would miss. They had never found time to do anything but think about making ends meet. They had not been to any of the many scenic coastal beaches or spent time relaxing by the Swan River.

Besides not having the money to appreciate the water, Lilly was fearful of oceans and rivers. She respected their dangers. She was aware she could not keep herself afloat in the calmest water having not learned to swim. Fredrich's only interest in the Swan River was to fish, mostly a past-time dream.

The naive relocation process naturally led to expectations in this unheard-of town, expectations hurriedly accepted in the belief problems would be as distant as the township itself.

Conventional opinion was that rental prices outside the larger towns would be next to nothing. Besides the likely affordability of housing in Boogardie,

Fredrich held unconscious expectations about his adopted town. He assumed nearby Mount Magnet would compensate for what Boogardie probably could not offer—shops, church, school, health clinic, bank and more.

In the back of his mind, Fredrich imagined there must be some kind of bus service linking Mount Magnet and nearby townships. If town water was not supplied in Boogardie, ground water surely would be available for washing, cooking, growing vegetables and raising a few chickens and a goat or two.

His mind wandered further. He thought most country towns had a 'School of Arts', not that Fredrich had an interest in cultural matters. He had no appreciation of the reality that such establishments were now virtually not exigent.

In fact, such 'schools' were generally without purpose these days, many not even used as community meeting places. Mostly they were from long past township development periods filled with hope and expectations. Today, many were merely curious planning elements, little more than symbolic.

Such innocence washed away the realities of remote country life. It even supported his belief Boogardie might hold attractions above and beyond affordable cost of living.

Fredrich had some experience as a labourer in coal and iron-ore mines and as a station hand outside Perth but had no schooling and no trade as such; although, like many country folk, he was handy, if not skilful in some trades work. His quiet disposition and persona more than compensated for his lack of education and social interaction. He was the typically honest outback character, well-intentioned and hard-working, always doing his best. His bush morals were evident to those with whom he worked.

As practical as he was in many ways, he had developed a dream-time interest in gold. Although, this had nothing to do with his moving from Perth, Fredrich was prone to be optimistic and believed in luck subconsciously. For him, gold was synonymous with luck and Boogardie happened to be in the middle of gold country. The blind process of selecting Boogardie may have been a matter of luck.

While the process that led him and his family to Boogardie was bizarre, he was mindful enough before leaving to visit the Perth city library to find out anything he could about the township.

Without purposely looking for gold prospects, he learned there were many old tailings in that part of the country once famous for gold production but largely abandoned by individual gold seekers. Mining licences in many areas were not necessary for fossickers. Prospecting licences were irrelevant for small-time operators throughout the country providing they stayed off fenced or company land.

At the library, Fredrich browsed through a few picture books of Western Australian townships but Boogardie was not recorded. He understood little of their written content and relied on photographs and drawings of towns in the area.

The library was socially uncomfortable place for him. He was not so much embarrassed being among readers but felt he was out of his environment completely. Unlike most adults in the State, he could barely read and could not recall ever attending school in his native Norway where he was born and spent most of his childhood on a horse farm before coming to Australia as a young man. In the library, the pictorial history of gold mining fascinated him. Fossicking was well represented in photographs and sketches.

Recognising his disposition, a library official explained to him some aspects of the area. The official told him Mount Magnet produced 30,000 ounces of gold a month in its heyday.

Photographs of two other villages further north caught Fredrich's imagination. They were Cue and Meekatharra, about 120 kilometres apart. Both were on the Great Northern Highway that linked Perth to Wyndham and joined up to the coastal highway to Darwin, the capital of the Northern Territory; a total of more than 3,500 kilometres, according to the official, not that Fredrich had any concept of such distances.

Nevertheless, in his own way Fredrich appreciated the relationship of physical effort to manageable distances. In Boogardie, Fredrich's mode of transport would be his bicycle while Lilly and the girls would have to rely on buses. There must be buses; there had to be buses, he assumed.

The library official picked up on Fredrich's particular attention to Cue which was about 80 kilometres from Mount Magnet. He explained that Cue had a fascinating history. It was said to be relatively popular among visiting and local fossickers as the area offered many abandoned diggings.

One story was that early gold seekers welcomed the summer storms as the rain exposed specks of gold creating the rumour that the streets of Cue were paved in gold. Large banks of tailings were at the main Cue site known as Monte Carlo Bank. Slightly south-west many tailing banks remained and there were a number of old metal vats and timber shaft mountings, according to the official.

Gold ran out in the 1930s and the entire population of 13,000 vanished virtually overnight.

The official explained further that Meekatharra, about 200 kilometres from Mount Magnet, was a large gold mining township and had been redeveloped by mining companies. It currently had a clinic, church, bank, high school, government buildings and a locally famous hotel.

The day to leave Perth arrived.

Fredrich settled his bills, packed their few belongings and hitched a ride on an iron ore truck to Mount Magnet, some 450 kilometres away as the crow flies. It was a dusty and tedious trip but the driver, like all iron-ore truckies, wasted no time. The family was reserved and uncommunicative in a friendly way, very much like many country folk, but the driver was happy to chat away, largely to himself.

The driver was pleased to have company, as one-sided as the conversation was, and to help out. He thought he was doing a good turn for a young family that probably had experienced hard times and surely were in for more hard times in a place like Boogardie. He dropped the family off outside a bank in Mount Magnet and near a real estate agency.

The five ventured into the bank where they met a most understanding manager who asked to be called KT. They opened a modest savings account, the smallest the bank had seen.

Next, they visited the real estate agency and met the manager who was the antithesis of KT but produced a listing of a long-time unoccupied Boogardie house in need of some 'tender loving care'. There were no photographs or drawings but the agent assured Fredrich the house was liveable and included the 'basic necessities'. The agent seemed not to know what was in the house but was adamant power and water were available. He could not recall the name of the owner but was so happy the house was to be occupied, he lowered the rent to a nominal amount.

To Fredrich, the deal was odd, perhaps a little suspicious, but suited the family. Fredrich told himself this was probably the way people in this part of the State did business. With a false smile and a limp handshake, the agent accepted the rent, handed over the keys and bid the family farewell.

While a relatively short distance from Mount Magnet, it took the family a long time to hitch a ride to Boogardie as very little traffic went that way and the bicycle was awkward to transport.

Without even inspecting the timber clad and corrugated iron roofed house, they deposited their luggage and hurried off to the only shop in Boogardie. It was a general store about a kilometre from the house. They were tired and it was getting late but they needed food, kitchen utensils, bottled water, batteries, candles and toiletries.

The store was large, typical of general businesses in remote townships. *It might have been an old converted 'School of Arts,'* Fredrich thought. Profitability did not appear a priority.

It featured a huge untreated timber floor. Walking around the store created echoes noticeable only to the odd visitor. Long timber counters along the entire length of the room on both sides were in front of ceiling-to-floor shelves. They contained an extraordinarily diverse range of items from canned foods and toys to medicines and tools arranged in a seemingly unorganised manner; although the store-keeper, a fit elderly Chinese man, seemed to know where everything was.

There was an unfamiliar odour, not unpleasant but certainly odd. After a while the family noticed the source—incense sticks on a small altar located high on one of the rear shelves. The altar displayed a miniature skeletal figure in a small ornately carved box. The dark carved timber doors of the box revealing the figure were relieved by gold painted sections that reflected the light.

Fredrich supposed the ornament was somehow related to ancestors or perhaps mystical beliefs. Clearly, it was not for sale. For the girls, it was the most interesting item in the store.

Fredrich whispered to the girls who were staring at the altar: "Don't stare. I know it's strange but we must be pretty strange to him."

Strange also was the store-keeper's attire. He wore a dark-coloured, light-weight, full-length tunic with concealed buttons down the front and a full rounded collar buttoned to the neck but not tightly.

He introduced himself to Fredrich as Chin. His focus was on Fredrich but he did not fail to notice Lilly's demure and the girl's fascination with several Asian artifacts.

Little did the family know that Chin was to become for them much more than a remote Western Australian store-keeper; he was to be involved in the girls' occupations as adults overseas.

The family could not help but notice peculiarities in Chin's speech but these did not inhibit their exchange. Chin had a tendency to begin sentences with 'yes', very much like many Westerners subconsciously mutter 'hum', a habitual prefix, meaning nothing. He also dropped his verbs occasionally and had some difficulty in pronouncing certain words, particularly those beginning with 'l' and 'th' but he seemed to pronounce some words in ways difficult for others using sounds like 'sz' and 'tz'.

As Fredrich introduced his family, Chin repeated the names in acknowledgement. "This is my wife, Lilly," Fredrich said firstly.

"*El*," Chin replied.

"And this is my eldest daughter, Angelina," Fredrich continued to which Chin repeated reasonably accurately. "And these are my second and third daughters, Theodora and Lucinda," Fredrich said. Chin's acknowledgements were *Tzda* and *Czunda*, both sounding very similar.

Addressing Fredrich, he said: "Yes. Out back…small café. I serve tea Fridays, some weekends for customers. You…invited to have tea with me. No cost. Just let me know earlier, please. Food…not too spicy for girls, some cushions on the chairs…comfortable, eat together."

Family life for the Folvigs began anew in their small three-bedroom house.

Matters requiring attention depended on Fredrich earning an income—where to find handyman work and begin fossicking, how to travel to the most suitable locations and how to sell any gold he found. Fredrich soon learned that a trader visited Mount Magnet monthly to buy gold and precious stones, mainly opal and sapphire.

These questions would have worried most people but Fredrich did not become despondent easily. His antidote to becoming disheartened was a combination of family loyalty and a strong work ethic that saw him persist with whatever he was doing, successfully or otherwise.

Added to this was an instinctive feeling of improved circumstances in the future based somewhat on his feeling lucky. Real excitement for him would be finding gold, tantamount to winning a lottery.

The absence of real excitement to date, derived largely from his lack of community interaction and his narrow life experience, did not translate into boredom as long as he had things to do. This disposition helped him maintain a healthy mindset in the context of making the house liveable.

Lilly was different. She worried silently. She contributed quietly by cleaning the house and ensuring everyone was well fed and adequately clothed. She had enough material to make clothes for the girls and soon became proficient at cooking on a country stove.

Regardless of their ages, the girls assisted eagerly in their own ways combining work with play.

As in the past, Fredrich and Lilly created a happy family environment; the hard work making their combined effort all the more satisfying and their interdependence stronger; particularly Lilly's reliance on Fredrich whom she regarded even more now as the strong core of the family.

In a relatively short time, the basics were established. Maintenance of the house, food, bore water, infrequent town water, power generated by a series of batteries, schooling and bus transport were managed.

A novelty was the infrequent appearance of Aboriginals and occasional camel traders who sometimes passed through the main townships with wild dromedaries which were rounded-up and sold to businessmen who would transport the animals to Geraldton for shipment to the Middle East. Otherwise, the camels were a pest. Many years earlier they were an important form of transport of goods throughout central Australia, a service then controlled largely by Afghans.

Welcome companionship came by way of a new acquaintance, Steve Rabillard, who rode an old Ducati racing motorbike modified to handle the rough terrain. After dropping in for a cuppa a few times, he offered to transport Freddo, as he called Fredrich, to and from Mount Magnet and even Meekatharra whenever he could. The nickname stuck and was accepted by Fredrich as a sign of camaraderie.

Steve expressed an interest in fossicking.

One day, he suggested Fredrich and he work together on a so-called profit sharing basis. It seemed an idle remark and the matter was not taken further at the time.

Like Fredrich in the past, Steve survived on rouse-about jobs to pay for food, fuel and lodgings. He seemed to have no ambition. Nor did he seem to have family or local responsibilities but surprisingly was highly educated, as far as Fredrich could tell.

He seemed indolent when commitments were involved but always willing to work on projects of his choosing and to lend a hand spontaneously to others.

The Folvigs were not the only people Steve called on from time to time supposedly thirsting for a cup of tea, the consumption of which he managed to draw out until sandwiches appeared. There seemed no purpose in his neighbourliness other than to have a yarn. He was accepted by Fredrich as an honest, exceptionally educated, somewhat lost person.

Nevertheless, there were contradictory aspects of Steve's personality.

On the one hand, he looked generally untidy. His appearance was consistent with the way he moved. He walked with a limp due to a motorcycle accident. The injury was not attended to at the time. It was now too far gone to correct without expensive surgery in Perth. It gave him a little pain but he did not complain. In fact, he joked about his leg and fascinated the girls by being able to swing the lower part backwards and forwards as though his knee was on a swivel. It did not inhibit him on his Ducati.

On the other hand, he seemed familiar with certain classic subjects and was inclined to recite brief extracts of poetry. Without vanity, he demonstrated his knowledge of history occasionally referencing all kinds of topics they discussed to distant historical events. Fredrich had no idea of their relevance to their conversations but pretended to be impressed.

Steve seemed to have firm views about religion but Fredrich avoided taking part in any discussion about religion because he was out of his depth on such a topic. Still, it was hard for Fredrich to avoid accidentally.

Steve's views emerged when Fredrich asked if he was really serious about a joint fossicking venture. They agreed to go ahead and Fredrich remarked with idle enthusiasm: "With God's help, we'll find enough gold to make us all rich one day."

Steve's reply was friendly but less idle. "Maybe you're right, Freddo, but it will take more than God for us to succeed. To paraphrase your own namesake, Fredrick the Second of Prussia, in the mid-1700s: 'Religion is the idol of the mob; it adores everything it does not understand'. But we understand how hard it can be here don't we Freddo?" He asked rhetorically.

The abstruse quote and question went over Fredrich's head. He could not see what brought the reaction on or the connection with fossicking, other than indicating Steve was an educated, out-of-place, non-religious if not atheistic, friendly person.

Time flew happily, albeit not without a struggle to make ends meet.

A few years on, life's red light had turned amber. Hopefully, it would be green soon.

The family had survived on meagre earnings from fossicking and frugal home spending. It had established relationships based on mutual respect with Chin, KT, Steve, and a few others in Mount Magnet, as well as a couple of neighbours on the outskirts of Boogardie.

When fossicking seemed promising, Fredrich and Steve camped out for up to a week at a time. Sometimes they would overnight at Hope Creek, only 20 kilometres from Meekatharra, when the fish were biting. There was a high rock outcrop above a deep water-hole where they preferred to fish for red bellies, a favoured fish. There was plenty of water in the deep hole under an overhanging rock, even during the dry.

By now, Angelina had completed her primary schooling. Theodora was close behind and Lucinda well on the way.

Steve proved useful in assisting the girls with their homework whenever he was at the house after school time.

He encouraged them to take an interest in foreign languages as a novelty, not to understand any but to recognise different sounds and inflections in the hope this would assist in time with their English. Combined with this he taught them something of the history of the Western Australian outback, especially the part Afghans played in camel trading. The girls were curious to know more from Steve about the first arrivals of Afghans in the 1830s and their part in the British development of the outback.

All this he did in a fun way, without instruction or direction. Fredrich and Lilly welcomed Steve's interest in the girl's schooling.

Steve got hold of an old short-wave radio and showed the girls how to switch to foreign language channels. The girls spent time listening to foreign language broadcasts, particularly Dari, a common Afghan language. They also listened to the world news from the BBC when they tired of a language they could not understand. They played games based on recognising Afghan sounds they remembered and subconsciously dreamed of knowing something about or even visiting the country from which the Afghans came.

They even kept a toilet roll of words on Angelina's bedroom wall. Whenever they heard an Afghan word clearly enough on radio or in the street, Angelina would write it phonetically on the roll. After some months, a metre of the roll contained almost 50 sounds. The aim was to finish a role in a year.

All the girls had exceptional teachers in primary school and were successful. There were a couple of reasons for good teachers working in remote areas. One was that some of the up-and-coming teachers from Perth accepted contractual or part-time work in so-called hardship postings to accumulate extra work credits enabling them to apply later for transfers to permanent work at their preferred schools elsewhere.

Paradoxically, primary and secondary schools in places like Mount Magnet attracted some of these younger, brighter, and more enterprising teachers.

Another reason for the girls' success was simply they liked school. They were academic naturals. For all three, study was exciting. Each encouraged the others by example. This attitude was reflected in results.

This instinctive work ethic and persistent curiosity germinated into a single-mindedness of purpose indicated in their preference for some of the more difficult optional subjects offered in secondary school. Their latent interest in languages, geography and technology led to their selection of some subjects considered the tougher by many of their friends and generally avoided.

Theodora excelled in basic mathematics due originally, in part, to her playing constantly with an abacus given to her by Chin. As rudimentary as this was, her ability with an abacus became a talking point in the household. By the time she entered secondary school, she was quite skilled in rapid calculations of product prices and various costs associated with Chin's store. She even tried to make her own abacus using coloured balls and adding rods to broaden the scope for calculations but this did not succeed.

Nor did it impress Chin. He asked her rhetorically: "It was made in Chun Gur—Middle Kingdom, China—2,600 years ago. You, little girl…want to improve it?"

In secondary school at Mount Magnet, the three consistently topped their classes in English, mathematics, physics and geography.

In addition, they always were on the lookout for short-time after-school jobs, particularly any involving computers since the school had only a few reserved for final year students.

They also wanted to learn languages conversationally as well as grammatically other than French which was the only foreign language option. The more intriguing languages for the girls were not taught at Mount Magnet.

At this stage, Angelina, Theodora and Lucinda had little social interaction with students of their own age other than at school. Socialising was the one area they missed.

Every couple of months, a black-and-white ball was held in Mount Magnet. It brought together young iron ore workers, station hands and township girls. In earlier times, and currently elsewhere in mainly rural areas throughout the country, bachelors', and spinsters' balls (B&S 'shindigs') were held in large sheds on stations. Industrialisation of the Mount Magnet area attracted industry people to such events that were held at town venues.

Although, the boys usually wore dinner suits or tuxedos and the girls dressed up in home-made gowns, dress became less important as a typical ball night progressed and more beer and whisky were consumed by the boys. The cloths Lilly made for the girls generally stood out for their cut and quality, even though some were reworked and swapped until Lilly had to make new ones.

Angelina, Theodora, and Lucinda were underage and participated but did not drink. They were excited by the social rapport but were shy, sensible, and looked after each other.

For some of the older boys and girls, the evenings extended into all-night outings at particular places, mostly out of town. A favoured place to spend the night after a ball was the abandoned township of Lennonville, about 12 kilometres north of Boogardie.

Lennonville was a gold mining town established in 1896. At its height, it boasted 5 hotels and a population of 3,000. A fire wiped out a large part of the town about the same time as the gold ran out resulting in the entire population vanishing. What remained of the township were several small buildings and a railway station platform. Other than occasional B&S ball-goers, no one ventured there.

Besides the obvious, a common excuse for such a night was that there was avoidance of drunk driving charges as the police at Mount Magnet kept a close watch on these events within town limits. They extended no leniency to township offenders but did not bother with what went on beyond, unless it was serious.

For a modest price, a truckie would deliver groups of couples who wanted to spend the night under the stars at Lennonville and collect them at a set time the next day, weather permitting. Relationships were generally steamy at the time but not long lasting as distance was a barrier and many of the boys and girls had time-consuming jobs.

Nearly sixteen, Angelina met Bob Davis at her third B&S when she experienced her first kiss. She would never forget it. A jackeroo on a relatively small 50,000 square kilometre cattle station north-west of Mount Magnet he was a strapping young man of seventeen with a privileged public-school education. He was learning about station life before going to an east coast agricultural college to study for a degree in large animal husbandry.

They were attracted to each other and agreed to attend the next ball when perhaps they would consider visiting Lennonville together.

Soon enough, the next ball came around after which they spent the night at Lennonville. Angelina made arrangements for Theodora and Lucinda to be escorted home after the ball and informed her parents she would be spending the night with friends.

It was her first family fib but the prospect of being alone overnight with Bob was irresistible. She excused herself by regarding it as an inconsequential private mental restriction. She knew she was not going to drink or lose her virginity. She just wanted cuddles and kisses throughout the night.

That is all that happened.

Because of Angelina's uncertain future and Bob's likely move interstate, they promised to try to meet at the Royal Exchange Hotel in Meekatharra each year at noon on 2 December if and when one or both left the area. If they could not make it one year, they would try the next. It was a fairy-tale promise made in youthful exuberance but agreed seriously and coincident with academic and likely employment breaks. The fact that December generally was a particularly hot and stormy month did not matter.

About this time, the hotel became permanently linked with the Folvig name because of an incident involving Lilly.

The incident did not involve Angelina or her sisters directly. They were bystanders. In any case, they were underage, did not drink and were well protected by the publican from any patrons inclined to get amorous or offer drinks. The incident became fixed indelibly in the minds of patrons and put the retiring Folvig family in the forefront of Meekatharra social folklore.

Prior to this, Fredrich and Lilly were thought of respectfully as hard-working loners, mainly by necessity rather than intent. Their surname also was not Australian. It was Norwegian, meaning horse breeder, although no one knew this. In addition, residents were not considered 'locals' until they had spent most of their lives in or near the town.

Lilly was walking outside the hotel after shopping one day. She was dared half-heartedly by a group of would-be drinkers to ride a horse they had with them into the bar and order a beer for it. There was no inducement, other than assuring

22

her the horse was placid and 'partial to a drop'. It was a light-hearted suggestion, an impossibly incongruous challenge made in jest by a group that had not yet had a drink, and not expected to be accepted.

The proponents, hotel staff, patrons, Fredrich and the girls were astonished when this diminutive lady wearing a long dress and scarf appeared at the saloon door side-saddled on a horse. Everyone applauded softly so as not to spook the horse as Lilly led it cautiously to the bar. Looking down sheepishly at the muscle-bound bar attendant, she asked: "Sir, may I have a beer for my horse, please?"

"You can ave anythink yous like, Luv. And you can ave me job too if the boss seez me," the bartender said, as he offered Lilly a soft drink and placed a bowl of beer on the bar for the horse which made short work of the offering.

After being assisted to dismount, the publican intervened. He whispered to Lilly: "If your family ever wants to overnight here, they are welcome. It's on the house. And if you ever want some easy part-time work in the restaurant or lounge, all you have to do is ask. You would bring this place some class and help the patrons behave better than my guerrilla can," he said looking at the bartender.

On attempting to hand back the reins to her darers, they refused to accept and told her the horse was hers to keep for 'being such a good sport', if she wanted it. Before she had a chance to decline, Fredrich came forward and thanked them for their offer and accepted on Lilly's behalf.

The family now had two home-based modes of transport, a bicycle and a horse, in addition to the municipal school bus and Steve's motorbike, when he was around.

Over the following year, the girls matured rapidly. Now all teenagers, they studied diligently and enjoyed the life the family had made for itself.

The family was comfortable.

Chapter 2: Tribulation

While riding to town, Fredrick's horse was frightened by a snake on the road. He was thrown and fatally struck his head on a rock.

A short time later, the driver of an iron ore truck found the horse which led him to where Fredrich lay. The driver quickly relayed the news to the ambulance station in Mount Magnet.

The girls were devastated when they heard the news and horrified when they saw their father's body. They had not seen anything like this before.

Lilly's reaction seemed extraordinarily stoic for someone who depended so much on her husband and so eagerly shared hard times before the girls were born and afterwards. Until this moment, she had become increasingly comfortable in Boogardie. Now, in an instant, the comfort vanished but she did not show it.

Her apparent composure puzzled observers. This slight, unassuming person did not appear to succumb noticeably to the distress of such a tragedy. Others seemingly more robust emotionally and physically would have appeared grief-stricken, even behaved uncontrollably for a time.

The registrar at the hospital where the body was taken for coronial examination was accustomed to serious injuries and death due to road accidents and the reactions of next of kin and close friends. As a middle-aged male doctor, he was quite familiar with the psychological consequences of trauma. But he was nonplus about Lilly's apparent acceptance of what had happened.

He wondered: Was she really so emotionally strong? Was she struggling to conceal her emotions to protect her daughters? Would post-traumatic stress set in soon? Was her composure a symptom of some as-yet undetected disturbance? Did she need medical attention and, if so, how would she accept help?

Steve agreed to liaise with the police and look after funeral arrangements as soon as the death certificate was issued. He took charge of the horse as well.

At a small gathering of family and friends outside the hospital, Steve held an impromptu ceremony celebrating the life of Freddo. Keeping his eyes on Lilly and the girls, he delivered a surprisingly eloquent eulogy given very little information about the family's pre-Boogardie lives. It had those present in tears, except for Lilly.

At the same time, he held his motorbike helmet in one hand, the reins of the horse in the other and shuffled from side to side as though his leg was painful. The horse remained motionless, some kind of sixth sense making it aware of the communal stress. It was a surreal occasion that could not happen anywhere other than in this part of the outback.

Although, an atheistic, perhaps even an agnostic, Steve concluded by shouting, "denique caelum, Freddo." He did not attempt to translate or explain the meaning of this exclamation which was made in Fredrich's memory and in the likelihood of his early Christian beliefs.

Those present assumed it was prayerful. Only he knew it was a cry attributed to European Christian soldiers during the Crusades of the 11th and 13th centuries, meaning 'Heaven at last (for you, Freddo)'. It was a private salute in a Christian context.

Lilly's resilience was demonstrated practically when she and the girls returned home. The first thing she did was to comfort the girls. In a combined hug she whispered to them quietly, with normal inflection and a steady voice that they must be strong, would continue as a family and must realise death was inevitable for all of them at some time.

This seemed to have a sedative effect until the girls retired to one bedroom where they cried, sobbed, and spoke over each other without listening. They did not know what to do with themselves. Lilly could hear them and knew what was going on. There seemed nothing she could or should do but to leave them alone hoping they would exhaust themselves and rest. Eventually, they were silent.

In the privacy of her own room, Lilly diarised her life as best she could in the form of a scratchy letter to her two cousins in Adelaide, Beth, and Judith Robinson, with whom she had not communicated for nearly three decades. It was a therapeutic exercise, an involuntary means of ameliorating her inner stress. It was lengthy, not intended to inform, a one-way conversation with two distant people primarily for her satisfaction. It did not seek sympathy, support or understanding.

It kept her busy from the time the clot of red submerged in the west and the flaming orange rose in the east.

Lilly's reaction was asymptomatic of severe stress blocked by a lifetime of enthusiastic subordination. She concentrated wholeheartedly on family tasks which liberated her from the realities around her. Now reality emerged in the hardest way. Even so, she was able to fain composure.

Lilly did not know if her cousins were still alive but thought she might have heard if they had passed away. Nor did she know if they resided at the address she knew but expected they were still there. The Robinsons were an early free-settler family and well regarded socially and professionally in South Australia. Lilly recalled that their house was very large and in an affluent suburb. They were unlikely to have moved.

The cousins were elderly and wealthy spinsters. Lilly had been told they employed a full-time gardener, a cook and two housekeepers and occupied themselves by keeping in touch with a legal firm in the city run by the Robinson family for generations.

Lilly mentally laboured with the letter since she had not written anything more than a shopping list for years. Her scrawl would have put to shame Banjo's thumbnail dipped in tar. Like Fredrich, Lilly had no formal education since she left Norway as a teenager but her personality was reflected in her written expression that was primitive and meaningful, more engaging than if she had been able to write an erudite expose of her life.

Steve photocopied and posted the letter early the next day. Seemingly buoyed by the letter-writing exercise and still not showing distress, Lilly asked him to accompany her to Meekatharra to visit Chin and the hotel proprietor. She then wanted to visit KT in Mount Magnet and the gold trader who had become by then a family friend. The reason for the visits was to thank her friends for their support. Lilly wanted to travel by the school bus. Steve accompanied her on this slow whole-day return visit.

Chin assured her he would stand by to help in any way he could. The assurance was made with sincerity and was recognised as such.

She gave KT her photocopy of the letter to Beth and Judith and asked him to keep it in the bank. It was to be given to Angelina if Lilly was unable to do so for any reason. "I'm not likely to be run over by a bus here, but one never knows," she said.

Lilly then asked KT if the family had any debts and if there were any funds in the family bank account. The account had been transferred to her only even without her consent, and was in credit but only by a few dollars.

They discussed what was to happen now that there was no family income and, in particular, how the girls would survive if and when she also passed away. The conversation was more difficult for KT than it seemed to be for Lilly whose friendly directness was disarming. KT knew this was her way. He thought her being impersonal at times helped her deal with unfamiliar matters. He thought also that after a lifetime of supporting the family silently and willingly she was now being tested and her true colours were emerging.

Whatever was going on, here was a woman whose strength of character was extraordinary. She could handle first-time issues and deal with obstacles simply and with dignity. *She was willing and able to take difficult decisions alone and was trusting completely in her friends,* he thought.

This kind of unintended exposition of herself and her unwillingness to ask for anything but advice had the effect of KT silently conversing with himself. What assistance, he asked himself, could he offer knowing that anything he could do necessarily meant bending bank rules. Lilly had children to support, no guarantor, surety, collateral or prospect of income and she had on-going household costs. She was a one-hundred per cent bad risk in terms of any loan criterion.

He wanted to suggest she talk to business people she knew in Meekatharra and Mount Magnet about assistance but this seemed like avoiding the issue and no normal loan would be possible anyway. Even if some form of compassionate loan from a business source was possible, it did not change the inevitable outcome. He suggested, however, that she keep at arm's length from the real estate agent with whom she had the lease.

He also gave her advice on government and non-government family support services but did not persist as she seemed quite an independent person unlikely to accept anything she perceived as charity. In a nicest way she was difficult.

His resistance failed. In a light-globe moment, KT suggested he set up a loan account for her if he could convince Chin, the hotel proprietor and the gold trader, to act as a unitary guarantor for a limited amount for a limited time, perhaps 12 months, based on the bank verbally guaranteeing the lenders.

The loan account would be in Lilly's name. Access would be given to Angelina, despite her still being under the age for such a facility, supervised by the guarantors.

Regular repayments would not be required. Withdrawals would be accrued and interest would be negligible. The loan application could be twigged to justify acceptance. After the expiry date, KT would forget to close the account with the silent agreement of the guarantor parties to continue replenishment. This meant that withdrawals could continue until the situation became untenable. It was not only against bank policy but was risky and illegal but he believed he could claim documentary errors and the three guarantors surely would help him out at a pinch. It was 'creative'.

Angelina would not be told the full story and hopefully would not realise that withdrawing funds from the loan account after Lilly's death or at any time was wrong, if withdrawals by her ever became necessary.

KT provided advice to Lilly about how to innocently avoid repercussions if and when the loan was cancelled and repayments were demanded by his head office in Perth. "After all, I may not be around forever," he said. He knew Lilly was a fair person and would not be party to defrauding the bank. He assured her that what he was suggesting was within his authority. She accepted what he said based on his assurance that bank policies relating to remote communities were extremely flexible.

After Fredrich's funeral, all these arrangements were made with the support of the guarantors. Lilly was grateful and relieved, although a little confused about the leniency of the bank and her privileged treatment by all those involved. In Perth it seemed never like this, but then Fredrich was the one who dealt with money matters there.

At home, Lilly scratched out a document detailing all of this as she understood it. The next day, she went to the bank again and gave the document to KT to look over. Again, it was difficult for KT as it was virtual evidence prepared innocently of his pre-planned wrong-doing, but he accepted it and agreed to hold it in safe keeping for whenever it might be needed. Anyway, there was time. Lilly was unlikely to pass away any time soon. She also held copies, addressed to Angelina and Steve in the event of some misadventure, along with a note to contact KT in due course.

As surprisingly logical and busy as Lilly had been to this point, she asked Steve if he would take her to a quiet place where she could wind down for a few hours. She suggested Hope Creek as he and Fredrich had mentioned it from time to time as a peaceful fishing spot and it was picturesque at this time of the year. There was no bus to Hope Creek which was at the headwaters of the Murchison and ran into a dry lake known as Lake Annean.

It was slightly more than 20 kilometres from Meekatharra. She wanted to go with Steve on his motorbike, not use the horse which now held bad memories for her.

Steve took her to Hope Creek. He agreed to pick her up in a couple of hours while he drove off to look at the surrounding area for possible fossicking sites.

The creek was quiet and beautiful. She walked to the edge of the rocky outcrop above the deep waterhole she had heard Steven and Fredrich speak about and reasoned syllogistically: "To break down now will distress the girls further. I'm of little use to them if I am depressed and weak. The solution is here."

She jumped.

Steve returned to the creek and was horrified to find her floating face down. He retrieved her body, covered it with heavy branches to prevent birds getting to it, and set off for Meekatharra as fast as he could to inform the police and paramedics at the ambulance station of her fatal 'accident'.

Part Two

Just as the girls had become accustomed to the colourful sunrise, daytime and sunset messages of the West, they accepted with similar complacency the maroon hues of the South without an inkling of the heavenly warnings they foreshadowed.

Chapter 3: Patronage

"Look what I have," Judith exclaimed to Beth. "It's a letter from Lilly Folvig sent from some outback place in Western Australia."

"Read it, please," Beth asked.

As Judith read it, their surprise turned to vague pessimism. Lilly's endeavour to record her life seemed to indicate unintentionally a present or emerging predicament.

Both cousins were sensitive to the intent of documents. They were familiar with innuendo, inference and concealment, mainly in legal contexts. Their propensity to scrutinise documents, particularly unexpected ones, had developed over years of association with the family legal firm, Robinson and Company, run now by Sir Jonathan Rowe.

Lilly's letter clearly was significant but how to interpret it was unclear. It meant something but did not seem intended to convey a message. Beth and Judith thought this could be because there was no practical intent. Why, they asked themselves. This worried them more than if a problem had been stated clearly. They felt it unexplainably fateful.

On re-examining the letter, they still could not detect a tangible reason other than passing on news of Fredrich's death. While Fredrich's passing was tragic news, it represented a relatively brief and early part of the text and could have been conveyed in a more concise way without the lengthy historical commentary on life. Nevertheless, it did not seem simply pleonastic; there was meaning, somehow.

While not associating with Lilly for decades, they interpreted it as a possible expression of ineluctability or perhaps a cry, but not for help. The letter was confusing.

In their early 80s, Beth and Judith were often at the firm's offices. They impressed the partners and legal staff with their wit and insight on paralegal matters. Neither had legal training, although some in their circle of friends thought they might have but never said so. Their inability to decipher Lilly's letter stumped them more than a senior council's clever manoeuvring to confuse and contest a case against a client.

It seemed clear that country Western Australia and city South Australia were worlds apart socially and commercially. The letter portrayed a clear distinction in time and nearly all areas of social life.

Other than in developed mining areas, residential circumstances in some of Western Australia's remote townships had changed very little since the 1920s, even earlier, while in South Australia, especially Adelaide, progress from old to new was reflected in the protection, preservation and practical use of old buildings, particularly churches, and in innovative design and building techniques. Now, South Australians argued that Adelaide was an educational, art and cultural hub of the country.

Beth and Judith knew they had to respond. The problem was how to do so without seeming to be condescending by offering assistance or insincere by not addressing the reason for the correspondence, which they did not know in any case.

The response had to be genuine and soberly sympathetic. It could not imply a problem other than coping with Fredrich's death. It could not be short as this could create a wrong impression. Beth and Judith could not see how it could be lengthy as Lilly, until now, had not shown an interest in the lives of her South Australian relatives.

They agreed to sleep on it and decide on a response the following day. They were unaware that Lilly wrote to them in a virtual coma, and that by the time the letter was received, she had met her fate.

It took all their combined guile to draft a letter disguising several queries intended to elicit further correspondence that might reveal what help Lilly needed and would accept, apart from comfort.

The letter was received by the girls who were confused about what to do about it. They showed it to Steve who, likewise, was confused and he gave it to KT.

KT phoned Beth and Judith to convey the news of Lilly's death. He was a little circumspect as their letter revealed there had been no communication between Lilly and her cousins for many years and he did not know why this was so.

Not knowing anything about the cousins, KT said there were several people in Mount Magnet and Meekatharra interested in doing what they could to assist the three girls.

He told them that a Steve Rabillard, a single, local fossicker and friend of the family, visited routinely. He saw to it the girls attended school, had no problems with their homework which he was competent to supervise when asked, had adequate food and clothing, easily managed the horse and chickens, and sought his advice when house repairs were necessary. But they seemed too young to be maintaining a house and looking after themselves, despite Steve's assistance.

KT painted a picture of care but expressed a degree of concern that the girls were on their own. He said the authorities might feel obliged to relocate them with a family or find another solution but there was no immediate indication of this. He also assured them that Steve was a trusted friend, known in the community and had looked after the funerals of Fredrich and Lilly.

Even so, he was not a family member and probably would not get approval to be their guardian, even if he wanted to be. In any case, the authorities would decide eventually that a live-in female guardian or an established family was more appropriate.

KT emphasised the girls' future needed planning. It was important they reached the highest level of school education they could in Mount Magnet before entering the local workforce.

He did not mention the bank loan arrangements entered into with Lilly.

This was all Beth and Judith needed to hear. They were particularly apprehensive about the girls entering the 'local workforce'.

The two soon arrived without notice at Mount Magnet accompanied by a senior litigation partner of the firm and all the necessary documentation concerning their relationship with the girls.

They planned on doing a lot in a couple of days.

Firstly, the lawyer, Beth and Judith met early with the municipal authorities to apprise them of the situation. The lawyer informed them of the intention of Beth and Judith to take care of the girls who they would meet for the first time later that day. This seemed acceptable to the authorities providing the girls agreed.

Then, the three went to the bank where they met KT and thanked him for informing them of the situation. KT then told them of the unusual loan arrangement he had proposed to Lilly but had not yet been enacted. He was delighted that the responsibility for the girls would be accepted by highly respected relatives and he would not have to proceed with the dodgy loan.

He expressed his opinion of the real estate agent. The opinion was noted.

The visitors proceeded to Meekatharra by car provided by KT where they met Steve, thanked him for supporting the Folvigs and told him of what they were doing and who they were seeing in the area. The lawyer assured him that every effort would be made to transfer the house lease to him, provided he wanted the house. In recognition of his support for the family, Steve would be released from lease payments for two years and for another two years.

Thereafter, any increase in payments would be no more than CPI. This would make repayments virtually negligible. This depended on the real estate agent but the lawyer said that would be 'no problem'.

The lawyer also offered the mining equipment, the horse, household furniture and all other goods gratis. All this was dependent on the girls agreeing to go to Adelaide with Beth and Judith and on Steve communicating with the lawyer regularly to ensure that no loose ends remained after their return to South Australia.

They admitted that this was a little like putting the cart before the horse as the girls, not Steve, were their main interests, but it was expeditious. At the time the girls were still in class at school. Steve recognised their priorities and thanked them for their forethought and planning.

The lawyer had prepared lease documentation before he and Steve called on the real estate agent. Beth and Judith waited outside. Learning that the agent was a belligerent fellow, the lawyer outlined what he wanted concerning the lease in very polite and quietly spoken terms.

The agent made the mistake of interpreting the lawyer's approach as seeking to negotiate. He objected strongly and loudly, as was his way.

This provided the lawyer with an excuse to be tough, although he did not need an excuse.

Still in a barely audible monotoned voice designed to annoy—a tactic often employed by barristers in court to taunt an opposing party—the lawyer specified that operational injunctions and restraining orders, trade practice notices, costly corrective claims, possible registration irregularities, even corruption charges relating to leasing properties without owners' consent and 'anything else we can dig up' could be initiated against the agency and the agent himself before the end of the day if the necessary documents were not agreed, signed and witnessed.

In almost a whisper, the lawyer added: "Remediation and other costs of a loss by you in a court contest would be significant if you resist. In a way, I urge you to resist. There is no negotiation. I know from experience an order for arbitration will not be forthcoming. Understand? So, it's your decision, good man. Concede now or pick up the phone and call your lawyer who probably will tell you not to be foolish."

Witnessing this, Steve was aghast at the lawyer's seemingly outrageous stance, his cool presentation adding strength to his threats.

With his blood pressure rising and bursting to shout at the lawyer, the agent realised there was no argument against this adversary and nodded agreement. At this time the lawyer produced the documents and a witness was asked in from outside.

The matter of the lease had been dealt with and the agent left to stew over his misjudgement of character and his inability to get his way.

Before leaving, the lawyer mentioned that Steve was now a valued client of his firm and would be reporting regularly on performance of the agreement.

Outside the agency, the lawyer said: "You did not hear any of this, did you, Steve?"

Steve replied: "Hear what?"

Steve and the lawyer went to the hotel for a well-earned beer while Beth and Judith met the girls at the house. The five of them got on well instantly. The girls eagerly accepted Beth and Judiths' offer and were relieved that there was now a degree of certainty ahead, especially educationally. In the back of their minds, the girls thought there may be an opportunity now to learn some foreign languages, use computers and get to know something about the world.

Several necessary courtesies had to be paid and arrangements finalised within a short time because the five of them had to travel between Mount Magnet, Meekatharra and Boogardie, possibly more than once. The distance was considerable for what had to be done.

They travelled to Boogardie and Meekatharra to say farewell directly to Chin and the hotel proprietor. They then went to Mount Magnet to see KT and the gold trader who was in town that day.

They also called on the school and thanked the principal. Beth and Judith were particularly interested in the girls' academic achievements and obtained school references and other documents.

A visit to the graves of Fredrich and Lilly was paramount. After this, the lawyer arranged for well-presented grave stones to be made and laid later. The grave stones at the time were modest and made with limited donations from friends.

Chapter 4: Evolution

A new phase of the girls' lives began.

All attended the same Adelaide ladies' college and settled in well. They had no difficulty with compulsory topics but there was much catching up with electives. By now other students in their classes had a head start but the sisters were not driven by competition. They wanted to learn for learning's sake and catching up did not bother them. Unintentionally, it made them appear competitive.

Basic college electives were grouped into technologies and humanities. Advanced extensions of these were possible for exceptional students.

The sisters were fascinated with Asian languages but the college emphasis on language electives was towards Latin, French and to a lesser extent German.

Beth and Judith encouraged the sisters to take two languages, Latin being the main one. Their preference for Latin was in understanding the derivation of many common English words and its use in English legal and business jargon and a wide range of botanical, medical and other scientific terms.

The sisters made known a common interest in Asian languages. Judith and Beth admitted to knowing nothing about these languages and carefully expressed doubt as to their value in Western society.

Nor did Beth and Judith consider technologies especially relevant. Computer science was of little interest to them. Indeed, they believed science and mathematics contributed very little to one's overall education.

"You only need a good memory to be successful in scientific careers, such as medicine, engineering and accountancy," Beth would say. "Ancient and modern history, classic languages, geography, music and generally the humanities contribute much more to one's broad understanding of the world. There is an unhealthy emphasis on job-related education these days," Beth told the sisters.

She explained: "Unfortunately, knowledge for its own sake is diminishing. Employment outcomes are the primary goals of secondary and even tertiary education. I know jobs are important but a well-rounded education in the humanities will hold up against any technical skill."

Beth philosophised even further: "A mind full of dreams acquired from books can be a sound intellectual investment in the future."

Eventually, Beth thought this line of opinion could be a little too advanced for school girls and implied a concession: "Culture and technology combined are important today but our priorities are clear."

Beth, however, under-rated Angelina's understanding of this philosophical explanation. Not wanting to conclude in this way, Angelina told Beth: "The three of us feel most languages are essential to an understanding of cultures just as philosophy is essential to an understanding of cultures because there are many ancient languages and philosophies that influence everyone everywhere today. Certainly, technology is relatively new but has become an essential part of learning about cultures too."

There was no argument but no agreement; no winner and no loser. The sisters hoped they could replace Latin and French in time. In any event, more than two elective languages were considered by the college to be excessive for any student no matter how bright.

The sisters' generalised Asian language preference crystalised over time into specific languages, some of which were even more surprising for Judith and Beth. Until now, an Asian language was taken to mean Mandarin or Japanese. Bahasa Indonesia was attracting some general attention also.

All the sisters were interested in Mandarin.

Angelina wanted to investigate Middle Eastern languages as well. She was aware that there were many and most seemed complex.

Theodora wanted to be fluent in South-east Asian languages. Her interest in Mandarin remained the most intensive. Its use throughout and well beyond South-east Asia encouraged her. She quietly set herself an astonishingly competency goal of writing at least 4,000 ideographs a year after starting to learn Mandarin.

Lucinda was curious about Pacific Island languages. These not only were absent from the list of senior college options but were studied mainly in social institutions that supported people who came from various Pacific Island States. The purpose was to retain native languages, especially for infants and young children so that they learned the languages of their parents and ancestors. Otherwise, such language studies were associated with university research into Pacific Island societies, politics and economics, and by a few anthropologists and linguistic scholars in academia. These languages were not for Western students but this did not deter Lucinda, quite the opposite.

The courtesy of the girls in discussing their preferences with Judith and Beth, together with respectful persuasion over many months and their obvious dedication to their other studies, resulted finally in a practical compromise. To the credit of the school management, exceptions were made for the three sisters.

A trade-off was struck. Latin remained, regardless of other choices. French could be replaced. German was a non-starter. In the Folvig sisters' case, up to two additional languages were tolerated by the collage and extra time was made available, some before and after college hours, even though the study load of three languages for each girl seemed far too heavy. The languages had to be specific and outside tuition available other than for Latin.

All the languages had to be pursued seriously and consistently. Their interests in unusual language electives could not be seen to be based on novelty or vanity and could not create disharmony among the girls' peer groups.

Competency in these languages had to be tested regularly by an appropriate authority whether a division of the South Australian Department of Education, a recognised industry group, a certified management education institute or a university extension board willing to examine college students.

College assistance would be given with these choices, including representation and character references to outside teaching institutions, but no school tuition or qualification could be provided. No promises would be made.

Here began the sisters' pursuit of languages for which they would later become internationally renowned.

Mandarin was not so much a problem for the three as there were several avenues for teaching conversational Mandarin and even written Chinese, including university language laboratories that could be accessed during university and school holidays.

Initially, Angelina's additional selection was an Afghan language but this seemed problematic initially. She knew there were many languages spoken in Afghanistan. Many Afghan nationals spoke more than one. She began her enquiry to identify a language and tutor by speaking with an officer on the

Middle East desk at the Department of Foreign Affairs and Trade (DFAT) in Canberra. The department was only too willing to advise a college student.

On advice, Angelina chose Dari, sometimes called Afghan Persian, which was one of the two most used languages in Afghanistan and could be understood in many parts of the nations surrounding Afghanistan, including Iran, Pakistan, Turkmenistan, Uzbekistan and Tajikistan.

Theodora opted to add Malay to Mandarin. Tuition in Malay and Bahasa Indonesia was not difficult as these somewhat similar languages were spoken among some communities throughout the country.

Lucinda researched Pacific Island languages through regional cooperation and friendship associations and legations. Of the 30 Polynesian, Micronesian and Melanesian languages of interest to relevant associations, legations, churches and social groups in Adelaide, the main ones were Samoan, Māori, Tongan and Tahitian. She chose another, an old type of Motu. A modern form of Motu was spoken a little in Papua New Guinea.

It did not take long for Lucinda to find a tutor and grapple with the essentials of the old form of Motu called Pure Motu. The modern form, known as Police Motu, was a simplified version. In fact, the Bible had been translated into Police Motu decades ago.

As time passed, Lucinda also took an interest in classical Greek philosophers but did not seek tuition. She self-taught using library textbooks from the house collection. Philosophers of particular interest to her were those who tended to ask questions of governments, religion and of themselves. A couple of these became famous for turning questions into theories. Some met untimely ends. They were her favourites.

In their hearts, Beth and Judith still believed these optional languages were little more than mumbo-jumbo. Nevertheless, they observed a lot of energy being expended learning them and they wanted their charges to excel as best they could. They thought it unwise to place obstacles in their way. The three also were well ahead of their other studies.

The girls were permitted to study IT also. The three recalled with intrigue the final year students in Meekatharra occasionally having privileged use of the few computers at that school. The Internet was of particular interest then and more so now.

On paper, the work load for the girls seemed enormous but they were intelligent, always attentive during tuition, curious enough to enjoy the learning experience and appreciated a home study environment. Each had a private room at home and there was a well-stocked home library, mainly containing books and documents on the humanities, history and law. There were no house chores to perform, although they pitched in whenever they could. Their meals were healthy and professionally prepared.

Their routines were arranged carefully to combine learning with leisure and to fit in with the habits of Beth and Judith who routinely engaged in discussion after dinner about college and current matters such as laws, legislation, politics and ethics. It was an educationally oriented lifestyle for the girls. Boyfriends and other distractions were not part of the equation.

By now, Beth and Judith acknowledged the girls' understanding of philosophical issues. During one routine after-dinner discussion, Beth put an oblique perspective on her previously expressed view on the value of humanities and history in education.

"For me," she said, "education involves two fundamentals. The first is peace of mind which makes learning desirable. If one feels at home, learning is like reading an interesting book that one cannot put down. The second is appreciation of the things around one, including culture; even if some cultures are completely unfamiliar or influenced by what seem to be remote historical circumstances.

"Knowledge of ancient history, particularly an understanding of the three most significant classical Greek philosophers, Socrates, Plato and Aristotle, as well as a few of the mediaeval philosophers such as Augustine and Aquinas, are of great value in learning about behaviour, and perhaps even oneself."

Not knowing Lucinda's interest in philosophy, she said: "I urge all of you to take an interest in philosophy as it highlights the basics of our world and our place in it."

This was a godsend for Lucinda. Until now, she had studied philosophy from books on her own believing that this may have been seen by Judith and Beth as excessive. Lucinda now had support and felt free to do as much as she could openly to educate herself about her favourite philosophers of the past and their relevance today.

Not entirely able to conceal a somewhat pained expression, Beth made another concession that pleased the three sisters: "I must say I have never thought of Mandarin, Malay, Dari or Motu as classic foreign languages as they are so different to Latin, Greek, German and French. However, I suppose they are classic languages in that they reflect the cultures of the countries in which they are used, and perhaps even other countries."

This admission by Beth made the path to secondary and tertiary language education considerably easier for the three sisters, particularly Lucinda. Now they had to gently convince Judith and Beth of the value of IT.

In time, the Asia-Pacific-Middle East language trinity progressed extraordinarily well, so much so that it surprised the college which did not object to the girls dropping Latin when it became evident that top linguists could be in the making.

This became evident to the college when Theodora acquired a Chinese language typewriter on loan. She toyed with it writing simple sentences but impressed everyone who observed her. Later, she was successful in writing 3,000 thousand ideographs, still 1,000 short of her target. This was no mean feat as one of her favourite old ideographs contained no less than 30 strokes.

In her final year, Angelina became captain and dux of the college and was ranked top in IT. Her free essay on fibre-optic cables used on land and in the ocean earned her first place in the State.

She had her pick of universities to study computer sciences and wanted to do an arts degree majoring in fibre-optic technology, an area becoming increasingly important in international law, admiralty law and in security areas.

Her concentration on languages continued but she wanted to study common law and international law which she realised may be too great a task if attempted simultaneously, despite compatibility between these topics in university courses.

Lucinda developed an interest in constitutional law as it applied to political issues in the Pacific. Next to climate change and consequent sea levels, constitutional issues were the bane of many Pacific Island States.

Naturally, Beth and Judith encouraged any interest in law. It was an area in which the sisters would receive considerable family help.

They knew, however, that higher studies in specialised sciences, languages, law, mathematics and philosophy may not be available in Adelaide. Some of these topics were taught as separate topics elsewhere, mainly in Australian Capital Territory and New South Wales institutions.

Beth and Judith thought Angelina's future seemed to be directed by her interests in fibre-optics, Mandarin, Dari and admiralty law, and was heading into a government occupation, probably in a legal area.

Theodora now had less than a year to go and was following Angelina with her success in languages and IT. She had topped her classes in mathematics consistently. She was already a mathematician, almost on a par with her college teachers. She looked forward to tertiary level studies.

As young as she was, she quietly looked ahead to post-graduate studies in pure mathematics, cyber security, quantum computing and even theoretical areas of quantum physics that seemed to be more a matter of fantasy than reality and, for that reason, was fascinating.

Consistent with Lucinda's preoccupation with languages, she took a casual interest in so-called secret languages.

Secret languages were used centuries ago and were largely of religious origin. Their purpose was to converse in secret through devised words and phrases. Most were used by a handful of people for no particular reason other than not being understood outside exclusive groups. The few people who used them today seemed to her to be either retired linguistic zealots with little else to do or people delusional about the relevance of such languages. She was critically curious.

Lucinda also began to take more than a hobby interest in geo-spatial issues. This interest did not seem to fit in with her dedication to Mandarin, Pure Motu and law, just as Theodora's interest in mathematics and Angelina's interest in fibre-optic science did not seem to fit with their dedication to Mandarin, Malay, and law and to Mandarin, Dari and law, respectively. Nevertheless, there was a curious compatibility in these combined scholastic pursuits. It supported their belief that culture and technology were not at odds in today's world.

The Folvig team seemed to be falling into place albeit a little haphazardly. Their skill sets pointed to Angelina being a lawyer, scientist and linguist, Theodora being a scientific mathematician and linguist, and Lucinda being a linguist, lawyer and home-grown philosopher.

While considering university options, Angelina asked Beth and Judith if she could take Theodora and Lucinda to Boogardie to visit the graves of Fredrich and Lilly, probably for the last time.

They also wanted to call on Chin, KT and Steve. She was certain they would be safe to travel together and gave an unnecessary assurance they would behave responsibly. They were to stay at the Mount Magnet Hotel.

Angelina's preferred date of arrival was 1 December so she could be at the Royal Exchange Hotel in Meekatharra the following day. She thought there was a remote chance Bob Davis might be there but did not inform Beth or Judith. It had been years since they agreed to try to be there on 2 December each year.

All this came about with the blessing of Beth and Judith. Early on 2 December, the three girls found their way to the Royal Exchange Hotel. Angelina stood in the lobby at noon while her sisters had tea in the lounge. At precisely the appointed time, Bob came down the stairs of the hotel. He had stayed there that night. Both were extremely surprised.

They kissed in the foyer on this hot day in full view of passers-by, not that there were many people outside at the time. It was a prolonged kiss but somewhat reserved, as long married adults might give each other after a few weeks apart. It was not the kind of intimate embrace and kiss one might expect to see in an exciting romance.

Without sexual intimacy in Lennonville—unlike most of the others there in those days—and in the absence of physical contact or communication over a long period, it was as though they had progressed independently from a youthful to a mature relationship.

Angelina felt that perhaps the libidinal instincts of adolescence had passed her by. She had been a student every day of every week of every year without mixing socially a great deal with male friends of about her own age.

"I'm sorry I could not get here until now," Angelina said, "but much has happened and I have been studying a lot, like you I guess. It was unreasonable to ask my guardians to let me come while the three of us were still at college." As she uttered these words, she sounded more formal than intended but could not help it.

"I thought you might be staying here," Bob said. "Where are you staying? How long have we got?"

"We are at the Mount Magnet Hotel," she said. "Can you come and stay at our hotel tonight? We have several things we must do here today and tomorrow morning, and will be leaving for Adelaide the day after tomorrow. But we have tonight."

"Try to stop me," he said with some urgency.

"I too have been busy. I've finished on the cattle station and am into an agricultural course at Queensland Uni. I've put funds into a small cattle station in south western Queensland but am a long way off having a management role or owning it, which is my ultimate aim," he said.

They chatted about their university prospects and how they might meet regularly later now that one was in South Australia and the other in Queensland.

Later that day, the girls accompanied by Bob visited their parents' grave sites and noticed the much-improved head stones before returning to Mount Magnet where they all had dinner, before Theodora and Lucinda retired to the passing remark by Angelina: "Don't wait up for me."

Bob and Angelina went to her room for the night. They left the lights on while there was some brief foreplay. He used a condom. It was Angelina's first coition but she left any inhibitions behind. It hurt a little but she enjoyed it, perhaps not as much as if he could have waited a little longer.

In a sense, her intimacy with Bob completed their long-awaited reunion. During the night, they tried again and it was a little better for Angelina and predictably ecstatic for Bob. For her, the relationship had matured a little too much.

At breakfast, they agreed both had to complete their studies before thinking further of what they would do together. They would probably meet in Adelaide, Brisbane or half way in Sydney, not in Meekatharra or Mount Magnet again. The West was now an enduring memory. During this conversation, Theodora and Lucinda behaved in advance of their ages.

Time was limited. Angelina bid farewell to Bob. The girls proceeded to visit KT. They then travelled to Boogardie to visit Chin about midday when they knew he would close the shop for an hour.

They found him in a shed behind the shop dressed in loose cloths practicing a form of martial art. He was concentrating on what he was doing and seemingly oblivious to the girls watching him. His movements were rapid and continuous, unlike the slow rhythmically movements the girls perceived to be Tai Chee. His surprise at seeing the girls was not convincing; they realised he had been aware of their presence but wanted him to complete what he was doing.

He exclaimed: "Angelina, Tzda, Czunda…"

Before he had a chance to say anything more, Theodora greeted him with a flurry of Mandarin using a highly diplomatic form of address known as the 'Peking dialect' that recognised him as superior. He bowed and replied in similarly courteous pre-Mao Mandarin.

Theodora was relieved. Had he spoken another form of Chinese only or found her Mandarin too formal, she could have embarrassed him.

He said he was astonished at how tonal and eloquent she was after such a short time. It normally took a foreigner ten or more years of regular study to attain an acceptable level of fluency, he said. She surprised him also by revealing that she had learned several thousand ideographs.

Not to be outdone, Angelina and Lucinda wished him well in Dari and Pure Motu respectively, all of which took him by surprise. He thought he recognised a few Arabic words but he had never heard Pure Motu.

Chin was elated to hear of their success at college and asked them to keep in touch, particularly about their studies.

"Where did you learn all this stuff?" Angelina asked Chin while mimicking his arm and leg movements.

He told her he started some five decades ago in his home town of Ch'ih-feng in Liaoning province of northern China. "Yes…be active. Keep warm, healthy. Exercise good for mind and blood. Temperature often 40 degrees below. We light fires under trucks to warm them in morning so they start. Not like here."

He paused a little and said: "Yes, popular concept of Tai Chee is Taijzhang. Known at home as Chen. Most traditional. I teach in China before coming here 20 years ago. Yes, in the beginning I teach Taijzhang. Assist students with breathing, muscle control, coordination, balance, relaxation, meditation," he said pronouncing his words slowly and deliberately.

"I advance to combat forms but these not liked by provincial or central governments in China. Here I practice these forms on my own. Not slow, not like Tai Chee most Aussies know. Yes, the particular form I specialise…very ancient. Cannot explain. It's Labokkatao, a Cambodian combat martial art. Very few know," he explained while again pronouncing the 'L' in Labokkatao carefully and with some difficulty.

"It sounds fascinating," Theodora said. "But 'Loboko' hard to pronounce for *Czunda* and me," she said feigning in a friendly way his grammatical peculiarity and mispronunciation of Lucinda's name. He took her expression in good humour.

"I wish I could learn it, not that I ever would want to use it in combat, of course," she said.

"It's Labokkatao, not 'Loboko'. You call it Bokator. Easier," he suggested.

"Yes, well," he said, "if you were here longer, I talk to you about some basics but it's not something you boast about. I appreciate…not mentioning it to friends. My interest personal, not public. Some young yahoos…like to test me if they knew. That…unfortunate for everyone.

"Bokator not sport," he emphasised. "Most moves expose kill points. Final movement always fatal. Accidents happen in sports but this no accident. Not defensive. Not fun but I like it. Good for the mind."

They agreed to say nothing and hoped there would come a time when they were in a position to benefit from his experience.

He encouraged the girls to follow up their interest in Taijzhang and even Bokator but was unable to identify a Bokator teacher in Australia. "If you in Singapore sometime," he said, "yes, I recommend a master. He not give public lessons in Bokator. Authorities against it. Very good friend, my best friend."

The girls exchanged phone numbers and addresses with Chin and left thankful they had an opportunity to meet him again.

Chapter 5: Litterae

Angelina had firm ideas about her tertiary courses.

During an evening discussion, Angelina told Beth and Judith: "I know this is a big ask, but I would like to do law and computer science as a double degree, if possible. They may not be compatible generally with university programs but I think I can handle them together if they are available in the one place."

This combination surprised Beth and Judith but not as much as what followed. Angelina added: "As an extension of my computer science interest, I would like to explore the security aspect of fibre-optic submarine cable communications, particularly the access to cable data by organised crime groups. This could fit reasonably well with my law studies because theft by hacking cyber protected communications is both highly technical and illegal. Unfortunately, studying law and science at this level probably involves post-graduate work."

Beth responded gently: "Sounds like putting the cart before the horse."

Beth and Judith were perplexed. They were amazed that Angelina seemed particularly interested in organised crime. They thought her main interests were languages, communications technology and consequently maritime law, not such a specialised area of criminal law.

Before they had a chance to query her expanded direction, Lucinda expressed a similar view. She supported Angelina's comments by suggesting that dishonest use of communications technologies seemed an interesting and integral part of the study of both computer science and international law.

Lucinda elaborated: "In studying anything in these areas one needs to know about the motivations of people, especially evil motivations. Learning about successful dishonesty in this area may be very helpful in revealing weaknesses in particular technologies and lead to scientific solutions and criminal resolutions. We simply want to know what makes cyber criminals tick. Then, maybe, others can do something about it."

Lucinda was particularly curious about corruption, poor governance, neglect of ethics and standards and mistreatment of peoples in the Pacific Basin and elsewhere. "I am reminded often by historic man-made tragedies resulting from these behaviours." She referenced art that portrayed horrible scenes of wars, genocide and crimes against humanity. Research revealed all kinds of dark events and books told stories so bad they were hard to believe.

Knowing about these things from books was important but, in the end, to fully understand such events, and especially to apply that knowledge to solutions, could not be based on the written word alone.

"It requires hard evidence supported by practical observation, credible hearsay, forensics, and experience with the arguments used to accuse and defend perpetrators…in my humble opinion. This practical side of these things must be fascinating to you, Judith and Beth, if only from legal perspectives," Lucinda concluded.

Lucinda caught her breath and bowed slightly while quipping apologetically: "Sorry. Here I am, not yet a graduate and sounding like an experienced professional looking into the troubles of the world. What do I know?"

"Well," said Beth, "the two of you certainly have given this some thought. I assume Theodora thinks the same way." Theodora nodded agreement.

"Let me get it right," Beth said. "Are you saying that you want to learn about the emotional and intellectual stimuli behind inhuman events and what drives individuals to evil actions internationally? If so, you are really talking about the psychology of evil, not so much about technology or law.

"So now it sounds like you want to be experts in communications technology, law of the sea, constitutional law, criminal psychology, and several abstruse foreign languages. Anything else?" She asked jokingly while holding a fountain pen to paper as if to add to the list.

Nevertheless, Beth knew the sisters were exceptionally competent in their studies. Their skill in analysing situations and predicting outcomes was impressive by any measure, even at this early stage. They were thinkers.

Beth added kindly: "You certainly have given Judith and me as much a surprise as when we saw you for the first time in Western Australia."

Angelina added: "And I might say as much a surprise for us as when we saw you for the first time there. That was a time we will never forget just as we will never forget all the love and guidance you have given us since and continue to do so."

Both Beth and Judith were impressed by the girls' heart-felt expression of appreciation. They felt they were engaging with their peers but of another age. The exchange revealed that everyone was learning something and all were benefiting. And Beth and Judith were beginning to feel their age.

"Well, that concludes our bucket list," Angelina said gently taking the fountain pen from Beth.

"Getting back to basics," Beth said to Angelina, "your desire to do law and computer science in tandem may be difficult to accommodate in Adelaide. Indeed, if any university could help you, it probably would be the ANU or Canberra University in the ACT.

"As for legal studies, admiralty law and intellectual property law, these are not integral parts of the standard law degree anywhere in Australia. They are covered only marginally. I will try to find out what specialties are available," Beth said.

Several scholarships were offered to Angelina from universities in NSW and the ACT.

Within the week, Beth had advice that most of Angelina's primary study interests actually could be accommodated in any of the larger universities in the country using ANU Extension Board programs.

Advanced studies, however, would be available to full-time post-graduate students only, and in a limited number of institutions.

Angelina investigated three South Australian universities. One was a newly established Great Southern University (GSU) which had law and computer science faculties as well as others of marginal relevance to her specific interests. Most of the combined options were within the Faculty of Arts but Angelina was determined to study the two full degrees simultaneously.

Another was the Adelaide University where her topic preferences seemed to fit into its Faculty of Humanities and Social Sciences, one of five faculties at the university. It was an impressive establishment operating since 1874.

The third option was the University of South Australia, the largest in the State with a staff of more than 2,400 offering law and computer science in its Division of Education, Arts and Social Sciences.

She accepted the GSU scholarship on the proviso that two courses could be studied separately.

She settled in well.

From the beginning, Angelina was single-minded. There were no distractions. She did not pursue student causes, was not involved in student politics, was not a contributor to the student newspaper, did not participate in a university sport that required significant time and effort and avoided being tied into social groups or chase boyfriends. She was a studious, attractive, agreeable, inconspicuous loner. This disposition enabled her to handle the hefty double degree agenda.

At home, she also received consistently casual tuition in Dari and treated this as relief from her university studies resulting in her doing well in the language.

Time passed quickly.

In five years, Angelina received her general law and computer science degrees at the GSU, at the same time achieving high accolades for her fluency in Mandarin and Dari.

She needed practical legal work locally and sought extra tuition to extend her studies into the international arena, including admiralty and criminal law.

Her special interest in computer science covered infrastructure, security, network systems, tools and techniques.

She identified two specialist post-graduate courses with the help of a GSU lecturer in computer science, a former Australian Defence Force (ADF) communications expert fluent in Pashto, a popular Arabic language in Afghanistan.

He arranged for her to participate in the first one, an intensive, free, three-month course in advanced computer sciences conducted in Sydney. Attendance was by invitation. Attendees were post-graduate professionals.

The other course was in Queanbeyan in NSW near Canberra. It was for two-months several times a week and open to qualified and referred people on application. Many of the topics complemented those covered in the Sydney course. The cost was in line with industry standards. Defence College attendees received professional education credits on completion.

Neither course led to qualifications but seemed to promise the kind of skills Angelina sought. She no longer needed degrees. A post-graduate qualification was not an objective at present. She wanted knowledge leading to applied technology.

Being incorrigibly curious, she took both the Sydney and Queanbeyan courses. Some lecture times conflicted but she was able to adjust the Sydney schedule because sessions included repetitive elements, enabling a few ADF attendees to fulfil operational duties during some lecture periods. This meant she also was able to juggle sessions in Sydney with her Queanbeyan tuition.

Sydney course attendees included defence industry representatives and diplomats, as far as she could tell. There was little social interaction among them but problem-solving sessions were noticeable for the camaraderie of participants. Individual skills development was combined with team practice.

Queanbeyan course attendees seemed mainly academics and security consultants. Generally, they kept to themselves and lessons emphasised personal skills development.

Together, the course topics covered technical areas such as security document design, computer program design, State-sponsored hacking, code development and breaking, coded semeiology, cryptology, and transmission methods, including fibre-optic communication cable and satellite modes.

More broadly they addressed the various levels of cyber warfare, the norms currently agreed internationally for such warfare, including the United Nations Outer Space Treaty, vulnerability and deniability of cyber espionage, anti-satellite weapons and other counter-space capabilities, satellite collision prediction, space surveillance sensors, the prospect of indigenous satellites and generally what it takes to be a 'cyber warrior'.

Angelina's dedication and analytical capacity demonstrated in Sydney were noted by the defence and security community in Canberra.

On completing the courses, she received an invitation to meet a discussion group in Sydney seemingly unrelated to either the Sydney or Queanbeyan courses.

The invitation came from a group known as the International Conduct and Control Centre (ICCC) run as a Sydney-based non-profit security institution. There was little indication of the purpose of the group. It seemed vaguely associated with the ADF or the federal government.

Her invitation was for an informal meeting in the Sydney office of the ICCC. It was located on the second floor of a non-descript building above a coffee shop and small late-night supermarket in a lower economic area on the fringe of the central business district.

The meeting was brief and polite, almost to the extreme. Theodora and Lucinda were not included.

Angelina received a simplified explanation of the organisation and documentary evidence of its role in the form of a leaflet stating that it focused on predictive assessment and current case analysis of threats to national security. No details were given.

In the following days, she attended two lengthy meetings, again without Theodora or Lucinda. Both meetings were designed to make her comfortable while being questioned on a variety of matters, some intended to seem inconsequential.

It seemed to her the members comprised an expert group akin to a high-level executive search panel but this did not bother her. She participated naturally answering queries she could and admitting to not knowing the answers to other questions. In the back of her mind, she wondered if the interview method was of a type that could be used by international counter-terrorism agents or even terrorists themselves to influence and recruit people. Nevertheless, she had confidence in the patriotism of the centre.

Angelina was by far the youngest person there but not the only woman. Eventually, she was invited to join the group as a member and on acceptance was provided with a document for signature detailing her agreement to aspects of what was called the Official Secrets Act (OSA). She felt a sense of achievement in being accepted by a privileged group interested in national security without having to undertake all kinds of formalities or tests, although some seemingly casual interviews revealed an element of enquiry.

She accepted the centre's objective and signed. She was now a member and received a nominal payment.

Membership of the group was less than 100, all experts in various aspects of terrorism, revolution and corruption, as well as cyber strategies and tactics.

The board comprised consultants and retired senior officers of several services—the Australian Federal Police (AFP), the Homeland Security and Border Protection Service, the Australian National Security Agency, the Cyber Security Operations Centre and three security consultancies. There were a couple of serving ADF officers.

One consultant representative specialised in tactics used by organised criminals to destabilise weak sovereign States by targeting constitutional weaknesses, generally involving social mischief, pseudo-grants and various economic and personal benefits.

Another specialised in post-subversion remedial options.

A third was a female psychologist interested in terrorist motivation and indoctrination. She was central to Angelina's interviews prior to her being invited to become a member. Angelina admired the psychiatrist's ability to create an amicable and serene interview environment conducive to a lesser person feeling comfortable enough to be informal and even boast about skills. Angelina felt the psychiatrist applied some of the assessment techniques that could be applied to identify hidden weakness, radicalisation or latent hostility.

Angelina's predilections were precisely what the panel and the psychiatrist were looking for, a combination of agreement, restraint and reliability. She was informative and pre-emptive but not demonstrable, decisive but understanding of other views, intelligent but self-controlled, personable but guarded in being drawn into informality or controversy, and clearly respectful of the people around her. She came across as liking her new acquaintances and this, she felt, seemed reciprocated.

One aspect of ICCC's terms of reference that interested Angelina involved persuasion and influence employed by criminals, militants and fanatical groups hostile to democratic processes, an approach disguised as fair, charitable and socially sensitive. Fundraising for militant groups also was of particular interest as was militants' soft-sell of recruitment causes.

In an assessment to the ICCC board a senior member, Colonel Adam Weingraf, a serving army officer attached to the Australian Signals Directorate (ASD), noted that Angelina could be a useful addition to any one of several national security agencies because of her interest in admiralty law, communications technology and her probable ability to absorb complex issues of national concern. Her competency in Mandarin was evident to all and her interest in the law-of-the-sea was relevant.

He noted also that her sisters were highly qualified and might be approached in due course.

By now, Angelina was spending most of her time in Sydney. Very little time was spent in Adelaide and her Dari lessons were on hold, whereas Theodora and Lucinda were busying themselves in Adelaide and were seemingly out of the picture.

Angelina expected them to become involved in the ICCC sometime and thought it best to let any involvement develop without mentioning her membership. In any event, she was restricted in discussing the ICCC under the OSA.

Chapter 6: Resolution

Angelina's desire to develop her ICCC relationship was interrupted occasionally by Bob who would turn up in Sydney unannounced from time to time.

Occasionally, they would have dinner at a Chinese restaurant in China Town followed by a night in a nearby hotel. He was as keen as ever but she felt restrained partly because of her preoccupation with the ICCC and inability to discuss her interests. Time and distance also had changed the relationship. An enduring friendship remained but her adrenalin had diminished.

They talked about his studies and farm activities. She enjoyed listening to his animal husbandry and veterinary work, even though she did not know the difference between a fetlock and a femur.

The relationship for her varied from quite-satisfactory to not-so-satisfactory, depending on the intervals between meetings and the length of their meetings. There were no disagreements and communicating remained easy. She enjoyed intimacy with him in a hotel occasionally in a slightly naughty way. She hid her passivity well while he remained ever the enthusiast.

She side-tracked any discussion of them living together or settling down. She imagined such a future being one of a married couple growing old together with separate interests and rapidly decreasing libido. This could not be.

Several times Bob invited Angelina to Brisbane to meet his parents. Eventually, she felt she had to accept.

His parents left their country property and booked several rooms in a Brisbane hotel. The meeting was an amicable family gathering that included several of Bob's interstate relatives. From the beginning, a detectable assumption was that Angelina was part of the family. Angelina was not bothered by this and chose to regard the amity as reflecting courtesy and curiosity, rather than certainty.

Out of respect, Angelina and Bob stayed in separate rooms for the few nights they were in the hotel.

Nothing of their future together was discussed directly. Angelina was respectfully vague so as not to encourage talk of marriage or her own parents' hardship and demise. Bob's parents were aware of the absence of discussion about such matters and discreet in avoiding them. Bob did not pose any awkward questions. The tenor of the visit was genuinely polite, albeit more formal than Angelina expected of country folk. It was decorous.

While Bob and Angelina were at Brisbane airport awaiting her flight to Adelaide, Bob finally asked her to marry him. Angelina agreed to consider the offer after she had examined additional post-graduate opportunities and secured a job, even though her ICCC engagement looked very much like a permanent job. Both understood this could take years, probably quite a few.

Angelina had her degrees, was well established in her advanced IT studies, had post-graduate studies in view and was a member of a significant defence and security group in Sydney. Her Mandarin studies continued at a highly advanced level and her Dari studies now were back on track, albeit occasionally interrupted by her absence from Adelaide. She knew it would soon be time to gain admiralty law expertise and had expressed her desire to get started.

She also detected a heightened ICCC interest in her admiralty law ambitions. She wanted to pursue this area of law and other interests. Bob was not in this picture.

At home, she again sought Beth's and Judith's advice and discussed admiralty law with Sir Jonathan, the senior partner at the family law firm. Angelina had received help from the firm while studying for her general law degree but had not broached the topic of maritime law in any detail.

The firm did not promote admiralty services. Indeed, no South Australian law firm specialised in this area, although the relevant legislation existed and services were available on request, mainly from national firms and those based in Sydney, Melbourne and to a lesser extent in Perth. Angelina was familiar generally with this branch of law but far from satisfied with her practical knowledge of it.

"I am really not aware of the many intricacies of this specialty," she told Sir Jonathan. "I need advice on getting involved, getting experience."

"If I recall," Sir Jonathan said, "I believe our federal court deals with admiralty law under the Blue Ensign and within the Admiralty Act of 1988. Most ships visiting Australia are foreign owned and so it's obvious that we need laws dealing with claims against these ships and cargoes. This is so also for people, particularly owners, captains and crew.

"There are a couple of primary admiralty law actions available, although we have never had to apply them," Sir Jonathan said. "The most common here is known as *rem* which involves claims for liens against a range of subjects, including ships. Within *rem* there are *proprietary maritime claims* involving mortgages and even possession. And then there are *general maritime claims* which relate to a wide range of matters such as personal injury and damage to cargoes, and so on."

Angelina acknowledged she had seen the textbook definitions of these but knew of no practical examples. "I cannot see why there are not many more actions in Australia as the law involves international conventions signed by Australia. They cover drilling rigs and undersea cables, and there are plenty of these around our coastline."

"Be that as it may, Angelina," Sir Jonathan replied. "We have never had an admiralty law claim in any of these categories, perhaps because the main ports are elsewhere and the main cargo destinations and markets are in other States."

Picking up on her reference to undersea cables, he said: "And I am inclined to think there are few undersea cables off the South Australian coast. There's little need for communications cables to Kangaroo Island and the Antarctic," he added sheepishly.

Not distracted by this, she continued: "We have international fishing problems within or near our territorial limits. We are near internationally recognised wilderness areas and protected research and exploration zones. And the most direct shipping route from the west coast to the east coast is across the Bight this end of which is under our navigational control."

She could not help herself expanding the topic to her favourite hobby—horse. "A neglected area of great importance is the theft of data carried by fibre-optic submarine cables by criminals. I know it is complex and often has more to do with governments because much of the data is secret. I have never heard of a government or private case but the crime exists and it seems to fit into the purview of maritime law.

"Over the past few months, I have been thinking that this area of data theft could be pursued successfully if an investigator could establish motives for such criminality. Knowing the motives could be as important as finding evidence and could assist governments and private organisations prosecute these matters. I know all this suggests too broad an interest in admiralty law for a firm like yours at this time but it could be a niche market in future."

Concluding her pitch, she said: "What is preventing Robinson and Company testing the market by setting up a small admiralty law unit? It would only be a test. It would require no more than updating current legal staff and establishing a working agreement with a couple of associates in main maritime locations such as Singapore, Indonesia, India, South Korea or Japan.

"It might be useful to get more involved also in the maritime affairs of the associations and forums covering South-east Asia and the Pacific, particularly Melanesia and Micronesia. Certainly, this would require more time but no more personnel and little additional investment."

Sir Jonathan said he would speak with some of his colleagues and clients about the idea, providing it did not impinge on the firm's core interests. If responses were positive and an immediate cost-benefit assessment was not too negative, Angelina could join such a unit.

"Angelina," Sir Jonathan said, "I will enquire with our associate in Singapore and get their opinion as to the value to them and us extending their admiralty services to cover Australia, particularly South Australia, or at least, signalling to the market that a service could be available here. At the same time, I could speak with our shipping clients. They are interested primarily in matters relating to insurance, customs, and finance. What they have to say about other admiralty services may be interesting but they have not expressed any interest to date."

She said: "There is, however, a relationship between insurance and risk assessment when it comes to routes that cross territorial limits and international boundaries of countries prone to regional dispute. Piracy is also something we could look at but we are relatively free of this in our region, although small-scale piracy is evident in the north-west of the country. Flags of convenience from rogue States and smuggling also are matters worth examining. And eventually, all kinds of disputes requiring legal representation may arise in the South China Sea, already in regional turmoil."

"This is getting bigger than Ben Hur," he said as he tried to restrain Angelina from pressing further.

Eventually, Sir Jonathan contacted the firm's legal affiliates in Singapore. The conclusion was that there was probable value in formalising joint efforts in admiralty law. At least no harm would be done.

He arranged to discuss his findings at a meeting with senior staff, Angelina, her sisters, Beth and Judith. "To begin with," Sir Jonathan said opening the discussion. "I believe there are a couple of very different service areas we could concentrate on. And there is room for market and corporate identity promotion by judiciously addressing issues that occupy the minds of lawyers interested in maritime law internationally.

"One service area is to do with trade since nearly all of our resource exports are carried by sea and a fair percentage of our domestic trade involves shipping. It appears that damage done at sea or in ports to our minerals and other exports can be redressed legally. The same applies to our imports and domestic cargoes.

"Most ships servicing Australia are foreign owned and can be arrested and held pending resolution. This not only gives surety of recovery but may prompt highly favourable settlements because of the high cost of vessels lying idle. In some cases, a vessel may represent the entire asset of an owner. In these circumstances, the chances of recovering compensation quickly may be better than it seems.

"The key to this would be effective working agreements with associates. In our patch we could look after local ship arrests as a result of claims while an appropriate associate elsewhere may provide intelligence and advice relating to foreign owners. We may also share investigative resources into fault. Sharing costs could be attractive.

"Other service areas may be more competitive and may depend even more on associates, particularly in the United States. One is a service representing passengers and crew on cruises ensuring that claims relating to injuries are settled. Australia is now part of a high growth cruise industry due to the tourism value of our port cities. Cruising, however, is an international business and maritime lawyers servicing this sector are largely in the United States and Europe. So, here again, shared interests with associates could be the way to go," he said.

Beth chipped in and suggested that these areas seemed to fit conventional legal services anyway particularly insurance claims. "I wonder why we have not visited these areas before?" She asked giving Angelina a nod.

Sir Jonathan replied that the firm had been engrossed in other business but had the capacity to be flexible.

"As for opportunities for promoting our corporate identity," he said, "there seems quite a lot of room to do so. We may have been somewhat complaisant about our image to date but times are changing and we could give some thought to promoting ourselves domestically. A new service may help. Before any hard and fast promotional plans can be formulated, the new admiralty unit has to be structured, working and successful.

"Then we should understand something of the history, culture, noncompliance in certain countries and the uncertainties of admiralty law in compliant countries. Let's face it, admiralty law is basically a debt collection business, as are many areas of the law. We have to be clear about the *collection* aspect of the law, as abstruse as many lawyers would like it to remain."

Theorising slightly, he said: "Admiralty law often personifies ships as having caused damage, colliding with something, and so on. Even the term *ship arrest* carries an element of personal cause, whereas the guidance of ships is the real cause. Not only is the legal phraseology absurd but the meaning is as well. This could be a matter inviting professional curiosity publicly," he said directing his attention to Angelina.

"We may wish to enter the fray when we have a firm grasp of these intangibles. When we have developed the expertise and experience in maritime law, we could present ourselves as commentators in the same way some academics promote themselves as experts in particular fields through speaking engagements, published papers and public debate," he said. "Sometimes to the neglect of their real jobs."

"And sometimes carried away by self-importance," Angelina quipped.

She qualified this: "Only a small number of consultants are like this. We certainly would be factual and responsible."

Over the following few months, the unit was established. On average, Angelina spent a day every month in Adelaide providing legal advice and servicing clients as a part-time admiralty lawyer.

For the rest of her time, she was engaged mostly in Sydney at the ICCC and the remainder at the ANU's language laboratory where she conversed with her tape recorder in advanced Mandarin. She even played games with the laboratory recordings by making comments in conversation that were deliberately ambiguous or argumentative, very much like doing the opposite to a motor vehicle's GPS voice direction unit to make the unit work harder to recalibrate the situation.

Col Weingraf took particular interest in her developing maritime law work, as well as her criminal law interest relating to the theft of intellectual property and data carried by fibre-optic submarine communications cables.

He occasionally mentioned to Angelina his interest in Theodora. In particular, he admired her expertise in pure mathematics and quantum computing, as well as her language proficiency. However, her engagement with the ICCC was best developed step by step, as it would be with Lucinda. One expert was enough at a time, he would say.

Chapter 7: Connectivity

By now, Theodora also had achieved a double degree from the GSU, one in linguistics, majoring in Mandarin, and the other in pure mathematics, majoring in computer science.

Her pure mathematics degree was with honours because of her thesis on quantum computing. The thesis was developed over a year during which she corresponded frequently with experts in quantum mechanics in the US where a small quantum computer had been assembled and a number of ambitions concepts in quantum cryptography were under experimentation.

She was on expert interview lists of newspapers, radio stations and television networks. Requests for interviews increased after she was assisted by some of her US correspondents in having several papers published on the role of quantum computing in counteracting rogue States using sophisticated codes to hack into Western government entities, especially those controlling infrastructure and military projects.

She also had developed a reputation within academia as one of the leading foreign Mandarin scholars and was an accomplished calligrapher.

Theodora maintained contact with her main GSU tutor in Chinese languages and history, Professor Lee Ng Swee. An Australian citizen, Prof Lee had some contact with the PRC Embassy in Canberra, despite the politely—sometimes no so politely—tolerated diplomatic stand-off that characterised the bi-national relationship.

Unaware of the ICCC's interest in Theodora, Prof Lee wanted her to move from academic pursuits to business professions. He would say to her: "After spending so much time as a student, don't spend the rest of your life in the classroom, like me. If you must, stay a scholar but don't go into closet teaching."

He said there were many avenues for development. "Perhaps I can help. I may be in a position to facilitate a post with the United Nations in New York or the Office of the Director-General of Interpretation (UNODGI) in Geneva, as a senior simultaneous Mandarin translator. As contradictory as it sounds, my Chinese Embassy contacts may even help, although they would not want to be seen to assist.

"The United Nations Educational, Scientific and Cultural Organisation (UNESCO) has an ongoing interest in people whose skills combine high-level Mandarin and advanced computer science. There may be an opening in a security environment but this is not an area in which I have any contacts and the Chinese Embassy would not be interested in helping, quite the contrary. But I am fairly certain introductions could be arranged," he said.

He added casually: "Of course, our near neighbour, Singapore, is among the most advanced in many technological areas, including computer development. I have friends there."

Outwardly, the professor was well-meaning and modest intellectually with an enduring interest in Chinese and other Asian art. Like other art lovers, he seemed unable to restrain his enthusiasm among his peers when an issue arose about authenticity, quality or value.

This characteristic appeared at odds with his proclivity towards disarmingly quiet traditionalism in certain circumstances, particularly with strangers. When in unfamiliar or uncomfortable company, he could assume a position of the inscrutable Asian traditionalist, polite but noticeably unresponsive.

He never initiated criticism or even offered an admonitory response to an erroneous or critical comment. He always remained courteous and retiring, even when offended by vulgarity, gross ignorance or mischief. To initiate a gratuitous rebuke did not seem to be in his nature.

However, he occasionally amused those who knew him well by retiring from unavoidable argument initiated by strangers by referring to obscure historical events using Asian sayings, particularly ambiguous Confucian quotations that seemed to have only fleeting relevance to the subject at the time. Changing the pointedness of a critic's argument in this oblique way generally necessitated a pause presenting difficulties for the critic to maintain a position. This was mistaken mostly by those who annoyed him as bizarre.

Theodora suspected Lee was as strong mentally as he was skilful in disguised polemics.

Prof Lee and senior diplomats in the Chinese Embassy in Canberra displayed a degree of respect publicly but concealed their dislikes of the other's disposition. Trust was not mutual. The legation infrequently sponsored in-house social events but preferred formalised appointments for meetings. This did not inhibit appointments being made regularly but they had to comply with established protocols.

Quite the opposite was his social engagements with the Singaporean High Commissioner who enjoyed chatting with him informally about art, poetry, literature and music, some of these engagements arranged spontaneously. Meetings were arranged easily with the Japanese ambassador also.

During a casual conversation with Theodora about the fastidiousness of particular forms of Japanese and Chinese address, he asked if Theodora would like to accompany him to informal drinks at the Japanese Embassy in Canberra where he would introduce her to a visitor there contracted to the Singapore High Commission, Conrad Wong. A private sector Singaporean, Wong was a defence adviser to the Singapore High Commission and a regular invitee to the Japanese Embassy.

Their host would be a senior Japanese 'counsellor', a term commonly used for 'intelligence officer'. Lee and Theodora would fly to Canberra together and he would explain the mateship of the three of them—the Singaporean, the Japanese and himself, an Australian. She accepted.

The drinks had the secondary purpose of meeting a visiting Japanese musical group well known in traditional music circles but unknown to most Western music aficionados. The group would give a private recital prior to a public performance later in the week.

The professor asked Theodora to call him Lee, not use the title.

In a typical understatement, he said he knew very little about Japanese music. He said the group would play several old instruments. Two were of special interest to him.

Lee said: "One is the *taishogoto,* a kind of zither with metal strings and keys. The other is a *kagurabue,* a seven-hole, birchwood and bamboo flute. Unfortunately, the *taiko,* a large noisy drum, will not be played probably to the relief of many but often accompanies the *taishogoto* and the *kagurabue.* The *taiko* was used in some traditional settings for sounding a warning of imminent danger but it is never used these days as a siren. It was replaced for the performance by a more acceptable type of drum.

"The *kagurabue,*" he went on to say, "has a relatively low register and is used in Shinto rituals. Both traditional instruments are made in the customary way and seem somewhat primitive compared to replacements used these days for international recitals of classical Japanese music."

Lee introduced Theodora to the Japanese 'counsellor' and Conrad Wong. She was offered a cocktail while the others drank beer. Most Asians Theodora had rubbed shoulders with preferred single-malt Scotch, aged Cognac, some kind of national spirit or tea, not beer. The three downed a couple before she could finish her much smaller cocktail.

Before the musicians joined them, the group conversed in English and Mandarin. They talked about trade treaties and defence policies and particularly developments in the South China Sea, without referring to the Peoples Republic of China (PRC) or the Peoples Liberation Army (PLA).

Addressing Theodora, Wong asked: "It's difficult these days to find ways of mitigating current political disturbances and multi-national concerns in the South China Sea and the Indo-Pacific region generally. There may be prospects of using social and economic means to soften defence and security concerns. What do you think?"

This seemed an extraordinarily wide and unexpected question. It may have been semi-serious, but certainly not casual. It was her second surprise, a more sober one than her companions drinking beer in a typically Australian way.

Although asked in a simple way, Theodora felt initially she should be guarded even though she was with her professor friend who she thought would support her if made some kind of diplomatic *faux pas*.

In the back of her mind, she knew Lee was a cunning conversationalist and she did not know the 'counsellor' or Conrad Wong. Two of them could be summing her up, perhaps even the three of them, for some unknown reason.

Taking a big breath, she decided against being guarded. She responded in Mandarin using a form of address indicating she was among equals, a somewhat risky move when two of her three companions were strangers and older. It could have been offensive but she thought this might give some balance to the conversation. In any case, they had left themselves open to a discussion among peers by asking for her opinion on such a significant subject.

She said: "Don't know about the wisdom of combining vastly different policies—economic and defence. I don't think many people have a well-informed opinion on this. I would value your comment."

She really did not expect their opinion, so quickly explained: "For me, it seems problematic for diplomats and politicians of democratic societies to attempt this game with non-democratic diplomats and politicians. It would be hard to maintain a two-policy balance. Emphasising one policy may mean de-emphasising the other. I think the very least it would do is create confusion. The likelihood would be it would lead to defence policy planners of the non-democratic party being suspicious. I would be in their position.

"Having said this, there could be a common problem in nearly all countries and it's about personalities. Regardless of the democratic or non-democratic nature of the country, I believe ambassadors and high commissioners are very different people from trade commissioners, even though all may have the same national security interests at heart.

"I am the least among us here to know this for certain," Theodora said, "but since you asked me for an opinion and I am in the hot seat, I may as well be direct. These two policy issues are separate and too important for any country to try to attempt this kind of experimental diplomacy with another.

"The interpretation of policy issues is critical, especially if they are mixed. The words, construction, mode and tone of policy messages at home are important, and even more so when dealing with other countries that have different cultures, languages and political sensitivities."

She added: "Let's be straight forward—if I could have another cocktail, please—we are talking about the USA and the PRC hypothetically. Even if bi-national defence issues and bi-national economic issues are considered separately, both parties can end up between a rock and a hard place. And there are interpretation matters to consider. For the PRC, there may be no clear distinction between a message *for* them and a message directed *at* them. Both could be offensive.

"So, to answer your question, Wong, any kind of diplomatic message to the PRC involving defence tied to trade would be like sounding the *taiko*. In other words, it could be a warning or, at the very least, an ear-bashing," she said.

During the conversation, Theodora spoke briefly about her sisters and their qualifications. In a veiled response to Lee's offer of assistance concerning UN and UNESCO job prospects, she indicated she could be interested in organisations providing simultaneous translations for large scale events, particularly those involving defence or economic development.

She added that her elder sister was more interested in the admiralty aspects of international law and was also highly fluent in Mandarin. Both she and her sister had an intense interest in a range of computer science specialties from satellite and fibre-optic communications technology to cyber security.

By this time, Theodora also had the attention of Lee and Wong in her younger sister's interest in constitutional law and Asian, Middle Eastern and Pacific Island languages. Their Japanese host was similarly interested.

After the impromptu musical performance, Theodora and Lee left the Japanese Embassy with Theodora wondering what she had gotten herself into.

On the way to the airport, he tried to resume his push for simultaneous translation prospects. He said that many translators in the UN were highly qualified in several of the five languages covered by the UN.

"Firstly," he said "you need accreditation. This will qualify you for membership of the International Association of Professional Translators and Interpreters and or the International Association of Conference Interpreters. With your language skill, you should barely need to apply. You will breeze through both. I may be able to arrange a range of interviews with global executive search executives working for the UN and private organisations."

He added: "There are generally up to 14 simultaneous interpreters (SIs) at any one time servicing the General Assembly, the Security Council and the Economic Social Council of the UN. A general requirement of these SI staffers is to live in or near New York or Geneva where UN offices have a total staff of 1,600 or more, not all translators or interpreters, of course. So, residency may be an issue. But you do not have to be a staffer to be an SI. The UN has about 100 permanent SI staff and hires about 120 accredited freelancers. So, there may be a freelance opportunity if residency is a problem.

"Besides conference work, there is judicial, escort and public service work. Escort work involves interpretation of one-to-one and sometimes one-to-several conversationalists. I might say there is a wide range of well-paid and satisfying SI work in the private sector, perhaps more remunerative than in the UN, but I hope you will be interested in international relations work where your skills will be more broadly useful."

He concluded his sales sermon saying: "I leave it to you."

In any event, Theodora had enough of the hard sell which was uncharacteristic of Lee and, therefore, must have been highly well intended.

Theodora, Angelina, Lucinda, Beth and Judith agreed to hold a cocktail party for current and old contacts. It would be at the Robertson house and would be paid for by Beth and Judith. Angelina invited Col Weingraf who suggested to

Angelina that Theodora and Lucinda be asked to call into the ICCC office for an informal meeting soon after the party.

Theodora invited Lee and Wong to the party. Angelina thought it useful to brief Sir Jonathan about Wong who could have useful legal and defence contacts in Singapore and could even be familiar with the firm's new Singapore admiralty law associate.

The invitation list was considerable. It included ICCC board members, the senior lecturer at the Queanbeyan cyber security course, the vice chancellor and pure mathematics lectures of the GSU, the head mistress of the Adelaide college the three sisters attended, and the various Mandarin, Pure Motu and Dari tutors.

Beth and Judith agreed to meet the travel and accommodation costs of Steve and Chin from Boogardie making the group quite diverse.

A particular friend of Lucinda on the list was Associate Professor David McMahon, a constitutional lawyer who assisted her in her post-graduate constitutional law studies.

Of distinct Irish descent with a donnybrook attitude to debate, Prof McMahon was particularly familiar with Pacific country histories, traditions and politics. He had been appointed a visiting fellow of the Papua New Guinea University and adviser to several of the 16 members of the Pacific Islands Forum.

He also had been an invited Australian observer to a number of meetings of the Association of South East Asian Nations (ASEAN) which, at the time, comprised Thailand, South Korea, Indonesia, Singapore, the Philippines, Vietnam, Myanmar, Brunei, Cambodia and Laos, and was expanding, although some members were accused internationally of dictatorial governments.

Of dubious distinction was his deportation from Fiji after several long-term teaching assignments there hosted by the Fiji Government. On more than one occasion, his views on military government and constraints on the judiciary became intolerable and earned him a one-way ticket home.

He was now virtually persona non-grata as far as working there was concerned but wrote profusely on Fijian politics, law and economic development in ways his peers in the West and, indeed, most Pacific nations, thought were well reasoned. The Fijians even had a kind of love-hate relationship with him but had to maintain his exclusion.

He advised an Australian national security think-tank which prepared occasional position papers for the government outlining Asia-Pacific policy options. He sometimes was taken into the confidence of the Australian Secret

Intelligence Service (ASIS) and other relevant areas of the Department of Foreign Affairs and Trade (DFAT).

While the union between Prof McMahon and Lucinda was due, in large part, to their common interest in constitutional issues of several economically unstable Pacific Island States and the influence of the PRC on their sovereignty, there was also a delitescent likeness between the two. This was mainly because of his forthright attitude and her single-minded approach to investigative study. He did not suffer fools and she stuck to her views until proved wrong. This commonality formed a bond.

Both grew up in poor households but she had a happy upbringing while he lived in a loveless family. They knew very little about each other but did not speak openly about their childhoods. Despite the bond and her curiosity about what type of person he really was, she wanted to know less about him than she suspected. She thought getting too personal could have distracted from their professional exchanges.

He suffered occasional epileptic fits which Lucinda witnessed a few times and provided assistance which necessitated fairly close personal contact. She supposed these may have contributed to his readiness for robust argument and what some of his colleagues regarded as a chip on his shoulder.

He was one of the extraordinarily mixed and varied personalities invited to the party.

Earlier on the day of the party, Beth sent a car to pick up Chin and Steve at the airport and take them to their hotel before waiting to deliver them to the house.

Col Weingraf arrived early and asked the sisters to meet him in an adjoining room where he announced that the ICCC would like to meet Theodora and Lucinda accompanied by Angelina at a precise date and time, even though he expected Angelina would have forewarned her sisters of the invitation to meet. They would gather at the ICCC's office in Sydney to 'discuss a confidential matter of likely common interest'. Clearly, it was about career prospects and was not to be spoken about until their Sydney meeting had concluded.

They agreed and returned to the living room where they continued to welcome guests. The pre-party meeting took less than a few minutes.

The three sisters spent considerable time speaking with their old friend, Chin. "I still want to learn *Bokator* even though, as you say, there's no teacher here," Theodora told Chin.

"Yes, I said before…no teachers here," Chin replied. "You take holiday to Singapore. I introduce you to master. Not give *Bokator* lessons openly but you convince him give you lessons privately. You need plenty time."

In the evening, the sisters took Chin and Steve to the ethnic food centre of Adelaide where there were many Chinese restaurants. Steve said he could 'handle any kind of Chinese food'. After some Mandarin discussion with one restaurant owner, they were given an under-the-counter menu and selected a relatively hot range of Szechwan-Gansu Kansu dishes.

Spectacular was a traditional three-times cooked duck with sun-dried black chilli, a dish Chin had not tasted for many years as it took a long time to prepare and needed ingredients not easily available where he lived. Steve bravely suffered the consequences.

Chapter 8: Syntony

At the ICCC meeting, the Board's attention was focused kindly but intensively on Theodora and Lucinda.

Angelina was there but unaware of the impending interrogation since she was not subjected to particularly strong questioning. Observation of her at the specialised courses in Sydney and Queanbeyan provided sufficient information as to her suitability to join the ICCC.

Both newcomers felt the meeting could be to assess their suitability for membership but had no oracular appreciation of what they were in for. Being more than academically competitive in their individual and collective fields, they were comfortable in any group. If employment was the issue, they could pick and choose any organisation within limits and in their own time. They were modest but, more than anything, their own women.

They approached the meeting as an opportunity to enquire about the ICCC, largely as a matter of curiosity. They did not worry about the ICCC enquiring about them.

After being informed of the objectives of the centre, they became less inquisitive and more interested in its relevance to them.

The ICCC psychologist opened the batting. Applying the same introductory technique used on Angelina, the interviewer raised a number of miscellaneous issues in an informal way beginning with every-day matters leading to a more formal approach after lunch. To this point, it was not strenuous questioning.

Lucinda was questioned first. Theodora was invited to respond if she wanted to elaborate on Lucinda's answers or disagreed with Lucinda.

Opinion was sought on a range of issues. They covered likely reactions to witnessing at close range a major accident such as an aircraft crash, risk assessment and reaction when confronted alone with one or more armed villains, actions on observing an elderly woman being assaulted by a robust hooligan, order of reaction on being the only witness to a hit-and-run incident particularly in regard to retention of detail, attitudes to apparently lenient sentences given to convicted drug dealers, bail given to repeat offenders charged with violent crimes, actions arising from an opportunity to catch a thief in the act in public, handling and disposal options on finding a large packet of money or drugs.

Also, decision to save a life of two similarly aged persons in a suicide pact when circumstances indicated only one could be saved, the right or otherwise to carry a firearm in public, whether females should be trained in front line combat within the armed forces and comparative performance of women and men in high stress military environments.

These theoretical situations were intended to draw out attitudes about the balance between reason and emotion, natural justice and the law, gender equality and such intangibles as fairness, compassion, sorrow, resolve and temptation.

They were mixed intentionally to interrupt thought processing by limiting time and by distraction so that responses were delivered spontaneously without much time for deliberation.

The exchange with Lucinda took some time but nothing was too difficult for her. She was composed and gave sensible responses to all situations posed. To the irritation of the psychologist, Lucinda deliberately slowed the process down by deliberating on responses.

Since Theodora was silent noticeably, the psychologist thought she might not be as explicit as Lucinda and decided to press Theodora directly using even more complex questions the answers to which might indicate a degree of firmness, capriciousness or concealment about race and religion, topics not raised directly in the questions put to Lucinda.

An early one was: "Do you feel, Theodora, there might be a serious anti-Islam diaspora in Australia?" The psychologist wanted an opinion, not so much as to whether an organised collection of activists intent on anti-social actions existed, but whether Theodora thought such activists might be justified in some way.

Theodora's response was safe. Later, the psychologist framed a lengthy question still pinpointing Islam. "Theodora," she said, "let me ask you a question based on three related situations.

"Firstly, if you were a panellist at a public meeting televised here nationally in which an Islamic devotee tried to rationalise the benefits of Sharia law in a generally secular country outside the Middle East but where Islam was growing against a recent history of civil disorder and a backdrop of race, religious and social disagreement, what would you feel, say, or do?

"Secondly, let's say you were an audience participant in such a meeting, not a panel member, and able to remain silent, would you then say, feel or do anything? And, if the dialogue deteriorated into a general audience conclusion that an Islamic caliphate could be a solution to criminal behaviour and serious social inequalities, would you react?

"Thirdly, what do you think the international media would do with all this? Do you think any responses from you could be helpful or not?"

Recalling her discussions at home with Lucinda about Lucinda's studies of Greek philosophers of the fourth and fifth centuries BCE, Theodora replied: "Well, let me say, such questions, when boiled down, have a philosophical not just a religious base.

"Were I to reply in like manner to the questions, my answers might be as voluminous as Plato's *Republic,* Aristotle's *Organon* or, better still, Socrates' many unresolved and unrecorded discussions on justice. It's a pity dear old Socrates didn't document his discussions as much as his brother philosophers of the time, because many of his conclusions are true generally today, in my opinion.

"As Socrates would probably have said: 'I really don't have a clue', or something like that. While admitting ignorance and asking questions of himself and his peers, he established behavioural norms no one had thought of previously. As you know, he was put to death for his ideas by being made to drink poison, so I hope your questions are not a *venenum calix*," Theodora said with a wry smile assuming the psychologist knew the term meant a 'poisoned chalice'.

Lucinda gave Theodora a smirk in silent acknowledgement of an equally convoluted reply to the wordy interrogation.

"To be serious though," Theodora said hurriedly while seeming gently apologetic in case her comments were taken as acerbic. "I would think of what is just and right. I would act and speak diplomatically. I would hope to retain the truth but not inhibit a better understanding by those who hold differing view."

"That is all very well," the psychologist said, "but how would you do this?"

Theodora said: "Admittedly, this could be difficult when commenting on laws that are decidedly inflexible and completely incompatible with my beliefs, culture, and the legislature. While I would recognise that beliefs and practices reflect different environments, I would never give ground to those who believed in unjust or inhuman laws. That includes policy makers in some South-east Asian governments which have allowed provincial administrations to introduced Sharia law to otherwise secular provinces.

"In all sincerity, I would be interested in how you would answer your own questions," Theodora suggested, not knowing if the psychologist would take offence at the throw-back question.

As there was no immediate reply, Theodora was polite enough to desist. Instead, she gave the psychologist a way out by addressing a military question to everyone: "Can I ask the board a hypothetical question, perhaps a little more in line with the centre's interests. What would anyone feel, say or do if an accredited journalist embedded in a Western fighting group in the Middle East passed on restricted information to the public internationally through publicity against an agreement not to do so, an action that could be interpreted as informing the enemy?"

Theodora softened the question by saying that any response might be instructive for her, a less than truthful suggestion her audience appeared to accept. The tables had been turned, not intentionally but by extension of the interrogative process.

Before a board member responded, the psychologist said: "A fair enough question, Theodora. Others may have different views but I do not think so. For me, interrogation of the individual would be aimed at establishing whether the person made a mistake or communicated intelligence deliberately and whether others were involved.

"My position would be to assume the worst that is to treat the action as deliberate until proved otherwise. I would keep any investigation quiet. I would restrain and detain the person and inform my commanding officer.

"If I were given authority, I would try to ascertain if the person did so mistakenly, identify the source of approval for the person to be embedded and penalise the officer or officers involved, charge the journalist with an appropriate offence depending on the nature of the disclosure, close ranks against media enquiry and inform the relevant Australian secret service. If I thought for one moment the action was deliberate, I am sure the secret service would take care of matters."

Then the psychologist said more quietly: "This internal investigation may piss off the media but what's more important—a headline and follow-ups based on denial of the rights of a journalist or the safety of troops?"

She asked Theodora: "Did I pass your interrogation?"

"Thank you for that," Theodora said.

Addressing the psychologist directly, Lucinda chimed in. She asked about the media being pissed off. "As for your remark about the media, I agree and disagree, as odd as that sounds. As you have indicated, the fault for such an incident might be largely that of the ADF and the particular Service, not merely the person or publisher involved. In fact, it is probably mainly the ADF's fault, unless the journalist is a professional spy and the publisher a foreign hostile group which surely is not possible.

"I assume the authorities would have researched the training and political allegiances of the embedded person as well as his or her professionalism. Previous published articles, particularly commentaries, would have been instructive. If the person was a leader writer, opinions expressed in leader columns would have revealed not only the writer's attitude to certain topics but the publisher's as well. This would not be difficult today as reportage and commentary are so mixed and attitudes easy to read.

"If the ADF applied such checks, it failed to analyse the results professionally. If it did no checks at all and relied on by-lines and reputation, this also was a mistake," Lucinda suggested.

She added: "On the other hand, the ADF may be excused in some respects as defence forces of several Western countries, including the USA, do not seem to have a consistent policy on embedding journalists. The process often seems to be experimental and sometimes influenced by politicians who could be more interested in supporting publicity and not upsetting major media organisations.

"As well as this—and please excuse me for saying—the ADF does not have a great reputation in public relations. Advice from their PR departments may not be wholly reliable," Lucinda said.

"How so?" The psychologist asked a little defensively.

Col Weingraf listened attentively.

Lucinda explained: "Traditionally, former journalists form a high proportion of public relations and information staffers in public service and defence. The suspicion of many media journalist today is that those who decide to change to public service or defence work do so because the jobs seem safer and easier.

Tenure is relatively assured and the real news world has become highly competitive requiring new technological skills, a broad knowledge base and high education levels, including one or even two degrees.

"Regimentation of the public service and defence does not include the need or flexibility for serious investigative journalism. I'm not sure many Service PR people work at home or at odd hours to meet deadlines these days but I suspect media do, particularly agency reporters.

"There is also long-held animosity by news media organisations towards journalists who switch to business, defence or any other kind of public relations.

"That's not to say public relations expertise within all armed forces everywhere is ineffective. I am fairly sure military information officers in Russia and the PRC are professional propagandists guided by senior officers, some of General rank with technical, diplomatic and intelligence training.

"Again, please excuse me for saying that Western public relations chiefs in defence forces attain no higher than captain, a rank achieved by many with only one university degree, so I believe."

She said hoping she had not offended any board members but since the board's questioning conducted by its psychologist was contrived, she felt justified in speaking directly.

"But I digress. Sorry," Lucinda said apologetically.

Theodora's long-winded answers and inverse questions together with Lucinda's gratuitous opinions about ADF investigative processes and the media impressed the board.

The tone of the meeting now changed as Col Weingraf took over. He pointed to the extraordinary fit between the sisters' computer science, legal, language and regional interests and those of the ICCC.

"It is as though we were made for each other," he said with a grin.

"Ladies, our aim today is to see if we can reach agreement whereby, we help each other and our nation apply your remarkable academic skills to the field," Col Weingraf announced.

He continued: "We would not have dared to write a job description featuring your accomplishments because we would not have expected such an outcome."

He then moved closer to the two and said: "To deal with procedural matters first, we are offering three security positions dependent on all three of you accepting. We offer water-tight long-term contracts with the ICCC, guaranteed indirectly by the federal government.

"This may seem premature because job descriptions have not been outlined. Indeed, specific descriptions are not possible for what you may be asked to do. We are going a long way towards this by telling you as much as we can, perhaps more than we should.

"Let me explain firstly, the contractual nature of the positions with the ICCC is necessary because the government must be in a position to distance itself from some of your likely activities. At the same time, you need to be protected. Structured appointments, union representation, health and safety restrictions and other regulatory constraints could complicate our working effectively together and are irrelevant in the circumstances.

"Let me add that a contract is needed also because of historically poor human resource regulatory planning within government. In other words, they—I mean government—never foresaw our mission, nor could they handle documentation directly associated with complicated appointments such as this. Thus, your contracts will be with the ICCC and the prime security agency whose accounts are secret, not directly with either houses of parliament or departments.

"In effect, you will be permanent employees with all the benefits associated with permanent government positions. At the end of your contracted terms, all contracts will be renewed automatically. This is understood; it is not spelled out in small print or anywhere else.

"As counter-productive as it seems, if any of you ever wish to leave, you will have to resign as a team and will remain bound by your confidentiality agreements under the OSA. If one goes, all go. If one dies or is incapacitated, all contracts will be reviewed. Is this understood?" He said.

"As far as contractual arrangements are concerned, that's fine with us," said Theodora, "but first, what on earth are we getting into? What will we be doing? I assume we won't be like Ferdinand sniffing daisies in a paddock."

"All in good time," he replied with a smile about her fairy-tale analogy, and continued: "All expenses will be met and you will have special insurance to cover inherent risks. Insurance is not something you should be concerned about. The risks are something else. We cannot define them but we expect them to be significant personally.

"Your salaries will be identical and set initially at departmental head level," he said while holding his hand up to prevent any amazement being evident. He hastened to add: "This may seem disproportionate in relation to standard government pay levels but your work will be far from standard and in many ways unregulated.

"Now, to answer your question, Theodora, about what you will be doing, let me explain that there is a global problem behind the difficulties we face, but we are able to focus on regional difficulties only. These will be repetitive. There is likely to be little rest. I will define the global problem later but for now, you need to know something about your tasks.

"It's important to emphasise that you will be working regionally against corrupt officials of other countries, organised criminals with suspect national affiliations, would-be subversives with terrorist proclivities and, most importantly, malicious communications experts able to hack into global systems.

"While our task will be to counteract their activities as best we can, it is unlikely we will be able to achieve this without eliminating some involved…and I mean eliminate. Of course, this is not written into our terms of reference and is not recorded here…and I did not say what I just said. There will be a range of projects, or crises, that arise. These projects may not be what they seem. We have just finished dealing with one and we lost an agent as a result.

"A new and extraordinary project is ahead of us. The PRC is quietly behind the criminality we face. All I should say presently is that the project will be directed at our deceiving and otherwise neutralising certain computer technicians tasked by their leaders to acquire sensitive information and lay the groundwork for their influencing or even taking over governments in our region. And, again, the technicians may not be the only ones we have to neutralise.

"These technicians require immediate attention but so do other operational members of their team including subversion specialists, smugglers, money launderers and even corrupt foreign government officials who may appear friendly and are, therefore, among the most dangerous.

"They are parts of an organisation intent on raising funds, creating chaos, threatening their opponents and eventually replacing or controlling legitimate administrations of weak sovereign States. Ultimately, these States will achieve international *legitimacy*, courtesy of the UN, and greatly extend the PRC's place in the world, not that it is slow currently in getting there anyway by its economic and military development policies.

"A primary element in the PRC's growth is a *territorial policy* demonstrated by the South China Sea matter but strengthened in no small way by the influence of weak sovereign States, unless we can do something about this. At the very least, we have to interrupt this process. Now, the downside," he said with a smirk, "a major one is personal risk. Many government resources will be available to you but you may have to make fundamental decisions quickly, subjectively and without direction.

"Your main contact will be me, although ASIS operatives will work in-country with some of you from time to time. A couple of other national security agency chiefs will be aware of your work. Relevant ASIS operatives and security agency chiefs may be contacted in code when necessary, particularly in desperate circumstances and when I am not contactable. A dummy contact will be available for any of you to call if ever you are coerced to make a call to your team leader. When you call, you will ask for *Senior*.

"When you call *Senior,* that person, a man, will know immediately that you are facing a life-threatening situation regardless of what you say and will assume the conversation is being monitored by those threatening you. This person will be well informed, able to speak as though he is your boss and in a position to deal. I may identify that person later. It will not be me. If you are calling in a non-threatening situation and concerned about the security of the communication, you will ask for or address the message to *Junior.* That person will be me or my replacement at the time.

"Most departments will not know of you. You will not be listed in in-house government or departmental contact lists or any private, defence or political directories of any kind. Now, as for speaking with others about our discussions, I can qualify slightly what our psychologist has said. We have spoken generally—I mean generally—with Sir Jonathan about some of our common interests and told him we were meeting with you. He was checked out earlier. He knows nothing about your likely work or even that you have joined the ICCC at this time.

"Sir Jonathan is curious and knows we have an interest in your careers but he is a professional and will not press the issue until we are ready. If you agree to our offer, which I repeat, is one full-time contracted career package for the three of you, we will make him aware of your objectives and inform him that Judith and Beth are not to be informed.

"We are comfortable in letting Sir Jonathan in on some of the details of what we will be doing in due course. We do not expect him to be at risk. He is geographically, occupationally, and organisationally remote from the ICCC and is unlikely to be exposed in any way. Nor do we expect Judith and Beth to be vulnerable at any time.

"We will advise you at the right time about communications with Sir Jonathan and a particular Singapore associate of his firm who, incidentally, has been cleared locally by ASIS but not yet contacted. That contact will be advised appropriately by our high commissioner in Singapore after consultation with the Singapore foreign affairs minister and whoever the minister says should be involved in Singapore's Interpol office and the Singapore Secret Service (SSS).

"The Singaporeans are good friends and have some of the best brains in cyber technology and investigation internationally, as you know."

He added: "It may be fascinating to know you will be Australia's first covert female task force. You should be aware you will be posted separately, a couple of you outside Australia, and find yourselves in remote locations in hostile circumstances. Postings have been considered already; just needs to be twigged a little.

"Another matter is structure. There has to be a chief. The other two will be of comparable seniority, but a structure is necessary for operational reasons and will not affect salaries, conditions and decisions. It should not have a bearing on your personal relationships. I'm sure it won't. The chief will be Angelina. To rationalise her status, it may be said her position is because she's the eldest.

"Familiarisation with some of your likely offshore situations will be undertaken in Sydney and Canberra. We cannot help with your many skills, of course. Most are superior to ours and among the highest anywhere, but you will need field knowledge which is not taught at university.

"Any questions so far?" He said.

Angelina said: "Two matters I want to know more about. One is your comment on eliminating criminals in certain circumstances. To put it bluntly, this means killing people, does it not? This is beyond us. It is not a skill we have, nor one we want to have. Even if we agree to it, how do we train for it? If killing has to be done, I assume it will be absolutely necessary and done by professionals who have the skill or, if by us, in self-defence."

"Yes and no," he replied. "Of course, you may have to use lethal force to protect yourself or your sisters from being seriously injured or killed. I am sure you accept that.

"The matter of eliminating a non-threatening criminal will depend on the circumstances and whether assistance is needed. It may be that a decision to eliminate someone, who does not pose an immediate threat but is certain to pose a threat later when suitably enabled, may mean a decision has to be made and acted on spontaneous.

"Just think about it. There may be a situation that threatens national security but not your personal security at the time. Is assistance possible? Would you look the other way? It's a difficult matter which we may talk about later. Frankly, there may be no 'if and buts' involved. What is the other question, Angelina?" He asked quickly avoiding further discussion of assassination.

"The second is less concerning," she said. "Communications between the four of us may not be as secure as it should be all the time, especially if we are all in different locations and our systems are vulnerable to hackers.

"We are familiar with cryptography. We are as skilled in this area as any technicians I know here or most experts overseas. I am confident that coded messages between high-tech locations can be made highly secure but communications to or from remote places where equipment is unavailable could be time-consuming and possibly compromised before we start," Angelina said.

Before Col Weingraf had a chance to comment, Theodora suggested: "A high level of security may not be necessary in every-day communications anyway. For not-so-secret communications, we could perhaps use a secret language. It should not be difficult to formulate one. It could confound a hacker temporarily as it would not be based on mathematics, code formulae, algorisms or something ingeniously contrived in a language laboratory.

"After all, we have an affinity with languages and I'm sure we can come up with some crazy, short-term, general-purpose gobbledygook. In this case, Colonel, you, not just the three of us, may have to learn something new," she said in a barely audible voice.

He pretended to ignore the comment. Theodora continued: "I would be happy to look into this. There are a number of interesting mediaeval languages I have heard about used to communicate secretly within religious sects. It would be fascinating to modernise one of these, especially one without a grammatical base."

Col Weingraf agreed, with a little less enthusiasm than Theodora.

The sisters indicated their interest in the job offers. After a private five-minute conversation, focused largely on their concern about eliminating opponents, they accepted.

Only then, Col Weingraf revealed that a primary Singapore contact was Conrad Wong, visiting defence adviser to the Singapore High Commission in Canberra.

"Well, I'll be!" Theodora said loudly. "As I now suspect you know, Colonel, I was recently introduced to Wong by Lee in Canberra during drinks at a musical recital at the Japanese Embassy. That was the reason we invited Wong to our cocktail party at Beth's and Judith's place. I just cannot believe he is involved with the ICCC. I must say though he did ask a few pointed questions in Canberra, mainly about the juxtaposition of trade and defence policies. I recall his questions surprised me and were not easy to answer," she said less loudly.

During a break in the meeting, the psychologist acknowledged privately to Col Weingraf that the sisters were extraordinarily academic, polite, forthright and truthful but these characteristics may not be sufficient in difficult times.

She said that they seemed to be physically fit, attractive and could attract unwanted male attention overseas. This alone could lead to problems. There was little immediate evidence they could morally or emotionally handle killing someone, even if seriously threatened. They may not adapt quickly enough to dirty tricks which often involve instinctive deception. They were nice not nasty and might have to be seriously flexible for their own good.

To the psychologist, they seemed more suited to senior planning duties.

"This is not a warning," she said, "merely an observation."

Col Weingraf called the group together and outlined to the sisters the global problem he had referred to earlier. "The PRC is the main problem but cannot be our focus as it is far too extensive for us, or even any one country. Russia is a problem also and a little less in-your-face than the PRC because its focus seems to be the EU. For the same reason, we cannot broaden our attention to include Russia, although Russian support for subversives in our region may have to be looked at closely when we have the capacity to do so.

"And then there is the so-called Islamic State which is widely diverse and a difficult target. It is definitely a target," he said. "Put bluntly," he said, "I am sorry to say, the overall PRC problem is entangled with a problem in the US in our region. This makes the PRC context more serious. Let me explain our problem with the PRC. It is all about expansion in all economic, military and social areas achieved by cleverly designed, multi-faceted programs. These programs even cover the Pacific Ocean States.

"This is exacerbated by the US's relative weaknesses in the same areas, particularly its constraints in defence and economic policies, as strange as this sounds. It is the dominant world power now, but for how long is questionable?" he asked rhetorically.

"Bear with me please while I indicate briefly the comparative policies and defence force strengths. They present a worrying situation. It is clear to objective policy commentators that the US has to change from its age-old posture of *domain dominance*, as one expert put it. The change may have to be from a superior *force threat* to a conventional *deterrent;* in other words, a strategy change from *punishment to denial.*

"It is essentially a chess game with different pieces. The PRC creeps forward without major military threat despite the occasional exchange about breaching international laws. An ancient Chinese philosopher once said: you can win a war without fighting. And that seems to be precisely what is happening. Experts suggest the international response to this should be based on squeezing China's resources to prevent it from creeping ahead," Col Weingraf said.

Angelina interrupted: "But there is so much reliance on the US in nearly every respect. If that cannot be sustained, what to do?"

"That's not for us to say," he replied.

"We have to be realistic and concentrate on projects in our region, the Indo-Pacific. The wider picture is something else and for others to resolve. It is evident the balance of power is shifting in an adverse way. This is not entirely because of the PRC's military capacity and adventurism. It is disappointing to hear from some recognised experts that the US seems to be an atrophying force.

"This is the belief of independent researchers who support democratic systems of government. It is largely the fault of Congress because of ideological polarisation, narrow political objectives and weariness of extended overseas conflicts, most of which have been very costly.

"All this is resulting in less funding for US Defence and a national policy of looking more inward while the PRC is looking outwards, to the east, and influencing territories near the US," Col Weingraf said.

Angelina interrupted again: "Where does this opinion come from?"

"I'll tell you where it comes from but first, let's look at hard military facts. Firstly, let's take missiles since they are the sexy weapons, the predominant ones in any future conflicts or wars.

"A couple of years ago, the Chinese People's Liberation Army (PLA) had probably between 80 and 160 intermediate-range ballistic missiles (IRBMs) and about 80 missile launchers. These missiles have a range covering Malaysia, Singapore, Palau, Borneo, parts of Indonesia, the Philippines, the parts of the Mariana Islands and Guam. It is significant that there are US military bases or access arrangements in the Mariana Islands, Palau, the Philippines, Singapore and Guam.

"At the same time, it probably had between 150 and 450 medium-range ballistic missiles (MRBMs) and some 150 missile launchers. These MRBMs have a range covering parts of the Philippines, the Ryukyu Islands and Japan. Again, a couple of years ago, the PLA had between 750 and 1,500 short-range ballistic missiles (SRBMs) and a likely 250 launchers. These SRBMs have a range covering Taiwan, South Korea and Okinawa where the US has military interests.

"Want some more?" He said while giving no one a chance to respond. "Well, at the same time, the PLA had between 270 and 540 ground-launched cruise missiles (GLCMs) and about 90 launch positions. Yet in 2004, it is believed the PLA had no GLCMs at all. This growth speaks for itself."

Col Weingraf did not attempt to put specific dates on these statistics but suggested that the number of all kinds of missiles would be significantly higher now.

He compared some other military assets. "As if this is not enough," he said, "let's look at PRC and US submarines. A few short years ago, the US had 53 attack submarines and the PRC had probably 55. This, however, is not the full picture. Of the 55 PRC submarines, there were 36 modern ones and 19 older ones, whereas in 1999, the PRC had only 3 modern submarines and some 66 older ones, a larger but far less effective fleet then. Today, the fleets may be comparable. Again, the growth speaks for itself.

"The same type of growth is seen in PRC fighter aircraft," he said. "The PRC had about 837 4th generation fighters and 752 3rd generation fighters, whereas in 1999, it had only 52 4th generation fighters."

"OK," Angelina said. "We see your point. But again, where do these statistics come from and are they reliable?"

"Let me finish," Col Weingraf said. "The growth in PRC principal surface combat ships should be alarming. A couple of years ago, there were 48 modern combat ships and 39 older ones. While in 2004, there were no modern ones and

62 older ones. I realise these statistics have little to do with us," he said. "The ICCC is attacking hostile Chinese influence in the Asia Pacific region in our own limited way but it is instructive to know the change in US-PRC capabilities militarily."

Angelina took the opportunity to restate her question: "That's fine but I would still like to know where these statistics came from?"

"The figures are not secret, although the very latest ones would be," he said.

"The estimates I have mentioned are contained in an excellent report, 'Averting Crisis: American Strategy, Military Spending and Collective Defence in the Indo-Pacific', issued by the United States Studies Centre at the University of Sydney, 2019. The centre is known for its rigorous analysis of American foreign policy, economics, politics and culture. Some of the material comes from the Heritage Foundation. Missile range estimates arose from the (USSC), the Office of the Secretary of Defence (OSD) and the Centre for Strategic and International Studies (CSIS).

"Although four or more years ago, the report remains significantly indicative. One cannot get a more reliable unclassified source. OK?" He asked.

"Yes. Thanks," Angelina said.

Col Weingraf said: "Before we finish, I should repeat that the Russian bear is in the background. The love-hate relationship between the PRC and Russia has been going on for some considerable time with neither party giving anything away, but the PRC is by far the most noticeable and the most successful, not only in our region but internationally.

"While the Russian strategy includes taking advantage of any mistakes the PRC makes in the Pacific, its main aim is to play the PRC game by pretending to be supportive but covertly disrupting PRC Pacific projects. By creating distress and then overtly easing that distress, Russia hopes Pacific Island nations will conclude that the PRC's assistance is far from honest and Russian assistance is reliable. It's a complicated game which disregards Australia, and in some ways the US also.

"It's paradoxical in that the Russians sometimes do what we want to do in relation to the PRC, but beware of the enemy in friendly clothing. The clothing can change quickly as Russia cannot resist starting wars. It's engrained in its political psyche. Just look at the Ukraine, Crimea, Syria, Georgia and Afghanistan. It's even more theoretically paradoxical than this. If ever Russia combined with the PRC in a common pursuit, it could be catastrophic for

Western democracies. The restless bear and the cuddly panda could be a fearsome couple."

He added: "The PRC, however, has a lead as it has been pouring money into the Pacific for some time. Certainly, this is a costly method of developing influence and eventually controlling certain sovereign States. Russia cannot as easily buy influence. It is also a long way from our area of interest, although Vladivostok is within striking distance of the Pacific Ocean and is a major port."

Chapter 9: Tongues

After telling Judith and Beth they had accepted job offers with the ICCC, they asked not to be questioned about their duties until a further meeting with the ICCC. Judith and Beth appreciated there was a need for secrecy.

The next day, Angelina met with Sir Jonathan. She began by telling him cautiously about the meeting with the ICCC but he interrupted her: "I have been contacted by the centre already and know something of their interest in the three of you. They may even have an interest in the firm. In what way I am unsure.

"As far as the firm is concerned, you know I cannot change its direction fundamentally. What I can do, with your assistance, if you have the time now, is fine-tune our limited admiralty law service in association with our Singapore partner and whatever duties you have with the ICCC. Let's hope you have the time and there is some revenue in all this."

Accepting the changed circumstances, he continued: "At present, our admiralty law agreement is limited and reasonably promising but it cannot be all-pervasive because there are various national and multilateral conventions involved."

Sir Jonathan added: "If a serious international incident occurs in waters between Singapore and Australia and we are asked to assist, we must consider the relevant conventions and territorial and legal limits involved. Areas in the South China Sea could pose international complications. There are two countries between us, both with their own territorial limits and judicial systems that differ from ours.

"As I understand it, Australia's position regarding South China Sea disputes is based on negotiated settlements, adherence to traditional rights for innocent passage and access to and through international waters. But some countries such as the Philippines, which tend to be hot and cold on the PRC and even the US, have tried to muddy the regional situation to distract attention from itself by claiming Australia is too outwardly hostile towards the PRC."

Sir Jonathan concluded: "Our Singapore associates are happy with our few shared clients but they must be quietly puzzled about the whole arrangement, as indeed I am at this moment now that the ICCC is involved."

The sisters were enthusiastic about their new tasks and wondered about what precisely they would be doing and where they would be posted in the not-too-distant future.

At the same time, Theodora was eager to investigate several ancient secret languages mentioned at the ICCC meeting. All her previous language studies were intensive. Most carried goals. Her investigation of so-called secret languages was far less serious. She went about it in an enjoyably casual way. It was fun.

Many of these secret languages had unclear sources. They were not pure and had not changed over the years. On the other hand, Chinese was ancient and its derivation clear but political influences had changed it in recent decades, mainly in the creative simplification of script and in its popular spoken forms. The script changes in particular were unfortunate from Theodora's academic point of view, albeit better for the general population.

Her fascination with secret languages was due also to their vague mythical origins. A few were termed unknown languages, a contradiction in terms.

One, *Solresol*, had a musical basis. Another, *Ladan*, reflected emotions. Modern film makers had invented alien languages for use in the industry, some derived from these two.

Those that interested Theodora most were *Enochian* and *Lingua Ignota*.

Enochian, developed in the 1500s, was known as "the language of the Gods" and was referred to as an antediluvian language. A handful of occultists followed it today. They claimed it originated from Adam. Some words seemed to be from science and some from terms used in magic. A few scripts, written from right to left, existed today.

Several Finnish, Russian and Swedish songs had been written in *Enochian*. Critics believed it was a feeble English counterfeit and not a genuine language at all. It was all messy.

On cursory examination, *Lingua Ignota* seemed to be the most suitable to be used by the sisters when appropriate. Etymologists believed it likely to have been a private language. It was so old that it was barely applicable to present day communications.

It was said to be devised by Hildegard von Bingen in Germany around the 1100s and based on Latin and German. Hildegard was a Christian mystic, composer, writer and medical scholar. For some time, she ran an abbey where the language was used among nuns to discuss secret matters.

Theodora discussed *Lingua Ignota* with Angelina and Lucinda. She explained: "Complicating its current use is the lack of modern words not known in Hildegard's time, but this could be an advantage. We can add English, Malay, anglicised Mandarin and some Pacific Island words here and there and make it difficult for others to decipher. Some English words could be coded."

She revealed: "There are many words in *Lingua Ignota* describing known flora and fauna. Others are of no value to us, mainly because some plants and animals either no longer exist or descriptions are wrong in botanical and zoological terms. Hildegard was a highly skilled polemic person and was regarded as the patron saint of controversial debate, so much so that she was praised by the Pope at the time, Eugenius 111. This makes the language a little more fascinating than the alternatives," Theodora suggested.

"While inaccuracies and controversy are in our favour in reworking the language for our purpose," Theodora continued, "there are sufficient original words for us to work with. For instance, times, dates, days and numbers are available: *Archindols* is June, *Zigionz* is July, *Hoizka* is Saturday and *Dizol* is Sunday.

"Some key words of possible use for us are *Miskil* for sister, *Vrizeltin* for spy, *Durziol* for soldier, *Sarziz* for imminent military attack or battle, *Mazanz* for knife or weapon, *Sparfoliz* for investigator, *Cuz* for opium, *Zimzitama* for army, *Auiriz* for captain, *Dunschia* for dock or port, *Bisianz* for banker, *Iuriz* for judge, *Maliuzia* for whore, *Uirueniz* for fornicator and *Bizioliz* for drunkard.

"Quite a few words are of an ecclesiastical nature. Many of our common words have no clear equivalents in *Lingua Ignota*. So, when we use some ecclesiastical words, we really mean the most likely modern equivalents. For instance, there do not seem to be words for assassin or murderer but there is a word for executioner, which is *Moruzio,* and there is a word for exorcist which could be used for torture.

"And we can mix things up further, a bit like mulligatawny; it has many unknowns in it. What about using *taiko,* the Japanese warning drum? We could use it as a warning signal. I am sure we can add a few Dari and Pure Motu words to the recipe. I will take my hat off to anyone able to decipher a message easily and quickly in our version of *Lingua Ignota*."

Before Theodora had a chance to continue with more suggested translations, Angelina interrupted and said: "Hold on a bit. We should do all this in an orderly manner."

Theodora said: "I agree. We don't need an alphabetised English glossary of *Lingua Ignota*. As long as we are sure there are enough *Lingua Ignota* words available and we can replace or disguise meanings, I'm satisfied. After all, our purpose is not to develop an unbreakable code. All we need is a language for brief messages that temporarily confuse interceptors and provide sufficient time for us to undertake or respond to an event."

Angelina added: "If we are going to use code names for ourselves and the enemy, let us use *Lingua Ignota* descriptions. We are the 'angles' so let's use the translation *Aieganz* for ourselves. And let's use the word for 'devil', *Diueliz,* to refer to a collective evil or enemy. Thus, *Diueliz* is impersonal, not a person. It could be an organisation, a group, an entity, or a principle, but not a principal. People can become members of it. We should refer this to Col Weingraf for his opinion, but it sounds good to me."

Theodora and Lucinda agreed.

Angelina said that numbers could be used almost as commonly as words in some messages and suggested they use Dari and Motu numbers from one to ten, even though some were difficult for non-linguists to pronounce.

Dari numbers were: *yak* (for 1), *du* (2), *se* (3), *chahaar* (4), *panj* (5), *shash* (6), *haft* (7), *hasht* (8), *noh* (9), *dah* (10).

Pure Motu numbers were: *ta* (for 1), *rua* (2), *toi* (3), *hani* (4), *ima* (5), *tauratoi* (6), *hitu* (7), *taurahani* (8), *taurahani-to* (9), *gwauta* (10).

Angelina added: "If Latin words are to be used in coded messages, slightly inappropriate ones could be selected to add to the confusion of others while being clear to us. Full sentences would not be necessary."

Herein, *Lingua Ignota Excogitar* became the improvised version of the sisters' secret language.

Part Three

While awareness was aided by the colours of the skies, the seas were unknown; the sisters had to rely on the navigational skills of their nautical minders, all the time unaware of the ruthlessness of Ares and the necromancy of Circe.

Chapter 10: Deployment

An ICCC working meeting was arranged with the sisters. Most members attended. This time, Sir Jonathan was invited and asked to sign a confidentiality agreement. He did so and the sisters reaffirmed their allegiance to ICCC.

Addressing the sisters and Sir Jonathan, who were seated at desks equipped with monitors, Col Weingraf said: "Now let me tell you about your so-called *Diueliz*. I agree with you, *Diueliz* is an impersonal entity," he said. "All this is on your monitors. Please memorise. The hard drives will be removed after you leave the building but you can stay here as long as you wish."

After a pause, he repeated that the PRC was the ultimate enemy but it could not be confronted.

"Diueliz is a collective. Some members are organised and some are not. Thus, we have to know 'What, Where and Who' before we can do anything," Col Weingraf said.

"To establish 'What' it is evident we need to be definitive. We know already *Diueliz's* activities are designed to befriend, influence and control selected sovereign Pacific and near Indian Ocean States using a carrot-and-stick approach. Its approach includes, on the one hand, disrupting administrations, promoting revolutionary ideas, distributing untraceable propaganda, corrupting officials, disclosing Pacific Island associations and treaties as deceitful, intimidating certain organisations and even assassinating people seriously opposed to their interests.

"On the other hand, providing aid and grants, offering cheap loans that could never be repaid, making pseudo-philanthropic offers, assisting development projects, offering small business finance and providing a range of social community services. This kind of thing can lead ultimately to supporting Pacific Island States to consolidate into internationally recognised blocks critical of the West. Specific definition of goals will enable us to counteract effectively within our means.

"The 'Where' needs to be pinpointed for the same reason. We cannot be too diverse territorially. *Diueliz* sees target nations as those that are politically weak, economical fragile and socially diverse leading to community animosities of various kinds. The Solomon Islands is a case in point," Col Weingraf said.

He then categorised several target States, the modus operandi of *Diueliz* and countries unlikely to be targets.

- Known Pacific Island targets included: the Solomon Islands, Papua New Guinea beginning with Bougainville and New Britain, Tuvalu, Kiribati, Vanuatu and Tonga.
- Pacific Island countries unlikely to be targets included: Indonesian New Guinea for obvious reasons, Fiji because of its nationalism and strong armed forces despite continuing racial problems, Western Samoa because of its proximity to American Samoa, Nauru because of its desolation and inevitable demise, the Cook Islands and Tokelau because of their New Zealand links, the Wallis and Futuna group, New Caledonia and French Polynesia because of their French connections, although these connections seem to be weakening, and the Marianas because of their attraction to global oceanographic interests.
- Other unlikely were the Caroline Islands because of their federated arrangement despite their western extremity being close to the terrorist hotbed of Mindanao in the Philippines, and the Marshall Islands because of the presence of a US missile base there.
- Because of the structure of *Diueliz,* targets and non-targets were not set in stone because not all members were under instruction of a central body, and may act independently.
- Nevertheless, there was a regional modus operandi which was to form blocs of target nations, establish their strength, demonstrate their representative nature and demand seats in the UN. The blocs would replace existing forums which would be relatively easy to replace. Ultimately, these blocs would display antagonism towards Western capitalistic constitutions, support a socialist or communist approach to government and effectively share with or render control of the States' land and sea territories to the PRC.

- Indian Ocean targets included: the Maldives which already demonstrated popular discontent with their governments. Perhaps Madagascar would be a target in due course.
- Indian Ocean locations not of interest could include: Christmas Island and Cocos Islands because of their Australian connections, Reunion because of its French affiliations, and Sri Lanka because of its association with India, although the Indian connection may be fragile because of the continued concentration of Tamils in the north and their disconnection with the central government in Colombo.

Col Weingraf outlined a few of the many known capabilities of *Diueliz*. A highly significant one was PRC funded technology that enabled the group to tap into, collect and select confidential messages in real time from fibre-optic marine communications cables, something that had not been possible until now. This technology made *Diueliz's* arsenal of subversive weaponry formidable.

"*Diueliz's* spread of interests, particularly its threat to fibre-optic marine communications cables systems, calls for attention now," he said.

"It also indicates your postings, ladies, which have been finalised accordingly," he concluded.

Angelina would be based in Perth. She would have a watching brief covering the Maldives and nearby areas, as identified.

Theodora would be based in Singapore with a South-east Asian brief. She would pay particular attention to the Philippines.

Lucinda would be based in the Solomon Islands with a brief covering also Papua New Guinea, limited parts of West Papua/West New Guinea and certain other Pacific Island States.

"I will be available almost anywhere but will spend most of my time in Perth, Alice Springs (Pine Gap), Darwin and Canberra," he said.

He built on Theodora's secret language and Angelina's angle code of *Aieganz* and proposed the use of specific code names.

"I agree with the angles and devils codes but suggest the ICCC team to be known *Aieganz* 2; this number intended misleadingly to suggest two persons and only in the team should the code name be revealed. Angelina's Perth base could be known as *Aieganz* 5, a similarly misleading number. Likewise, Theodora's Singapore base could be known as *Aieganz* 3 and Lucinda's Solomon Islands base could be known as *Aieganz* 4.

"The simplified code name, *Aieganz,* would not be used on its own, other than if the code had been compromised or attempts were being made to break it," he said.

Theodora said: "Col Weingraf, the code names are clear enough as are the generalised threats, but can you tell us about specific *Diueliz* activities we must attend to? Is the attack on communications cables our first project?"

He replied: "Yes. For the benefit of others in our group today, I want to define the communications cable system and its significance first and later outline some counter methods and weapons we have, even though you ladies are familiar with the technology.

"There are significant connections between communications cable tapping and State subversion. One is revenue. Funds earned from one can assist the successful execution of another. It's as simple as that. Some retrieved data may be used to blackmail legitimate transmitters.

"Also, stolen data can be manipulated to demonstrate to target States that no one is interested in the welfare of Pacific Island States and near Indian Ocean communities, despite the rhetoric voiced in the UN and various regional forums. Not a lot of manipulation may be needed to achieve this. This is providing, of course, suitable information can be anticipated and separated by *Diueliz's* IT experts from the mass of data retrieved, even in a one-second transmission. We believe they have the technology from the PRC, as fantastic as this seems.

"There is no doubt that much confidential data is highly toxic. Pernicious messages are exchanged widely in the belief they are safe. Some are admissions of bad intentions or guilt. Others are indicative only or disguised in diplomatic language. The candour in such messages can be damaging.

"These messages cover a wide range of topics, such as neglect of the destructive effects of climate change, racial problems, a plethora of resources ignored by careless administrations, government corruption, cheap local labour used overseas by developed countries, forums set up to examine economic and social development reforms amounting to little more than talk-fests and trips for the boys and foreign economic aid and other funds largely returned to donor organisations in the form of consultant fees, travel costs and various perks.

"When incriminating messages are acquired, the argument can be put by *Diueliz* to target States that the paltry support and funding provided is meaningless, if not serving the self-interests of others," he said.

Col Weingraf explained further: "It is the offence behind this kind of manipulation that could be a major influencing factor in some Pacific Island States relying on *Diueliz* to reveal the *truth*. This strategy to subvert target governments is clever.

"Now," he said getting back to Theodora's question. "Let's look a little at the fibre-optic marine communications cables of interest to us. Of course, the main concern is the new technology *Diueliz* appears to have to tap into, separate and select data in or near real time. A particular threat is to a strategic undersea fibre-optic telecommunications cable system that links Perth to East Asia, Southeast Asia, the Middle East and Europe.

"Five commercial cables make up this Australian system that carries internet, phone, multimedia and a range of broadband data applications amounting to no less than ninety-five percent of all of our international phone and internet traffic, although most companies have no idea how their communications are delivered."

Angelina interrupted: "That's right. The volume of marine fibre-optic communications cable data dwarfs satellite traffic."

Col Weingraf allowed her to continue: "In total, there are millions of kilometres of these undersea cables any one of which can carry tens of terabits per second, whereas satellites carry higher latency and have a capacity of only megabits per second. Other Australian systems include a couple of cables that connect Sydney to the United States across the Pacific via New Zealand, Hawaii and Fiji, but I assume, Colonel, our immediate interest is the Perth-to-Europe system.

"Finally, our systems are part of 317 that criss-cross the oceans globally. Many are connected making the network structure highly complex. The cables through the South China Sea are of crucial significance in view of the PRC's development of military bases on newly built islands and the likelihood of requiring notification or approval for access. In fact, restrictions exist already, although they are being resisted," she said.

At this point, Col Weingraf held up the discussion to give Sir Jonathan time to comprehend the scope of the global cable system.

He went ahead: "Rightly or wrongly, interception of this traffic is sometimes undertaken by friendly nations one way or another but the conventional method is primitive. It is problematic, unreliable, imprecise and time consuming. More importantly, it requires a massive team of spies who handle data on or near land, know when crucial information is to be sent and have available funds for large pay-offs.

"I should say spying on each other is only revealed by whistle-blowers and is not admitted or denied, unless political pressure requires responses. But it is universally understood and silently accepted by most governments as a reality of modern international intelligence work even though it is highly inefficient. Of course, it does not involve *Diueliz's* new technology.

"Conventional wisdom has been that interception could be done only by nations with large funds. If deep-sea cables are targeted one would think the equipment needed would include submarines but *Diueliz* does not have submarines. Their new technology does away with submarines and does not necessitate deep-sea work.

"We know *Diueliz* is working with technical experts in or with access to the telecommunications companies that own and operate the cable systems. There is evidence to support this including bribes given to senior staff for information about transmission schedules. And we can cautiously predict scheduled times for important messages based on conferences, seminars, meetings, and other events in a given area," he said.

He said eliminating a threat could only be achieved in a limited way. It should be dealt with relatively independently. However, it was necessary sometimes to involve countries near susceptible cable links, particularly around Singapore, where fortunately government detection skills are good. Otherwise, we like to do our own counter-*Diueliz* work.

Trying to combine action by friendly nations generally against *Diueliz* could create a division of effort, may even lead to mutual suspicion about direction and leadership and might not have an easy passage through the political filters of government.

Summing up, he said: "Sometimes illegal methods have to be used to counter illegal activity."

"Our strategy is to use a small group with modest resources that can be concealed in national budgets. Costs mainly include offshore surveillance and staffing. The purchase of advanced technology is cost-prohibitive for us but we have the best brains in the business now," he said bowing to the three sisters.

Largely ignoring the compliment, Angelina said once a site was identified and an attack expected how much planning had to be done.

She then launched into a barrage of comments and questions: "It sounds like transfer stations and nodes are the obvious locations within identified sites we can manage. The management of these locations is the responsibility of telecommunications companies, hardly the most responsible organisations in the world. How can they be trusted? We have to know about the composition of the boards of these companies and whether the governments of the countries where they are domicile have adequate security.

"Are there any silent investors and, if so, are any Chinese? Do these companies out-source the security of transfer stations? Are there likely to be potential whistle-blowers on their boards; almost certainly not? Who undertakes sea patrols of cables and how far out to sea do these patrols venture?"

Theodora joined in: "Do we know for certain if *Diueliz* is somehow represented in the management of any of these telecommunications companies? Is their management local, regional, or international? If we are successful in counteracting a *Diueliz* attack, will this have a significant impact on *Diueliz's* operations or will it just move to another site?

"How do we distinguish a real cable attack to acquire data from a decoy attack without conducting a costly inspection? Can we trust others to inspect a potential attack site because we certainly will not be able to undertake routine inspections? How many attacks or instances of damage are recorded along our cable system?"

"Stop. Stop. Please, ladies," Col Weingraf said excitedly. "You have a habit of doing this: ask a question and expect an answer all at once. Your questions are very enlightening, but we have to remind ourselves of the background and consider one thing at a time.

"Before we examine these types of questions, we should define the fibre-optic marine cable system of interest to us. Let me describe the system for the benefit of Sir Jonathan and a couple of others here with us. I know Angelina knows all about this but all the same...okay?

"Our system is known as the 'South East Asia-Middle East-Western Europe 4' system, commonly known as *SEA-ME-W 4*. It covers Australia and Britain and connects either directly or through branches Indonesia, Singapore, Brunei, Thailand, Vietnam, the Philippines, Hong Kong, the PRC, Taiwan and Japan as well as Malaysia, Myanmar, Bangladesh, India, United Arab Emirates, Saudi Arabia, Algeria, Sri Lanka, India, Pakistan, Djibouti, Oman, Egypt, Portugal, Gibraltar and Britain."

Angelina stood up and seemed to assume a co-chair position momentarily adding: "The *SEA-ME-WE 4* system is massive. It is 18,800 kilometres long and is part of a 39,000-kilometre regional structure developed and managed by 16 telecommunication companies. It's massive. If I can pre-empt you, Colonel, we will be interested in less than one kilometre section of the cable likely to be attacked."

Col Weingraf tried to narrow the discussion. He said: "There have been attacks on our system in our area of responsibility recently but we are unsure precisely where, and yes, Angelina, it will be a very small area so we have to be precise.

"Somewhere between Penang and Medan, a stretch of less than 300 kilometres between Indonesia and Malaysia is a possibility. This is where sea traffic is heavy servicing commercial fishing and tourist communities. There are diving excursions for tourists day and night. It is also where territorial waters are constricted, where drug and people-smuggling is not significant enough to attract unscheduled naval surveillance, where port facilities with small to medium scale ship repair services are available and where all manner of vessels are located. Conditions favour attackers.

"A consideration is that key cable elements, such as nodes, are in shallow water near fairly large towns where plant and equipment are available. It is where cables could be accessed. This is far safer for criminals than the open sea," he concluded.

Angelina agreed. "*Diueliz* would surely focus on land based or exposed low-water repeaters and nodes."

She thought that, while thinking about possible sites, it useful for all at the meeting to talk a little more about telecommunications and technical aspects of cables. Knowing the answers, she asked Col Weingraf rhetorically: "With this huge infrastructure and the financial interests of the telecommunications consortia involved, quite apart from customer reaction to disruption, surely there are high-tech measures already in place to protect cables."

"Yes, Angelina," he said answering the question mainly for the information of others. "There is a degree of protection but it is inadequate. There are some armoured and alarmed cables but the best protection is surveillance, and this is not always practical. While undersea cables are flexible and traffic is less affected by environmental factors than satellite and radio communications, the main hazards are accidental breakages by ship anchors and submarine earthquakes, as much as one per week internationally."

Col Weingraf added: "Deliberate damage of cables as a distraction is likely to be in deep water removed from major sea lanes and fault lines where repair services are not so readily available. Work in these waters is time-consuming giving criminals a decoy option and time to attend to targets elsewhere."

He said: "Generally, most politically motivated attempts to cut cables to disrupt communications have been during wartime. We don't expect damage to be done openly by any government unless war is declared. Our cable system is exceptionally sophisticated and no one benefits in the long term these days by cutting cables simply to damage systems other than *Diueliz* which may do so for decoy purposes. Their primary interest is information.

"A few rat-bags have stolen lengths of cable and sold them on the black market but these guys are caught easily and prosecuted. It's not damage we are worried about. It's tapping into cabled communications using sophisticated technology," he said.

Changing the topic, he said: "I want to describe another highly sophisticated set of weapons of concern to us. It has nothing to do with fibre-optic marine cables but is even more indicative of the level of technology available these days."

While noticeably restraining himself from immediately naming the weapon, he continued: "This weapon is available to us but could be used against us in a recriminatory do-or-die act if we do not kill off *Diueliz* effectively. Another problem in using such a weapon against *Diueliz* is that it is most effective against large physical targets. *Diueliz* does not have a large facility or present a large tangible target itself. We do. We could use it against a relevant PRC installation but that would be upping the ante and most unwise."

Predictably reacting to Col Weingraf's restraint, Sir Jonathan eventually asked: "What's in heaven's sake is this mysterious weapon?"

"Thought you would never ask, Sir Jonathan," Col Weingraf replied.

"It started a few years ago with a system called Stuxnet which is effective today. Now there are two advanced forms of Stuxnet. Let's call them Stuxnet Mark 2 and Stuxnet Mark 3. As Angelina, Theodora and Lucinda know all too well, the original Stuxnet was used successfully to destroy industrial and infrastructural operations overseas. Stuxnet Mark 2 and Mark 3 are secret, just as Stuxnet was years ago. Over to you, Theodora," he said.

Theodora apologised for her following technical explanation but said it was necessary to appreciate the significance of Stuxnet.

She said: "Stuxnet was and remains a marvellous idea featuring a strange programming language used by the Americans and Israelis to damage Iran's nuclear program by infecting a major nuclear plant's program logic controllers (PLCs) that governed the operations of generators, centrifuges and such like.

"Stuxnet resided in these PLCs for months gathering control data. When it was ready, it sent centrifuges into overdrive causing significant damage. Later, it slowed centrifuges down causing even more damage all the time indicating equipment failure. The Iranians never located the faults. Their generators, centrifuges and PLCs were examined and found to be in order.

"An interesting feature of this extraordinary language was that when the operators tried to switch off the plant, the PLCs prevented operators from closing the reactors down, although the relevant instrumentation showed otherwise. It was nothing less than a magnificent hidden programming language. It frustrated the Iranians who abandoned the facility and relocated it elsewhere putting back their nuclear enrichment program about two years," she said.

"Since then," she said, "it has become available on the open market. It still has the capacity to infect PLCs that control power plants and all kinds of large facilities. It is now an important cyber weapon available to friend and foe for a price and has led to the secret development of Stuxnet Mark 2 and Stuxnet Mark 3."

Theodora feigned to be out of breath, paused a moment, and looking at Col Weingraf asked if she should continue. He nodded.

"Now, for the two Stuxnet upgrades," she began.

"The purpose of Mark 2 is to neutralise false Stuxnet readings by reversing false readings. Instead of allowing a malicious program to damage a target facility, it protects the facility from damage and returns false results to the intruder indicating the target has been damaged. It is virtually undetectable and does not cause complications with uninfected PLCs. Thus, it provides protection to the facility operator regardless of whether its PLCs have been infected.

"The purpose of Mark 3 is to identify the origin of any kind of Stuxnet-type device in PLCs. Together with other avenues of intelligence it may be able to provide some indication of the identity of the device operator but this is not certain. Clear as mud?" She asked.

Addressing the sisters, Col Weingraf said: "Just to conclude this Stuxnet discussion, I should add that if we are caught using questionable tactics we can claim national interest, although this will not necessarily save our bacon."

For the sisters he added a tantalising ADF parallel: "There is also a significant development which puts us in a leading position in jamming technology. As you know, there is an international battle in the electromagnetic spectrum for jamming a potential enemy's airplane radar sensors. Put very simply, we now have technology that may not only blind a potential enemy's sensors but actively mislead their radar by overloading their sensors.

"We can also merge jamming with cyber-warfare; a specially equipped aircraft can fire a coded virus into the energy beams of enemy planes or ships crashing or even taking over their systems. But this is about all I can say about these developments at present. The point is that *Diueliz* may possess the highest level of cable tapping technology but we have a few technologies up our sleeves. Such technologies are unlikely to be of any use to us in our work on the ground or in the water. We are a little more hands-on."

Chapter 11: Subversion

Having defined the submarine fibre-optic communications cable threat and Stuxnet, Col Weingraf wanted to comment on particular State subversion.

Col Weingraf addressed Lucinda: "An area of immediate interest to you comprises the Solomon Islands, but it doesn't stop there. Another area encompasses parts of Papua New Guinea, particularly the eastern provinces. Since some States are culturally and geographically related and have similar economic and political problems, we may be able to look at them simultaneously until, of course, circumstances require concentrated attention.

"Many communities within these States are unaccustomed and vulnerable to deceitful social incentives, handouts and entertainment. For example, most rural and remote village communities are unfamiliar with and attracted to organised gambling. Some leaders of large social groups welcome gambling because it seems to develop loyalty. Families may become dependent on it.

"This mix is conducive to *Diueliz* concealing its tactics as long as the criminals are not seen to be part of government, do not display items of a nationalistic or ethnic nature such as flags, do not seem to be interested in stealing national resources, do not pretend to be indigenous and the men do not openly fraternise with local women.

"Subversives like to be seen to provide basic products and simple services free of charge to low-income groups. These may include cheap rice and canned fish, kerosene, non-prescription medicines, sweets, toys, education materials and even new methods of building houses using native materials, low-processed timber and wood-fired ceramics. This altruistic pretence can be effective in generating support," Col Weingraf concluded.

"Sure, but can you be more specific, otherwise I will be spending most of my time travelling between islands trying to decipher what is suspicious and what is not?" Lucinda asked.

"I cannot give you names of *Diueliz* operatives but can indicate a few locations," he replied.

"In Indonesian West Papua New Guinea or 'Papua', for instance, some operatives seem to frequent Manokwari, the capital, but I suspect they operate also somewhere near a village called Wefari which is on another island and about 100 kilometres north-west, still part of Indonesia. They spend quite a lot of time in the Solomons, presumably in Honiara.

"Wefari and, to a lesser extent, Manokwari, are in wild, heavily rain-forested country. Between November and March, these areas are difficult to access. There are small hamlets scattered everywhere in the area. On the north side of the peninsula is a larger town called Sorong and south of that is Fak-Fak. There is a road from Fak-Fak to Manokwari of about 600 kilometres but there is a large bay, Berau Bay, between Fak-Fak and Sorong.

"Enough?" He asked pretentiously. "But this geography may not be as complex as it sounds. From a maritime point of view, the Pacific Ocean is off Manokwari and on the other side there is the Banda Sea, the Arafura Sea and further down the Coral Sea."

He added: "Indonesian areas can be particularly dangerous for everyone because of roving Indonesian police, many of them new recruits.

"The Indonesian Government usually sends inexperienced officers to remote parts because little national crime is expected there. The police cannot afford to have senior officers spending a lot of time roaming all over these places. The result is that inexperienced officers on their own tend to be trigger happy because they simply do not have the experience or confidence to deal with the unexpected. So, it is not because there are few Indonesian police that makes the area risky. It is because those who are there are not good at their job. *Diueliz* operatives face the same problem.

"Having said this, if I were a *Diueliz* operative, this could be an important area for me providing I was there for short stays only, able to avoid undue attention, knew a reliable exit route and had good communications with my colleagues elsewhere. If you felt it necessary to work temporarily in this area, you would have the same priorities…but you may have a communications advantage, would you not, Lucinda; you have *Lingua Ignota*," Col Weingraf said feigning a little cynicism.

"I mention West Papua New Guinea now," he added, "so you keep its importance in mind but I do not suggest we begin or stay long there. A fertile ground for *Diueliz* seems to be the Solomon Islands, named originally by the Spanish in the mid-1500s after King Solomon in the belief that the archipelago contained great riches, including gold. To an extent this was true. The paradox is that yesterday's invaders searched and found little but today's criminals, and I might say the PRC, recognise the political and material wealth to be exploited."

Lucinda asked: "Are there local government measures in place to stop subversion and exploitation, especially in land ownership?"

He replied: "There are legal and customary measures protecting exploitation by foreigners, but experienced criminals will always outsmart island governments, and when the going gets tough, the criminals leave. The only people who get caught are the nationals who support the foreign exploiters.

"Let me add to this observation, Lucinda," he said. "Three quarters of the population of the main islands in the Solomons group survive by subsistence farming and fishing but there is a bounty of resources that most of the population cannot access. In minerals, there is gold, lead, zinc and nickel. In timber, the Solomons have some of the richest rainforests in that part of the globe. Some gold and much timber have been extracted by foreign groups but many operations ceased years ago.

"A couple of international timber corporations ripped out enormous amounts of timber, and left decades ago. One main reason for their leaving the Solomon was civil unrest. But to the point," Col Weingraf said, "we have reason to believe that at least two Australians from Bougainville in Papua New Guinea visit the Solomons regularly. They may be the same *Diueliz* operatives who are known to visit Manokwari and Wefari in Indonesian.

"These operatives may have a base in the small Solomons village of Sepi at the eastern end of Santa Isabel. From there, they could manage local collaborators in Guadalcanal and Malaita. Sepi would be a strategic location because it is west of Malaita and near Guadalcanal where the capital, Honiara, is located. Civil war based on ethnic differences occurred years ago in these two areas. This means the location is close to two major islands in the Solomons but remote enough not to be identified easily. Escape from Sepi would be easy.

"The posting of Australians may be strategic also because Solomon Islanders do not have a problem with Australians generally. Westerners like us generally do not attract a great deal of attention, at least not as much as they do in the hot tourist spots of Indonesia and Thailand. Most foreign aid programs in the

Solomons are managed by Westerners and channelled through Honiara, although China is emerging as the main 'aid' supplier.

"As contradictory as it seems, being clearly conspicuous Australians go relatively un-noticed. This means a Western *Diueliz* operative would be relatively secluded in Sepi also. When such a person travels to Honiara, they would be relatively inconspicuous there as well.

"Of course, Honiara is where the action is. The parliament and departments are there. So also, are several commodity research institutes. The judiciary and police are headquartered in Honiara, not that they are particularly effective. The town is the largest allowing for all kinds of businesses, including the more nefarious ones," Col Weingraf concluded.

Lucinda asked Col Weingraf again: "What about the other large island groups in the Solomon Islands? Some are a long way from Sepi, if my geography is anything to go by."

He replied: "Besides Guadalcanal, Malaita and Santa Isabel, all of which are centrally located, there is Choiseul, a resource rich island at the western end and only about 70 kilometres from Papua New Guinea's Bougainville. San Cristobal also is a resource rich island at the eastern end facing a myriad of tiny independent island States in the Pacific Ocean. Others are in the New Georgia Group of about 20 islands to the central south.

"So, there we have it. We don't need to go into the geography of the Solomon Islands any more than this for the present. We are interested primarily in Honiara and Sepi. This is your territory, Lucinda. We will go through the details of your posting soon."

Col Weingraf said: "Your tasks are not clear presently but are as defined as they can be and your territories as narrow as possible in the circumstances."

Next day the sisters discussed an approach, particularly for Lucinda. They knew suspicion about them must not be allowed to develop. However, circumstances would arise when one would be needed to support the other or all three would be required at the same time in the same place making concealment of identity an issue.

In such cases, apparent innocent exposure would seem a better option than hiding. Something smarter than regular holiday visits would be needed.

They thought a credible business interest that did not require a lot of time and effort could be the answer. This could permit their coming together regularly without suspicion. They agreed a modest designer swimwear enterprise was an appropriate option.

The three would be taken to be business women. They were attractive enough to parade their swimwear during marketing campaigns, if necessary. As Australians, water sports would seem natural. Corporately their presence would be plausible.

A start-up company was established as Asia-Pacific Aqua Fit Pty Ltd (APAF) with Angelina as Australian director, Theodora as the Singapore-based regional CEO and Lucinda as a major shareholder resident in Honiara.

Its headquarters was in a private residence in Perth. This was an inexpensive arrangement and gave the entity an expected Aussie base. Designs would be sourced from ICCC contacts throughout South-east Asia, including Indonesia.

A possible fringe benefit of using cheap Asian production companies could be an accidental association with *Diueliz's* operatives who often exploited labour from South-east and South Asian areas as part of their so-called assistance to economically fragile Pacific Island States. For *Aieganz 2* to access *Diueliz* in this way was more of a hope than an expectation at this stage. It was not a defined plan.

Theodora and Lucinda visited their assigned locations. Theodora's Singapore unit was in Coronation Road (West), a relatively high-priced location. It was not far from several strategic government establishments, including the Ministry of Defence (MINDEF), the Military Security Department (MSD), the Centre for Strategic Infocom Technologies (CSIT) and the Joint Intelligence Directorate (JID). She was in the thick of it.

Lucinda rented a small place in Honiara and found a village holiday house in Sepi. Because of the need to be remote and the difficulty in travelling during the wet months, Sepi appeared reasonably safe even though it was where the two suspected *Diueliz* operatives from Bougainville were believed to visit occasionally.

Lucinda's choice of Sepi meant she would be noticed as soon as she took up casual residence but there was no reason local people would be any more curious about her than other foreigners, including any Bougainvilleans. Small Solomon villages like Sepi had unspoken reputations as safe places for foreigners wanting to get away from the big cities, avoid the authorities or live an alternative existence. It was in the interests of locals not to pay too much attention to such itinerants.

She believed some basic communications equipment could be integrated with a television receiver.

Lucinda's Honiara unit was above a group of poorly maintained shops. The shops were vacant often. The local landowner was short of cash most of the time and made a point of looking after tenants who paid rent regularly, particularly the very few like Lucinda who paid a couple of months in advance. This meant the unit was relatively secure.

It could be used to house a limited amount of stock and closed occasionally for lengthy periods without attracting attention. The unit was within walking distance of government offices and one of the two main hotels.

Angelina visited her new residence on the outskirts of Swanbourne, a coastal suburb of Perth. It was close to Campbell Barracks, part of the Special Air Services regiment headquarters.

The registered office of APAF was the office of a local accountant in Perth's CBD.

On returning to Sydney after visiting their assigned locations and finalising residences, the sisters were given final briefings and a little extra agent training in Canberra and Sydney, including instruction in self-defence. Linda wished she had learned a little *Bokator*.

They confirmed their code protocols and undertook some last-minute simplification of *Lingua Ignota*. They were realistic about the use of this secret language as the very name meant 'unknown language' in Latin, and most educated people knew some Latin.

A few people schooled in the arts and history might be aware that Hildegard von Bingen had composed 'Ordo Virtutum', perhaps the oldest surviving morality play, and that her complete works on health and healing, 'Physica', had been translated from Latin years ago and published internationally but her secret language was not a focus of even those who knew of her. Hildegard used her own cipher alphabet which no one today could use, including *Aieganz* 2, as it was not typeset in any current language. In any case, it was unlikely modern-day criminals associated with *Diueliz* would know anything about Hildegard.

It was soon time for the sisters to relocate.

Each also began making contact with known supporters and others thought to be helpful in one way or another.

The main new contacts were given coded designations progressively. Established contacts were given an *Aieganz* code preceded by the letter A.

Likely, but unconfirmed, assistants would be given an *Aieganz* code preceded by the letter B.

Suspected enemies also were graded. *Diueliz-A* represented subversives, *Diueliz-B* money launders and revenue generators, *Diueliz-C* social disruptors, *Diueliz-D* corrupt government officials, *Diueliz-E* criminals such as smugglers, drug dealers and assassins, and *Diueliz-F* technicians including those engaged in tapping submarine communications cables.

Now the sisters were good to go but they had to find their own way initially.

Chapter 12: Action

And go they did but in a somewhat unexpected direction.

Theodora's first meeting with her Singapore-based ASIS contact, Terry Webb, was intended to be a simple introduction but it was far from casual.

He asked to be called Terry.

She received time-sensitive intelligence about her first task. With none of the usual pleasantries, Terry told her in no uncertain terms to consult ICCC immediately about information from Singapore's CSIT revealing that *Diueliz* planned to attack the SEA-ME-WE 4 cable on Saturday, 2 July, a little over a week away.

He said: "General details only are available but specific instructions as to locations and precise timing will follow."

He explained that the generalised information came from hacked *Diueliz* messages that were consistent with an expected behind-closed-doors announcement to be made at an international seminar at the Singapore National University on that date.

Largely using the modified *Lingua Ignota* code, Theodora sent her first secret language message to Col Weingraf and her sisters, as instructed by Terry. The English translation read:

Colonel Weingraf, Angelina and Lucinda. Warning. Threat by *Diueliz* F. Planning attack on submarine cables. Saturday July 2 here. Team help needed. Lethal force, please. Best of luck. Theodora.

The actual code read: Junior, Aieganz 5, Aieganz 4. Taiko. Instans. *Diueliz F.* Consilium oppugnare. Hoizko. Ziguinz. Rua. Aieganz 2. Durua. Moruzio please. Best of luck. Aieganz 3.

A word-by-word interpretation of the code was: Junior (Colonel Weingraf in English). Aieganz 5, Aieganz 4 (Angelina and Lucinda, code names in Lingua

Ignota). Taiko (warning in Japanese). Instans (threat in Latin). *Diueliz F* (technicians for submarine cables in Lingua Ignota). Consilium oppugnare (planned attack in Latin). Hoizko (Saturday in Lingua Ignota). Ziguinz (July in Lingua Ignota). Rua (2 in Pure Motu). Aieganz 2 (team asks in Lingua Ignota) Durua (help in Pure Motu). Morizio (executioner in Lingua Ignota) please. Best of luck. Aieganz 3 (Theodora, code name in Lingua Ignota).

Theodora was certain an attack by *Diueliz* was certain but was uncertain where.

Her request for an 'executioner' was necessary as she thought there could be violence. The word, 'please', and the comment, 'Best of luck', gave the message a degree of informality indicating a low level of priority in case of interception.

This was a quick start. She met her ASIS contact for the first time, received her first intelligence, became engaged in her first project and sent her first coded message, all in a matter of minutes.

She was hopeful Col Weingraf would send someone experienced in neutralising an enemy. Perhaps Terry was able to attend to this. Her part in any raid on *Diueliz* would be lessened a great deal if this assistance was assured. She wished Chin was there.

In due course, *Diueliz* sent two messages that were hacked by CSITS and passed on to the Australian High Commission and ICCC. They specified the location of cable attacks.

It seemed likely *Diueliz* was unaware of the ICCC team's knowledge of their plans. However, as a precaution, they added more complexity and protection to their second coded message.

The first *Diueliz* message read: "Target (SEA-ME-WE 4 cable location 30kms west of Parit Buntar between Medan [Indonesia] and Penang [Malaysia]) to be actioned at precisely 1240hrs Singapore time on Saturday, 2 July. Protection provided. To be detailed further by courier."

The second message read: "Identify, monitor, isolate, action Terumbu Retan Laut node tap (SEA-ME-WE 4 cable location [Singapore]). Specific message needed from IASDC (understood as International Aid, Support and Defence Conference) at SNU (understood as the Singapore National University) on Saturday, 2 July. Behind closed-doors advice by key-note speaker prior to main presentation at 1200hrs. Precise time to follow, probably 1255hrs. Node exposed low tide, 1200hrs, 1.54m. Will offer cover. Further instructions to come."

The first hacked message seemed too generalised. It also indicated the Parit Buntar attack could be a routine decoy to be deployed slightly ahead of the main action so as to attract the attention of authorities a long way from the real action. Its brevity and generalisation indicated *Diueliz* was unaware it was being monitored. Clearly, the real target was in Singapore.

The sisters, Col Weingraf and Terry met in Singapore. Addressing her sisters, Angelina remarked: "Saturday, 2 July, will be the day we sink or swim." As she said 'sink or swim', she secretly felt a slight need to expiate her mother's watery demise, even though she had nothing to do with Lilly's passing.

They had a little more than a week to set a trap.

The Solomon Islands and Perth had to wait.

At the meeting, Terry revealed himself as the sisters' *moruzio.*

His adoption of this furtive role indicated to Theodora that he was probably a suitable person for any such role in the future. It seemed to her in keeping with his stance and firmness when they first met.

She felt somewhat comforted that Terry was a senior official with the confidence to be protective and ability to deliver a *coup de grace* in any confrontation between *Diueliz* operatives and the sisters.

His speech, presentation and physique impressed her. He was of average height and about 35 years of age. He seemed to prefer casual clothes. She thought his day-to-day apparel underplayed his build and probably concealed any bulky items he carried. She imagined him unclothed as a well-built person but not lean and fit in a gymnastic way. In her imagination, he was a resting tiger not a racy cheetah.

Until she had an opportunity to speak casually with him, her private assessment was based only on his appearance. He was a man who chose his words sparingly, a disposition that made those who associated with him cautions about engaging in informal conversation. Because of this, Theodora wondered about him, not in any negative way but rather in expectation of finding an honest comrade with a heart. This aimless curiosity engendered a kind of remote attraction.

Theodora's desire to learn about him was not dissimilar to her habitual yearning to learn in her early language and IT studies. She wanted to learn more about this Terry because, for one reason, she was not satisfied she knew enough.

She thought one of the team could acquire useful information about the proposed attack by visiting Terumbu Retan Laut ahead of the attack but in a way that did not give the game away.

A visit might provide information about the manpower and equipment needed for the attack, the mainland support needed and the structure of the node. Ideally, it might help find out something about the *Diueliz* technology used to extract messages selectively from cables.

Theodora suggested she could visit in the guise of an APAF representative researching the Singapore swimwear market. This seemed feasible as the IASDC and the Singapore University could be expected to be interested in exhibitions of swimwear and other clothing from time to time as part of their fund raising and student interests.

Alternatively, she suggested she could possibly infiltrate the conference as a simultaneous translator but there was little time to organise this.

Terry said: "No. Maybe next time. You live in Singapore. That's too close so your direct participation is out of the question.

"But your idea of a visit is sound. Indeed, you have pre-empted my strategy, although I was thinking about some other form of cover that did not carry the same exposure. I was thinking that perhaps a husband-and-wife cover would be safer, even a local honeymoon couple. But then again, this particular area is not the most preferred part of Singapore for overseas visitors."

Theodora jumped at the opportunity to take up this line of conversation in a personal and light-hearted way: "Theoretically, a husband-and-wife cover would be feasible but we have no credible husband and no credible wife. And if we were involved, Terry, it would have to be a little more than a one-night stand. What say you?" She quipped.

He ignored her.

Theodora thought she had injected a stimulus into his routine or at least diverted his concentration in a friendly way, although his reaction concealed this. She had used familiarity to create mild embarrassment. She could do so again later to get to know him better. Now was not the time to play games. Nevertheless, the exchange went some way towards Theodora forming a character profile of this friendly *moruzio*.

He remarked he suspected Lucinda's potential targets in the Solomons could have something to do with the planned Terumbu Retan Laut cable attack. He could not be certain but thought that everything seemed connected. Therefore, Lucinda should not be involved either.

Theodora suggested Angelina. "I know time is limited but Angelina is no slow worker. As an APAF director, Angelina could be researching remote parts of the Singapore swimwear market. She could have papers to support this while being on the spot.

"Additionally, she could arrive with some convincing tourism development plan which you could dream up and present in a glossy document, preparation time permitting. She could carry a directive from a Singapore tourism authority commissioning a small tourism research project. All this could be used in the event of any suspicion about her particular interest in Terumbu Retan Laut," she told Terry.

Without uttering a word, Angelina listened attentively and with surprise as Theodora talked about Angelina's undercover role. "So, I have nothing to say about all this," Angelina observed in a friendly way.

"Of course, you do. You are the star character," Theodora said. "I'm just making a few suggestions, but a tourism project is plausible as is an APAF's market research project."

Terry agreed and asked Angelina who was only too keen to help.

He explained to Angelina that the only node near the island was connected to a telecommunications management facility about one kilometre away. It was on the coast side of the West Coast Highway near the university. He would investigate the facility further.

When time came to raid the node just before it was hacked, he would arrange with his Singapore colleagues for simultaneous raids on suspects in the nearby mainland telecommunications facility.

Terry obtained a letter of authority from the government for Angelina to undertake tourism development research. She would look into tourism integration of a group of nearby islands—Pulau Merlimau, Pulau Ayer Chawan, Pulau Sakra, Pulau Bakau, Pulau Ayer Merbau and Pulau Serayae—and assess the capacity of the group to attract and accommodate Indonesian visitors from Sumatra and Kalimantan, as well as other regional tourists. The project had to be limited to regional markets and not create unwanted attention by looking too far afield.

One of only a few small hotels on Terumbu Retan Laut was selected as a starting point as it had the most dubious reputation. It was likely to be attractive to those interested in local goings-on there and elsewhere.

It was the Blue Bird Inn known by Terry to support such extra-curricular activities as minor black-marketing of electrical and electronic appliances from the mainland and the provision of escorts, many from parts of Kalimantan, locally renowned for their beauty. Mid-level officials and local military officers from Indonesian and Malaysia quietly frequented the establishment for weekend sex.

For Angelina, it seemed a relatively safe place to nose around the area, providing she did so carefully. She was not obviously promiscuous nor the type to be searching for sex trade staff. She seemed a legitimate researcher. If anything, her selection of this hotel could be seen by others as possibly not the best choice.

While checking in, Angelina alluded to her interests. Being an unusual guest, she expecting this information would be conveyed fairly quickly to those in charge.

Word spread quickly.

The next day at breakfast, the manager introduced himself as Felix. Angelina adopted a conciliatory, broad-minded approach, one with which he seemed comfortable.

Wanting to avoid any impression that the status quo of the establishment would be disturbed by her research, she said: "I really don't know how my research will pan out but from the couple of hours I have been here, it seems very little needs to be changed on this particular island, certainly not to the Blue Bird Inn. If I find there is scope for development, it will probably be on six other islands I have identified already and the services connecting them. What do you think?"

Felix readily agreed. Lying through his teeth, he said: "Yes, we operate in a private way and any improvements would probably involve extra costs which we could not sustain. In any case, I'm not sure we want any major changes. We are just a modest family group even though we enjoy a high occupancy rate at the weekends."

Angelina wanted to indicate she knew what was going on while seeming genuine. She wanted to cut through the guff without creating suspicion or surprise. She needed to be guardedly worldly.

With a twinkle in her eye and a degree of innuendo, Angelina said: "I know costs are all important and any little extra here or there must be a good thing for everyone. No one would want to do anything about that. Indeed, one might be inclined to help the inn earn consistently more income by simply improving current services without a lot of notoriety."

She added: "Quite apart from my tourism interest, I run a small swimwear company and hope to be holding activities ranging from normal marketing events to catwalk showings of swimwear using local and some Western girls. Who knows where this could lead?"

This suggestive line continued and a casual rapport seemed to be established.

Next day Felix asked her to dine with him in one of several private rooms. It was separate from the main eating area which was a large open indoor-outdoor space that could hardly be described as a dining room or restaurant.

During a few glasses of wine and talk about the natural beauty of the surrounding waters, Angelina cautiously raised a number of questions about regulations, immigration and taxation leading to an exchange on politics and management of the region.

At one point she remarked: "It seems to some there are regional authorities that conspire with big business to exploit their communities. On the other hand, it seems some authorities are exploited by big business. It must be hard to tell friend from foe. Just a casual observation, nothing I know or want to know about, but I would be interested in what you think, Felix?"

Felix displayed some discomfort with the direction of the conversation and said: "I don't know but there is someone better able to talk about politics than me. Just wait a bit and I will get a friend you might like to meet."

She emptied her third glass in a nearby pot plant and pretended to be finishing it when Felix arrived with an Australian friend, apparently a frequent but irregular resident of the inn.

"Hi, Angelina. I'm Bernic. Would you like another drop?" He said.

Looking at the now empty bottle, she said: "Thanks, Bernie." She drew out the Christian name hoping unsuccessfully he would give his surname.

"I don't use other names. Everyone calls me Bernie, and probably a few other names behind my back," he said.

"Felix and I were having a pleasant conversation. I guess you are a good friend of his. Are you a guest or do you live here?" She asked.

They both started on the new bottle while Felix excused himself and left. Without volunteering his surname or answering Angelina's question, Bernie pondered aloud: "I was going to ask about you, Angelina, but you seem to be asking the questions. You sound like a policewoman," he suggested not so flippantly.

"Do I look like a cop; I hope not?" She asked.

She was pleased Bernie asked the question as it indicated his suspicion that she could be looking into prostitution, black-marketing or taxation. He would not have asked the question had he any idea of her real purpose for visiting Terumbu Retan Laut. Could he possibly have an association with *Diueliz?* she mused.

"Who can tell?" He replied. "I must say you don't look like a police officer. You speak with an Aussie accent, you're not the right nationality, you're too attractive and the bulges are in the right places."

Angelina then told him about her dual tourism and company interests to which he asked what department gave her the tourism commission. She promised to show him the documents which were in her room. With a meaningful smile, she invited him to have a look with her but he declined.

At this point, it was not evident to Angelina that he accepted her commission was genuine, that he thought she was coming on to him or that he suspected some kind of trap. He could be the one laying a trap. Although, she had no concrete reason to suspect him of anything, the ICCC had taught her to view suspiciously everything out of the ordinary.

"Before your interrogation," she said with a smile, "Felix and I were talking about the need or otherwise of changing anything on this island. My feeling is that we should let sleeping dogs lie and not disturb establishments on this island. I would not wish to interrupt established income streams such as they may be.

"Maybe something can be done about integrating the other islands into a common tourism package but this is my first visit and I need to know much more about the other islands. We chatted about regional authorities and big business influencing the region. I don't know how Felix and I got onto this topic."

She paused after her explanation and said: "As for your earlier remark, who can tell, you may be a cop yourself, Bernie. You look more like one than I do, and you don't have a full name or perhaps don't even live here. In the movies, that could make a good undercover cop plot."

Without an immediate response, she now felt she was able to get away with being somewhat glib. Even though much of the informality was from her, she felt able to speak more seriously without risk of alienating Bernie and he did not react defensively.

After another pause, Angelina reverted vaguely to the matter of municipal influence: "What governments say among themselves may be very different from what the world hears from them. This seems to be the way things are these days everywhere. One either works with them or against them. There's little anyone can do about that.

"I wish there was. If there was some clarity, I could see my way with my swimwear business even more clearly. I don't know if you experience this in your business, whatever that is."

While she was doing most of the talking, she assessed Bernie as no friend, more possibly the opposite. He seemed well informed locally but certainly was not forthcoming. He was attentive and interested. His pretence of being amenable seemed cautionary.

While trying as adroitly as possible to draw him out on legal and illegal aspects of business, leading hopefully to finding out who he is and whether he could haplessly comment on anything related to *Diueliz,* she remarked: That's probably the wine talking…but what I do know without the need for a glass or three is that there must be enough red-blooded guys here interested in their ladies trying on my two-piece creations to establish a market, providing there is no interference from outside.

"It would be good if the business was one-hundred percent market driven in this region and had zero per cent government involvement.

"I will have to wait and see. I have not really started yet. It may be best to test the products in a small market. Singapore seems obvious but it is large. I hope to look at areas in Malaysia that are not strictly controlled by Muslim administrations, thus Kuantan and Malacca are not of interest. Nor are many Indonesian locations like Manado in Sulawesi and Ache; it would be hard to design and sell a niqab or burka as part of a two-piece swim suit.

"The best places to start may be non-Muslim Pacific Island States, such as the Solomons and even Tuvalu and Kiribati, although these two would be small," she said.

Angelina had put a lot of burley in the water. She hoped the bait would be taken and she would learn more about any nefarious activities on Terumbu Retan Laut that could involve *Diueliz* in some way.

Early the next day, Bernie knocked on Angelina's door ostensibly to accompany her to breakfast. He said: "I've been thinking about your swimwear project and would not mind knowing more about it. Maybe I can help."

Before he asked, Angelina showed him her company documents. She thought this was the reason for meeting her privately. She expected he might want to check even though he showed a degree of acceptance the previous day. As he did not ask about the tourism project, she assumed also he had checked the validity of her commission in the meantime and was satisfied it was genuine.

All this communication with Bernie was based on Angelina's completely unsupported supposition that he could be some kind of useful lead.

Her suspicion was circumstantial and presumptive, but instinctive. There was no real evidence, and their meeting was coincidental. It was not conclusive in any way.

Still, she had a good feeling she was making headway and that he was useful. Otherwise, their rapport would have ended early. If she detected his interest was sexual, this would have been evident straight away. She would now treat him as a potential source.

The breakfast was typically Singaporean and small but she managed to stretch it out enough to engage Bernie in her research. He was comfortable with this which prompted her to say she would appreciate being shown around the local islands.

He readily offered.

"Thank you. I would appreciate it very much," she said.

"If you have the time, perhaps you could give me some advice later on my swimwear prospects in the Solomon Islands and even PNG, although these prospective markets seem unimpressive. Do you know anything about them?" She asked.

He said: "I know nothing about swimwear but I can tell you PNG would be a waste of time. I cannot help with the Solomon Islands either."

"Well, you know much more than I do having been to these places," she said.

"Not at all," he said, "I have never been to the Solomon Islands and I have only been to Bougainville in the PNG group," he told her cutting short this line of discussion as though he may have said too much or the topic was of little interest to him. He did not seem suspicious about the conversation.

"She informed him she had to leave for a while but would be back on Saturday, 2 July, if that suited him."

He agreed to show Angelina around but said he had urgent business that particular day and suggested the following Wednesday, 6 July, instead.

This could have been coincidental or indicative of his possible knowledge or even involvement in the planned 2 July attack on the cable. If so, at what level, she wondered.

"The only reason I suggest next Saturday is because I have to meet some friends visiting Singapore on the previous couple of days. But Wednesday, 6 July, sounds great," she said.

They agreed to spend that Wednesday together visiting some of the islands. If he kept the 6 July appointment, her instinct was probably wrong and she would have nothing to worry about on the island. Her only loss would have been time spent with a generally disagreeable person. More importantly, she would have contributed nothing to the ICCC project.

On the other hand, if he was implicated in the telecommunications cable crime and remained a free man, she knew full well she would need immediate protection and would never be able to set foot on Terumbu Retaben Laut again.

Even if he was arrested and put away, her timely association with him would not be seen as coincidental by any accomplices who would surely get rid of her. She was mindful of Felix who had been conspicuous by his absence since introducing her to Burnie. In this case also she would need immediate protection on the island.

Angelina returned to the mainland and met Terry to report on her discussions as she did not think it safe to phone or even send a coded message from the island.

After listening to her, Terry excused himself and made several phone calls. He returned to inform Angelina that, "Bernie spends much of his time in the Solomon Islands. He is known in Bougainville. His real name is William John Mylan, not Bernie. He has no criminal record and the Singapore authorities have no reason to detain and question him about any recorded crime. He has IT qualifications from the Queensland University.

"The authorities are trying to match him with a similar foreigner photographed visiting the cable communications facility on the mainland meeting with two nationals, both dressed in white laboratory clothing who appear to be technicians of some kind. Normally there would be nothing untoward in this as the photos are part of routine area surveillance of the facility and its surrounds and meetings between people there are common. Nevertheless, now you can take it Bernie is dangerous.

"We think we may be looking at three people, the most important from a technological point of view being the two 'white coats'," he said.

Angelina quietly congratulated herself. Her instincts were right, and against the odds.

She also congratulated Terry, not only on his watchfulness but on picking the right establishment on the island in the first place. "There may have been a degree of luck on your side," she said, "but that does not matter. You have short tracked the investigations a great deal. I still could be wandering around the island trying to pick up leads and picking up more than I bargain for in the process. Thanks."

She then kissed him on the cheek but prolonged the kiss deliberately. She did not have an interest in him sexually, and was unaware of Theodora's latent interest in him. It was a kiss of appreciation, just a little longer than perhaps it should have been.

"If you can get your 'exciting' date with Bernie out of your mind," he told Angelina, "what about having an early dinner with me tonight? We can progress our moves from here on."

She accepted.

Over dinner at an out-of-the-way restaurant, Terry informed Angelina that, "We have a high probability of capturing these two technicians and observing their cable message handling methods when we raid the facility. The raid will involve undercover staff there and will not be heavy handed until we have eyes on these two and those at the node.

"If Bernie is on site, we will deal with him. If not, we will chase him down in our own way, without the formalities. Captured or otherwise, you should always now regard yourself at risk since he is clearly part of *Diueliz.*

"You can be absent from the island from 2 July or you can remain at the Blue Bird Inn until 6 July. If you stay, there is a good chance you will be safe, even if we fail to capture Bernie immediately. You will be seen at the Blue Bird Inn, not where the action is. It will appear you have nothing to do with the raid. We will be around you there unseen but I have to say there is no certainty about safety in this game.

"It's up to you if you go or stay. If you stay, just be aware we cannot be seen with you without putting you at risk. And cannot get to you faster than a bullet," Terry warned.

Angelina decided to stay through 6 July, perhaps even beyond if Bernie escaped and remained interested in her.

Terry said: "Okay. You are in till the end…sorry, you are in till *his* end."

He explained: "Our raid on the node is a little more problematic than the facilities raid because the node is in the open and there is a time lag in our getting there on foot and in the water. While getting quickly to the node at low tide may be a little difficult, there seems no chance of them getting away even if they see us coming. They cannot swim for it, but they may have a system of destroying their technology devices or the node itself. Or they may do something we do not expect.

"If you are at the inn, Angelina, you should simply show surprise about any commotion since we will endeavour to keep the public away and the raid should not involve the inn. Nevertheless, you may be able to alert us safely if any criminals miraculously slip through our fingers and try to exit the area through the inn. If so, do not try to prevent them. Just observe and report."

The land-based telecommunications management facility looked like one of many small power transmission buildings and was alongside a high-rise residential block. It had been observed from outside continuously. Since learning of the cable attack details of the facility layout had been supplied by an insider.

The off-shore node was accessible within the normal high and low water marks. The planned 2 July 1250-hours attack, based on the CSIT intelligence, was fortuitous as it coincided with a particularly low turning tide.

The one kilometre road from the shore to the telecommunications facility was to be manned covertly on the day, as well as routes to the highway in case any targeted people attempted to escape by car.

Timing was of the essence. There would be no time for confirmations or orders. Actions were to be precise, independent and conducted regardless. In particular, coordination of the Terumbu Retan Laut sting in Singapore and the Parit Buntar decoy sting between Medan and Penang had to be coordinated carefully.

The Malaysia-Indonesia pseudo-attack by a secondary ICCC group on *Diueliz's* decoy cable attack had to precede the Singapore action by at least 10 minutes. This would provide time for the Malaysian *Diueliz* people to contact their Singaporean counterparts and report that authorities were present, thereby confirming the authorities had taken the bait and concentrated on the wrong location.

Meanwhile, identification of persons of interest in Singapore proceeded. Terry established the main ones were Mylan, alias Bernie, the two technicians and a couple of known facilities managers who had access to computer rooms.

The SSS had a *pulse remora* as a stand-by for the raid, a device used to clog up mobile phone transmissions for a short time. It would be used to block warnings by *Diueliz* in case the ICCC raid was foreseen, not conducted fast enough or something else unfortunate happened. The *pulse remora's* value depended on knowing if the enemy became aware of their bluff being called.

In this case, the critical time was around 1247 hours, between the two raids and three minutes before the node raid when the ICCC operatives were likely to be visible approaching the node. The *pulse remora* would be activated at 1246 hours, just in case. This timing would not block the Malaysian advice of the raid on the decoy there.

The plan was in place.

Both raids were carried out in a timely manner.

Five technicians and managers of the Singapore facility were arrested before they had an opportunity to close down the intercept apparatus which was kept open while experts, who followed the raiding party, investigated the technology involved. Three criminals at the node were arrested. Details of the process of accessing cable information without disturbing the integrity of the cable were collected for further investigation by Singapore's CSIT and CSIS.

These eight, however, did not include Bernie.

The team expected to apprehend him. Now they were uncertain of his precise involvement until he rushed through the inn passing Angelina who was seated on the veranda looking at swimwear brochures.

When she saw him, she barely had time to shout that she looked forward to their outing in a few days before he left on the run waving an arm indicating their meeting was still on. "Anything I can do?" She shouted as he disappeared without reply.

The Singapore raid was regarded as successful and the Malaysia-Indonesia raid 'failed' successfully.

Chapter 13: Stratagem

In case Bernie returned secretly, Angelina needed to stay in the area for a time. Her presence would legitimise further her tourism research venture and ensure her safety.

Since Angelina had spoken to Bernie about her research before the raid, she found it necessary now to visit Pulau Merlimau and Pulau Bakau, two of the islands to be researched, to gather data about prospective attractions, costs, manpower, transport and other basic services, in case he did return and keep his appointment with her. It was a simple enough task. Evidence of genuine research was essential.

Should he return, there surely would be another opportunity for SSS to deal with him.

It was unlikely similar attempts to tap cables off Singapore would be planned for some time so the focus of ICCC attention turned to the Solomon Islands because of a possible Solomon Islands-Bernie connection, as flimsy as that seemed.

Even though the Malaysian criminals thought they had avoided capture, they were unlikely to risk another real or decoy attempt in the vicinity.

Angelina had been seen here and there but not identified by any *Diueliz* party as involved in the sting. Theodora was in the area regularly, although presumably not identified as an interested party either. Even if she had been seen with Terry or entering the Australian High Commission or one of the Singapore intelligence agencies, *Diueliz* was unaware of the impending raid and probably would not have paid attention to her.

Be all this as it was, the PRC spies in the area surely would have been scrutinising all cable hacking, government subversion and other clandestine activities, even without the knowledge of those conducting activities knowingly or unknowingly on their behalf. Spying on their own colleagues was commonplace among PRC institutions. They would have been spying on their South-east Asian and other surrogates for years.

While Lucinda was out of the picture as far as Bernie and the cable hackers were concerned, she was established already in the Solomon Islands. Her tasks, however, were as unclear as Angelina's when she checked into the Blue Bird Inn on Terumbu Retan Laut. The ICCC's new primary targets were in the Solomon Islands but it was difficult to put cross-hairs on specific activities. There was no clear bull's eye. Lucinda was starting from scratch in Honiara and Sepi.

For Lucinda, subversion of the State and corruption of officials by *Diueliz* and others had to be stopped or delayed for long enough for corrections to be initiated but there was little to go on. If Bernie turned up some time, he could pose a danger.

After consultation with Angelina and Theodora, Col Weingraf visited Lucinda in Honiara, acting as a business visitor interested in APAF's need to source stock. His intention was made known through the local newspaper but not promoted beyond small business news items. He needed some exposure to avoid apparent secrecy but wanted to minimise public interest.

He briefed Lucinda on a likely course of action. "Lucinda," he said, "we have two matters to take into account. One is the possibility of Bernie or anyone else associated with the failed Singapore attempt to tap the cables finding sanctuary in the Solomon Islands and asking questions about your working relationship with your sister, Angelina.

"The other is more difficult. It is how to become familiar with government officials and lobbyists so as to be confident about those to trust, those to doubt and those who are indigenous *Diueliz* members or shadowy PRC players. We are not interested particularly in common villains. It's a tall order requiring careful screening."

Lucinda told Col Weingraf: "I will need all the assistance I can get but you cannot remain here for too long. Business visitors would not be expected to stay more than a week and you don't really look like a rag-trader."

"I am happily aware of that," Col Weingraf said with a smile. "Any complications with Bernie and company will have to be dealt with by you in the first instance. It is important that you allay any negative interest or suspicion in Honiara and Sepi. The moment you detect a potential threat, you must let Terry know through Theodora. He will sort it out if you cannot do so yourself.

"There may come a time when you have to do what you don't want to do, that is neutralise a threatening person."

He continued: "The Solomons is very different from Singapore, Canberra and any Australian state or territory. You must be confident in yourself if you feel you have to solve a problem. Many serious community issues and even some legal issues are dealt with summarily here. It's cowboy country. Just look at the main community sport—boxing. If you see a boxing match here, you will notice the contenders may not be professional, but their intensity is extraordinary. The same with rugby; the game does not necessarily stop with the whistle. You know what I mean," he assumed.

For the first couple of weeks, Lucinda divided her time between meeting government trade officials and local business people, including the hotel owners who could be interested in swimwear displays and promotional events.

She also visited a Chinese operated casino in Honiara and three management schools that catered for students from several Pacific Island nations, as well as the Solomon Islands.

All kinds of interesting developments emerged during this broadly intensive exercise but she remained mindful of the task in hand. Some of her time was spent in vocational training colleges.

Most management students had unrealistic ambitions and wanted to obtain senior jobs in developed countries, particularly Australia, New Zealand and even the United States. They underestimated local job prospects. Some with mid-level government positions enrolled in unrelated courses simply because they believed the more qualifications they had helped in applying for foreign jobs. Many firmly believed any foreign job was better than a local one, and they failed to appreciate the contribution skilled managers could make to their own communities.

She met with the heads of schools and a management college interested in motivating bright students to examine their value to local communities and government. She even offered to consult gratis in the development of mathematics, linguistic and business courses.

She muttered to herself that this kind of educational development could be a rewarding career for the right educator as the number of students interested in contributing to the nation generally reflected an imbalance between supply and demand.

This interest by Lucinda was taken by observers to be an altruistic side-line. While it was genuine, it helped lead to identifying government officials who were unlikely to be corrupt. This did not create suspicion as it was likely most corrupt officials had little interest in students developing an appreciation of local community service, unless there was a dollar in it for them.

Lucinda was seen also apparently enjoying her 'time off' visiting the casino, although this was task driven because of its Chinese management and reputation. She was aware that the PRC in Beijing had publicly expressed an interest in strengthening diplomatic relations with the Solomon Islands which had recognised Taiwan as part of the PRC in recent years. This diplomatic excursion into the Pacific was welcomed by the Solomon Islands but received hostile publicity in the United States and Australia.

She was noticed as someone who visited the casino a little more often than most non-addicted foreign gamblers. Otherwise, she did not draw a great deal of attention to herself because she was well behaved, did not accept the excessive amount of free drinks offered to players and was willing to take advice about card and dice games from time to time. She was a modest loser and an occasional winner.

She did not use her Mandarin but listened attentively when in the company of senior staff members. Over a couple of visits, she formed an idea of who were the prime-movers.

Lucinda became increasingly convinced that there was a secretive PRC connection. Community disregard of a level of PRC visibility seemed to her a sign of weakness among some Solomon Islands authorities, unlike their counterparts in Singapore.

Most locals were uninterested in national issues. They were focused on the cost of living and ethnic grievances. This was not to say there were a few administrators, particularly at undersecretary level, and some community leaders, who honestly wanted economic and social reform, especially reform of government governance policies and processes.

Even so, Lucinda had to spend time noticeably on APAF's swimwear business.

She visited Sepi several times in the first few weeks mainly to show the house was occupied, not an invitation to robbers.

Col Weingraf pondered about the usefulness and safety of getting Lucinda some Chinese assistance to ascertain whether or not the casino was harbouring subversives interested in other Pacific Island States on behalf of the PRC or was some other kind of PRC investment. Neither was known at the time.

Furthermore, it was in Lucinda's interest not to reveal her knowledge of Mandarin for as long as possible but a Chinese assistant could converse in Mandarin openly and perhaps create some ethnic rapport with management or punters.

Col Weingraf raised the idea with Terry who was supportive. He suggested one Chinese expert assisting Lucinda could be noticeable. An innocuous group or at least two would be better able to assist her in her reconnaissance work if their visits did not seem unusual. He suggested further that any Chinese group should comprise extremely different personalities.

They must not be seen as a business, gambling or otherwise nosey consortium. They should come from different backgrounds, appear as divergent in their interests and skills as possible and arrive at different times. Known Singaporean government officials were unsuitable because of the risk of accidental identification.

Who could be more unlikely to be working together than Chin from outback Western Australia, Lee from an Adelaide University and the Singapore *Labokkatao (Bokator)* master who was not part of any business or diplomatic group and was a virtual recluse in Singapore.

Chin agreed without question. He assured Col Weingraf that he had continued his *Labokkatao (Bokator)* studies and practice, even though he was now considerably older than when he first encountered the three sisters and their parents on their first day in Boogardie, later when the sisters returned from South Australia for a visit, and later still at Beth's and Judith's cocktail party in Adelaide prior to the three sisters joining the ICCC. He was a little greyer on the sides but looked healthy.

Since Col Weingraf had trouble in pronouncing the martial art, Chin suggested he use the same pronunciation as the sisters—*Bokator.*

Lee and the Singapore *Bokator* master agreed also. Lee loved the idea of an exciting change working with the sisters, particularly Theodora, and the master was enthusiastic to work with his old friend, Chin.

This back-up team seemed ideal. Each member seemed middle-aged, unconnected and a threat to no one. Their combined skills included Mandarin, management, strategic conversational engagement and a highly lethal form of martial art.

Col Weingraf referred the composition of the team to the ICCC psychologist. She believed Lee's debating strategy and opinionation derived from a closeted teaching environment and hid a strength that could translate into accommodating and enjoying unfamiliar conditions, even exciting and dangerous conditions. However, this could not extend to his being a *moruzio.* Any violence would have to be dealt with by others.

In an on-the-spot search of Lee, she uncovered his expertise in accounting which was his first qualification before moving to teaching. As a result, he provided accounting advice gratis to various organisations associated with his university. He had kept in touch with State and federal accounting regulations in case he needed this skill in retirement. He also knew something about international accounting associated with the large number of foreign students at his university.

Although, no incentives were needed for Chin and the *Bokator* master, Col Weingraf suggested the master's closed-shop teaching could be given a safe degree of transparency by the high commission which could approach appropriate Singapore security groups. A suggestion could be made that the Singapore armed forces could benefit similarly from learning something of his specialised form of martial art. At the same time, Col Weingraf would agree with the Singapore Government to keep an eye on the master to ensure the training was not offered to the broader community.

Payment was arranged for the three.

The early brief was to form opinions of leaders of the casino and related businesses and assess any worrying ambitions. If these opinions supported suspicions that they were involved in subversion and corruption of parts of the government or assistance to the PRC to control government in due course, the resulting brief was to disrupt their work and hopefully reverse any demolition of the State's sovereignty.

This was a completely gratuitous brief, not a commission or request by the Solomon Islands government. It was without local authority and could be illegal but it was right.

It was hoped also that the main instigators could be neutralised so that they could not start again elsewhere but assassinations were not planned, at least not until the kingpins were identified and their activities left no alternative. Even then, there could be less blood-thirsty methods, including framing them and using credible misinformation to create internal mistrust in the PRC. It was better that distrust resulted in them removing each other than the ICCC having to remove them. This was a lesson learned from the Russians at the end of World War One.

The Solomon Islands government would not be involved until the criminals, traitors and collaborators were revealed.

Details of a hopeful engagement of the three individuals and Lucinda—not a team as such—with the casino were clarified. This would be based separately on common interests, such as the *Bokator* master offering to assist with the security of the casino if the opportunity arose, Chin chatting about his own interest in martial arts and various districts in China, and Lee observing out loud at an appropriate time that there seemed scope for the profitability of the casino being improved. Theodora would play an invisible part.

Language capabilities would be underplayed. One dialect only would be used by each if conversations had to be in Chinese.

In case checks were made, backgrounds would be massaged. The *Bokator* master would run a Singapore street shop and practice martial arts as an aside. Chin would have a similar story using a Chinese restaurant in Perth as a business with his martial arts interests generally used for health purposes. Lee would be a retired freelance teacher of Asian arts and philosophy with a home in Adelaide. These vague parallels made it easy for the three to stick by their stories and supported their credibility.

If and when the common Australian identity of the three sisters created unwanted curiosity, it could be explained firstly as coincidental and later by all being associated with the clothing business. Any suspicions that led to further enquiry in Perth, Adelaide and Singapore would be covered by ANSA rigging addresses. However, three Australian women and three Chinese in Honiara over a given period remained a potential weakness.

Terry would be seconded to the Australian High Commission in Honiara.

Any occasional meeting observed between Chin and the *Bokator* master could be seen as innocent enough because of their common martial arts interest but no formal meetings, particularly lunches or dinners, would be held between them. Terry and Lucinda would not meet regularly, although their common interest in the high commission would be understandable. Communications would be by mobile phone and messages would be deleted or locked. Any actions necessary would be coordinated by Terry and Col Weingraf who would be resident temporarily in the high commission.

How to do all this!

And what if Lucinda's belief there was a connection between the casino and the PRC and between the casino and corrupt government officials was all wrong? Still, investigations had to proceed as if Lucinda was right.

She would concentrate on the administration by meeting with commerce and trading officials, including the younger government undersecretaries overseeing commerce portfolios. She would be wary about liaising with some of the older and more senior ministers and commissioners unless exceptional opportunities arose. Some already were suspect; some presumed honest.

Expectations and assurances were conveyed to Lee, Chin and the *Bokator* master without again going into the PRC and *Diueliz* ambitions. The three were asked separately a second time for agreement to be involved and all agreed, after which they all met in Adelaide where the importance of their assistance was restated.

All then flew to Honiara separately, at different times and with different hotel bookings. Later, they met at the high commission.

Lucinda and Chin went to Sepi to check on her bungalow. The presence of Chin was comforting because of the potential for problems in this far-flung village. Terry had concerns also and decided to tag along.

Coincidentally, Bernie visited his bungalow the following morning and called on Lucinda whom he knew as Angelina's partner in the swimwear business.

Chin appeared to be a non-descript person in the background, possibly an elderly servant. Terry hid in case he was needed. Had the group been together in Singapore, Terry could have arrested Bernie but in Sepi, an arrest resulting in Bernie's return to Singapore was problematic.

"I am surprised to see you here. Is Angelina here too?" Bernie asked Lucinda.

"No. She is in Singapore I think but could be visiting soon," she replied warily. She knew she was now being confronted by a likely *Diueliz* member who had escaped the Singapore fibre-optic communications cable raid.

"We had some good times at the Blue Bird Inn a few weeks ago," he said, "but I think she got involved with some unsavoury Singapore characters there. If I knew who they were, I could have looked after her but it doesn't matter now. Does she have a lot of friends in Singapore?" He asked.

"Not many, as far as I know," Lucinda replied.

They talked about the Solomons and he asked why Lucinda seemed interested in that part of the world as there were few prospects for Westerners and there seemed a limited swimwear market.

He said he had friends in the city but worked elsewhere. That was his reason for setting up an R&R base, as he called it, in Sepi. His explanation was intended to get Lucinda to be more forthcoming.

His enquiry had the opposite effect. She thought his approach was contrived. It was not conversational but rather investigative, bordering on doubt and perhaps leading to a problem.

Lucinda tried to placate him: "If I am going to make a go of the swimwear business here, I too need a place away from the city," she said.

She continued: "It's not the same for men. There are plenty of recreation places in Honiara for men, not the least the casino which, I might say, I have visited once or twice out of curiosity, mind you not as a gambler. But there's not much else.

"I really don't think Angelina has many friends in Singapore and fewer here but I do not know. To be honest, I have none. Honiara may be attractive to some but not me. I hardly think Angelina would come to Sepi. I have not seen any foreigners other than you now," she said.

He replied: "You would be surprised. Many foreigners and others come here, including a senior government friend of mine tomorrow."

Realising this was a momentary slipup by Bernie, she risked encouraging him further. "But they would hardly come here by choice."

He insisted: "I just said so. Of course, they do."

Lucinda muttered a sound that gave the impression deliberately that she doubted any senior government official would visit Sepi, and by implication visit Bernie.

Resentfully, he responded: "You don't believe me. What do you know?"

Just as Lucinda knew she had gone too far, Bernie turned aggressive. He thought he would find out from Lucinda what she and Angelina were up to.

He grabbed her violently by the neck, pushed her against the wall and shouted: "I know why you are here. So why don't you explain, otherwise you're going to get hurt."

Even before Terry could respond, those were Bernie's last words.

Chin seemingly came from nowhere and applied two fingers to one side of Bernie's neck partially paralysing him. It was not a *Bokator* move which would have killed Bernie instantly. There was no real violence. Bernie just stood still unable to move his upper body.

"Czunda, You fine. Yes...you go to other room, please. OK," he said looking at Lucinda closely.

While Terry watched amazed at his skill, Chin released his grip and struck Bernie with a two-fingered punch under the heart resulting in Bernie remaining in a semi-paralytic state. With two hands free, Chin then applied a silent but lethal IRA technique that left no messy evidence. He placed one hand over Bernie's mouth and pinching his nose with the other. There was no resistance but for a gaze that preceded death in a few minutes.

Chin would have liked to practice his *Bakator* on an active, living opponent, especially a much larger and younger one, but this quiet method was more appropriate. Bernie was dead in six minutes.

"Perhaps I can join the party now," Terry said while addressing Chin and ushering Lucinda to a side of the room to collect herself. Then speaking softly to her, he suggested she send one of her secret language messages to Col Weingraf stating everything was progressing well and the escaped *Diueliz* had been taken care of.

The message was sent as a progress report stating that nothing further needed to be reported. It did not forecast the expected arrival the following day at Bernie's bungalow of a likely corrupt senior government official. This was partly because it was not known who the official was and whether he or she would be accompanied by others.

Nevertheless, Terry now knew he and Chin could cope with more than just a couple of others, if necessary. So, he typed a short unsigned note without names to be left in Bernie's bungalow asking the visitor to meet at Lucinda's bungalow as soon as possible.

In the meantime, they considered various forms of unconventional interrogation of the expected official or officials. They hoped to extract the names of other key corrupt government officials, *Diueliz* identities and, if at all possible, names of PRC overseers.

Bernie's body was concealed at Lucinda's place.

The official visitor's fate was sealed before he arrived, as were others if more than one came. Association with *Diueliz* was sufficient evidence of guilt, albeit circumstantial and based on association and hearsay. This was not a time for legalities and fact-finding. Fatal confrontation would occur.

Terry explained: "We will make it look like a murder-suicide. It will seem Bernie and the official had disagreed, presumably on some unknown corruption deal; Bernie had threatened the official, the official had killed Bernie and then killed himself.

"I know it sounds convoluted, but it's not too difficult to stage and there should be no loose ends with a police service that is largely corrupt and would want to avoid investigation of one of their own officials, regardless of what part of the public service he was attached to. Bernie's disappearance might even be welcomed by government officials."

Only one official called at Bernie's bungalow. After finding the note, he turned up at Lucinda's bungalow, again with Chin an inconspicuous house servant and Terry in hiding. When it was evident the official was alone, Chin easily had him on the floor unable to move but fully conscious.

Terry retrieved and destroyed the note.

There began a barrage of questions. The first was the identity of the visitor who was the defence advisor to the prime minister. Other questions were about corrupt officials, members of *Diueliz* and PRC kingpins in league with ministers and departmental heads. Chin came into his own by using a number of painful pressure points but the official resisted.

Terry revealed Bernie's body and said he had suffered an agonising death. The visitor would suffer the same fate if he did not answer the questions. He was promised his life if he provided the information they needed.

Combined with Chin's threat to intensify his pressure point technique, the visitor revealed that two senior Chinese casino officials reported privately on government diplomatic and political matters to the deputy prime minister. He said the casino acquired this kind of information from government patrons in exchange for sexual services provided in back rooms of the casino.

More significantly, the deputy prime minister received similar favours and considerable amounts of money regularly for providing security and defence intelligence to the two casino officials.

He said the information from the casino officials was used locally for political purposes but he did not know what the casino officials did with the intelligence they received from the deputy prime minister.

However, he did not know how deeply the PRC was involved politically, although PRC sympathies had been expressed publicly by many in government and had caused a degree of civil unrest.

The interrogation concluded with Chin rendering the official partially paralysed using the same technique used on Bernie. Still alive, the official was walked slowly to Bernie's bungalow by Chin while Lucinda and Terry carried Bernie's body back in an upright position.

In the bungalow, a ligature was tied tightly around Bernie's neck and wrapped around the official's left hand. Without resistance, the official's throat was cut using a sharp kitchen knife which was placed tightly in his right hand making it appear a murder-suicide scene. A typed note was placed in Bernie's pocket indicating that *another* payment was needed to keep quiet about the commissioner of police and the deputy prime minister, without saying anything about what needed to be kept quiet. The scene was made to appear the official had strangled Bernie and then cut his own throat.

The note would not give investigators any clue as to who and what the payment was for, how much was expected and what was the involvement of the commissioner of police and the deputy prime minister.

Chin said to Terry: "Yes…all this very logical but messy. I not do it this way. You sure it work?"

Terry explained: "I'm certain there will be no forensic investigation because of the likely involvement of senior government people in criminal activities."

Chin asked: "What about the commissioner of police and the deputy prime minister. Yes…you know they are bad people?"

Terry again explained: "I am sure the minister is a crook and the police commissioner is up to his eyeballs in it. In any case, there will be no real investigation because the police commissioner is involved. No one will know where it might end. Everyone will be afraid.

"It all seems watertight, Chin. One would hardly think Bernie was killed elsewhere. As for the Prime Minister's Defence Adviser, he karked it at the scene as his blood is everywhere."

Lucinda and Chin then returned to their respective accommodation and Terry went back to the high commission.

When Lucinda met Lee, the first question he asked was about her wellbeing. He was surprised she was not stressed after what had happened, not knowing her earlier ICCC training had prepared her for violent confrontation.

He explained he had time to liaise with the casino to the point where he was able to assist the casino reorganise some of its accounting practices. He had even suggested a few areas where *creative* accounting could be applied safely. Several suggestions had been adopted. The advice was provided occasionally, not in haste and not on a paid basis. It was friendly advice from an ethnically similar professional with vaguely common interests.

Lee reported: "There are only four Chinese managers in the casino. The main one is Yi. This a nick-name meaning the number 1 in Mandarin when using the correct tone, as we all know."

Lucinda asked: "What is his family name?"

Lee responded: "I don't know. He is called Yi by everyone and he prefers this name. He has not volunteered much but I can tell he is Beijing educated and may come from the north. Perhaps he has a record in the PRC, or perhaps he is a PRC spy. It does not matter at the moment, I guess. The main thing is I enjoy a degree of trust.

"I hope his confidence in me is genuine because, as you know, I am good at normal accounting but not as good at this kind of 'psychogenic rithematic'," Lee said alluding to his judge of character in not being able to persuade Lucinda to pursue a simultaneously interpretation career.

He added with a wry grin: "I have been advising Yi casually on how to improve the casino's accounting systems and the casino has benefited. In particular, I have been able to enhance significantly his money laundering account. So, I am making headway with my spying duties.

"Actually, Yi's laundering account has been operating successfully for years in a clumsy manner but I suppose clever accounting is not his forte. Most of the money is laundered locally, probably through government. After processing, it is simply handed out in poorly administered grants and corrupt cash payments on fake receipts. I have records.

"He has a load of receipt books signed and stamped for various amounts. The books can be purchased from any book store and the stamps can be made anywhere to show genuine purchases. All this will be so easy to expose in time, especially as offshore havens are not involved."

He remarked, however: "Yi is otherwise clever and should not be taken for granted. His education was not in economics or finance. It seemed to be in an area of geo-political science.

"I do not know the other casino officer. He is known as Qui, as in the Chinese number 7 which, of course, is a lucky number. He looks after casino security, including the security of funds. Our *Bokator* master has been getting to know him. They have been cooperating in training security staff but I do not think they like each other much. They come from different areas in China and there may remain historical prejudices among certain Chinese provinces," he surmised.

Except for Col Weingraf, the others met at Lucinda's rooms above the shop-front in Honiara to plan the next move. The quasi-Bougainvillian-Australian who seemed to run the Singapore connection and one corrupt Solomon Islands government official had been neutralised. There surely would be more needing attention, including the deputy prime minister and senior police officers. The group suspected there was another unnamed Australian from Bougainville no one had met.

There was no publicity of the murder-suicide indicating a cover-up had been launched successfully with the help of the deputy prime minister. He now needed close ICCC attention.

While all this was going on, Theodora had been liaising with the undersecretary of Trade and Training, a youngish man named Benny and concluded he could be an asset.

Her association with him began when both coincidentally witnessed a rowdy street demonstration around parliament house about public servant pay and conditions.

Theodora recounted a conversation she had with Benny at the time that led her to think he could be trustworthy. She had remarked to Benny that some of the placards and announcements seemed more about general dissatisfaction with the Solomon Islands government, not just about specific pay and conditions in the public service. He had agreed with her.

She reported that Benny said young people in particular looked at apprenticeships as too long and jobs in the public service socially lower than in other occupations. Public servants wanted more money and status. He acknowledged this sentiment had some merit but there was evidence of an orchestrated move to undermine the government using these grievances as a smokescreen.

He thought the aim seemed to make the government unpopular among the broader community, particularly school-leaver and apprenticeship groups. He suggested another likely cause of disenchantment was due to international elements that encouraged disruption to gain support for unstated causes, private wealth or public service influence. Of recent times, disruptive events in public seemed to have some kind of international and local coordination. This was a concern, perhaps even threatening the stability of the community.

Benny admitted there were animosities within the Solomons, but these were local and mainly tribal, not the cause of dissatisfaction with government.

The location of the country in the middle of the Pacific and its extensive natural resources attracted the attention of the wrong people, "just like the Spanish in early times who thought there were more treasures here than in King Solomon mines," he told Theodora.

Theodora's experience with this undersecretary was encouraging.

Terry and Theodora discussed with Lee and the *Bokator* master the routines of Yi and Qui at the casino.

This concluded with a broad three-pronged plan that was as presumptive of guilt of their targets as it was ambitious: Firstly, to get as much information as possible from Yi about Chinese lobbyists in Honiara before removing or disabling him in some way; secondly, to get rid of Qui in whatever way was appropriate; thirdly, to encourage Benny to formulate a collective of honest undersecretaries and other like-minded senior public servants to counteract foreign influence of government, a collective that also would expose local collaborators.

"This had to achieve results quickly," Terry said. "Already there had been two deaths. It was only a matter of time before there were more. Such outcomes could lead *Diueliz* to investigate the sisters just as Bernie tried to do, albeit in a clumsy manner. *Diueliz* could call for outside support from the PRC and its PLA's spy division or try to balance any setbacks themselves," he said.

Lee's first move was to reinforce his rapport with Yi. He did this the same way Theodora gained the confidence of the undersecretary—by expressing a common belief, the difference being Lee had to be deceptive in the extreme.

Lee asked Yi a leading question: "Do you think the casino could play a greater role in giving the Solomons a more secure future by extending community and administrative support through advice and leadership?"

Lying through his teeth, he added: "Even though we have some squabbles sometimes with China about provincial differences, the PRC has gained a lot economically and socially by consolidating its national administration, improving its governance and generally benefiting the people. Perhaps the Solomons and other Pacific Island States could benefit likewise with this kind of guidance.

"After all, China has many more centuries of experience in government than any other country which is willing to help, and other countries able to help are few and far between."

This factitious patriotism did not seem to surprise Yi, so much so that Lee was unsure if Yi had missed something.

He thought Yi's reaction, or lack of it, could be comforting or discomforting, hopefully the former. Eventually, Yi replied in what seemed to be a practiced political narrative: "It is the PRC's aim to provide needed assistance to needy countries, particularly in economic management and infrastructure support. We want to help."

Coming from a financial controller of a casino that targeted some of the most vulnerable in the community and did not present as a PRC supporter, Lee accepted Yi's mendacity and even encouraged him to elaborate.

He said to Yi: "China already is doing a lot in Pacific Island infrastructure, such as in Vanuatu where support for that country's sea and air ports is impressive."

"That is so," Yi replied, "because there is a need there, and in Tuvalu, Kiribati and Tonga where we hope to do the same."

Yi's use of the collective 'we' on several occasions placed him fairly and squarely in the PRC camp.

They both discussed various needs in the Pacific before Lee risked extending the conversation even further. "It seems China is going it alone. The US seems quiescent militarily while China is expanding quickly. I understand the Middle Kingdom and the US have approximately the same number of large submarines, whereas China had only three or four in the early 2000s while the US has been building them since the end of the World War Two.

"The same applies to principal combat ships of which China has 48, whereas in the early 2000s it had none. Of course, China had all kinds of war ships earlier but they were obsolete. This just goes to show the rapid pace of shipbuilding development China."

Yi accepted these statistics without comment or expression or even surprise that Lee had such statistics at hand. They continued their conversation about the altruistic intentions of China. Therein, lay another surprise for Lee; apparently, Yi was familiar with the PLA's military capabilities.

Did Yi see me as a soulmate? At least they seemed to be on the same page. Heaven's forbid, Lee thought to himself. *I am siding with a person who sounds like a PLA propagandist, or worse.*

Lee's subconscious comments sounded like an application to join the CCP. He was horrified at his own lies and the assumption they were virtually comrades in arms. But his deception had achieved its aim. He had gained more ground than he ever expected and in a much shorter time than he expected.

This mode of discussion was the reverse of Lee's customary style when in the rarefied atmosphere of Adelaide academia. Instead of being withdrawn and coming back with confusing remarks to confound those who either questioned his ideas arrogantly or praised themselves patronisingly, he was now encouraging the kind of person he disliked even more than those who irritated him previously. But he was enjoying it perversely.

Now Lee was comfortable in assuming he had unfettered access to the casino books. He already had a degree of access. It seemed complete now. Instead of getting rid of Yi, he could set up Yi as an embezzler of PRC funds and corruptor of the host State and the CCP. *This could be a much more torturous outcome for Yi than a few minutes suffering before departing this earth,* Lee thought.

The consequences of legal action against Yi were likely to expose more criminals, providing there were enough honest officials in the judiciary.

The casino books could be adjusted secretly by Lee to show monies going to a new private account of Yi in Honiara, to another account of a private Australian company in which Yi was registered as sole director, and to a private account in Australia for the deputy prime minister as well as a new local account set up for him. None of this would be too difficult to fudge with Col Weingraf's help.

At the right time, the accounts would be leaked to several news agencies and Chinese language newspapers in Hong Kong and Australia, the ASEAN Secretariat and the PIF Office, the Chinese Consulate-General in Honiara and to the Chief Ministers of Tuvalu, Kiribati, Tonga, Papua New Guinea and Indonesian.

Timing would be critical to ensure there was no opportunity for Yi or the deputy prime minister to be informed by the account-holding banks of their unusual deposits or for Yi to notice large casino withdrawals until too late.

Deposits would be no problem. Documentation would be collected by Lee at the time he opened Yi's local account and by Col Weingraf when he set up Yi's

Australian company and opened its account. Theodora would depend on the undersecretary Benny's support in establishing the Honiara account and authorising the deputy prime minister's Australian bank account under his name with Col Weingraf overseeing the transfer.

Timing would coincide with the *Bokator* master's access to Qui and two casino CCTV operators at about the same time. When the timing was right, Qui would be neutralised.

Theodora was given a day to double check Benny's resolve to help. It was a big decision for him but his support was certain when Theodora revealed the deputy prime minister's private dealing with the PRC. This was not just criminal. It was treasonable.

All tasks were coordinated by Angelina from a remote location. Preparations had to be made for last-minute adjustments if something went wrong. If something unfortunate happened, Benny would be protected.

The sting was to have:

- Angelina: book and confirm flights to Australia and Singapore for all, except Terry, as close as possible to the completion of the sting;
- Angelina: ensure all tickets would be at the airport for collection;
- Lucinda and Chin take Yi for a long lunch in town the day of the sting, if possible;
- Benny: open a personal bank account locally in the name of the deputy prime minister, initially with a small amount so as not to attract attention or require the minister's presence at the bank;
- Benny: open an Australian bank account for the deputy prime minister, with the assistance of Col Weingraf, also in a modest amount;
- Col Weingraf: open personal accounts for Yi in Australia, also in small amounts;
- Lee be informed of progress of all bank accounts;
- The *Bokator* master: keep close to Lee and either kill or disable for a long period the two casino CCTV operators and leave a message in the control room that both had a touch of food poisoning and would be back in a 'very short time';
- The *Bokator* master: then assassinate Qui and hide his body with the two CCTV operators in a casino location Lee knew was rarely visited by staff;

- Simultaneously, Lee would transfer from the casino's main account the equivalent of US$40,000 to each of all the new accounts, including those in Australia, later the same day the accounts were established;
- Lee: phone Lucinda and Chin at the Yi lunch to quietly advise them of progress and Lucinda would advise Yi that the casino was operating normally and he need not hurry back;
- Chin would excuse himself and depart for the high commission while Lucinda entertains Yi as best she could for as long as she could safely;
- Col Weingraf and Terry share the job of leaking to regional and local media details of Yi and the deputy prime minister conspiring to help Chinese interests control the Solomon Islands government while benefiting themselves financially, work that could be prearranged by secretly using the Australian High Commission's press office without identifying the source; and
- Terry: arrange private transport to pick up all members of the group at the Australian High Commission and proceed to the airport without delay as soon as the 'All Clear'' was given by Angelina, but in the event of the plan not working, everyone proceed to the commission as quickly as possible and stay there.

If everything went well, Theodora and Lucinda would proceed to Singapore. Terry would remain at the high commission. The others would fly to Sydney.

Yi accepted Lucinda's invitation to lunch.

Chin came to lunch as well. She sent Chin back from lunch and stayed as long as she could with Yi. She reasoned that the longer Yi was delayed, the more time the group had to complete the sting and get out of the country.

Everything proceeded as planned except that Lucinda remained too long.

She could not get back to the commission at the appointed time and had to catch a taxi to the airport on her own. The others had gone.

On the way, the taxi driver recognised Lucinda as one of the attractive foreigner ladies who promoted skimpy swimwear in town some time earlier. He stopped the taxi and called over a friend, a policeman. Very soon several onlookers arrived. She could not hurry the taxi driver without creating suspicion.

She knew she was going to miss her flight and even the next one. The others had left.

In due course, the body of Qui and the two anaesthetised CCTV operators were found. The *Bokator* master had decided not to kill the CCTV operators because Chin could not confirm their direct involvement in corrupt dealings or PRC connections.

The bank scams were emerging as news agencies and foreign correspondents began contacting the casino and the Serious Crime Squad of the police.

All this was going on while Lucinda was in the taxi. To the driver and his police friend, she seemed suspicious in a non-descript way. Her explanation that she was going to the airport to catch a flight she had missed already and for which she had no ticket was puzzling. Being in a wrong place at an odd time and seeming now a little nervous, she was worth questioning.

Eventually, she was taken to the Central Police Station. A senior officer took over. Surprisingly, Yi was waiting there with another senior policeman who was a regular at the casino.

Yi and the senior officer came to an arrangement that they would use Lucinda to extract a ransom from her friends whose whereabouts was unknown but thought still to be in Honiara. A ransom would help Yi, his police collaborators and others in government shown to be corrupt to flee the country. They needed the money.

They decided to hold off charging her until the next morning because the opportunity for a ransom would disappear as soon as she was charged with something, probably murder. They had to work quickly as she could be inaccessible in remand.

Yi and the officer took her to a shed next to the station and informed her she had no way of avoiding one murder charge and various kidnapping and assault charges if she did not do as they asked.

"The charge will not be the only problem you face," Yi told her. "You are a pretty woman now. What you will look like after a time in remand is nobody's guess."

The officer explained: "We want you to phone your boss and have him deliver US$100,000 to us at this shed tomorrow. If they fail to do so, we will leave you to the mercy of the court and the pleasure of our jailers. You understand? We don't need to do anything to you. The jailers will do it all."

She agreed and dialled the phone number she had been given by the ICCC. "Can I speak with *Senior*?" She asked.

"How do you know him?" The harsh reply came.

"I'm Lucinda and I'm near the Central Police Station," she said knowing the recipient would respond to this emergency as planned and that the call was being recorded and triangulated through the Australian High Commission.

Eventually, a softly spoken male voice responded: "Hi, Lucinda. What's up?"

She said: "I'm in trouble and need a large amount of cash tomorrow if I am to get out of this trouble. It's a matter of life and death. I need $100,000 US. Don't ask questions, just give it to me and I can more than justify the payment."

"That is lot of money, even for us, especially in cash. We can do it but it would be better paid over a week, not all in one day," he said stretching the rapport as much as possible.

"No, you can't do that. I need it tomorrow at the very latest. In fact, I need it by…" Lucinda said mocking an alarmed disposition while looking at the officer for an indication of delivery time.

Yi interrupted and said in Mandarin: "No later than 8.30am tomorrow. Understand?"

"Did you hear that, *Senior*?" Lucinda asked.

He replied: "Yes. That is a very tall order. It means we will have to raise the funds today. That early in the morning makes it even more difficult."

She said: "That's right, if I am to see this through."

Senior said: "Who is with you?"

She said in an even more alarmed voice: "Rau, don't ask me that. It does not matter. Just bring the money…"

"What's all that about?" Yi said to Lucinda threateningly.

She replied: "*Rua* is his name. It's friendly. He's more likely to help."

In Pure Motu, it meant the number 2 indicating two people were with her, including Yi. She knew *Senior* would refer the word to Terry, Angelina or Theodora. Anything unusual in such a conversation would be analysed.

"OK, we agree. I'll see you at 8.30am tomorrow, But where?" *Senior* asked.

"Near the Central Police Station," she said while looking at Yi for agreement to say more. He nodded. "A shed on the south side," she explained.

To give her position credibility, she added: "There will be a virtual army in the shed," she lied, although *Senior* knew there would be two only.

Yi and his colleague believed she was speaking with her superior and were taken in by her performance.

Before the end of the conversation, Terry had found the precise location. He assisted *Senior* doctor the phone conversation to incriminate Yi without giving any indication of where it came from.

He and another ASIS operative planned to pre-empt the delivery. A female ASIS operative would pose as the courier. That made three—the female ASIS officer, *Senior* and Terry—more than enough to take care of Yi and his police companion.

The operatives would overnight unseen in the scrub near the shed.

Yi and the officer were expected to stay with Lucinda since they needed to secure her and did not know if they were under investigation themselves by now.

As the decoy parcel courier approached with the supposed money, Yi and the officer looked out the half-closed door of the shed. They were sitting targets for Terry and his colleague.

Terry burst in. He killed the officer with a silenced pistol and subdued Yi who was given an anaesthetic injection that would last at least half a day. It was important that Yi, as well as the deputy prime minister, survived when their treachery was publicised regionally.

Terry, his two colleagues and Lucinda then went to the high commission as fast as they could. In time, Lucinda was escorted to Port Moresby in transit to Sydney where the sisters met with Col Weingraf to review what had happened. They expected to hear from Terry, who remained at the high commission, about local and regional repercussions of Yi's support of foreign government subversion of the Solomon Islands government and his corruption and treachery, as well as the corruption of the Solomon Islands Deputy Prime Minister and the murders of Qui and Bernie.

Benny was given protection locally and instantly became a whistle-blower hero.

Lucinda had posted a letter to her Honiara landlord handing over all the APAF stock to him gratis.

The ICCC paid for Theodora's Singapore residence for six months in case it was needed again. It would be kept under surveillance by SSS to detect any unwanted interest. The *Bokator* master's home and business were protected.

Angelina was comfortable in retaining her Perth accommodation. She also maintained the APAF business address, just in case it became useful later.

Despite Lee's exceptional academic background, he returned from the Solomons an even more informed pansophist. Chin also was more experienced than before he left. Both expressed an eagerness to assist again, if needed.

Chapter 14: Suspicion

All were relaxing in Sydney when Sir Jonathan casually informed Angelina of two unusual cruises from the west coast of Russia to Australia and South-east Asia travelling, in part, through the South China Sea.

He had learned of these during conversations with his Singapore associate while reviewing joint prospects for admiralty law services. His associate mentioned privately that something seemed odd with the cruises but could not elaborate.

Both cruises were for high-end passengers, mainly Asian, who could afford the relatively high cost and the lengthy time involved.

Angelina mentioned this to Col Weingraf. There was nothing untoward about the cruises other than their peculiar embarkation point and a particular destination, a Kalimantan port city. The cruises could seem to most Western observers a risky Russian attempt to cash into the global cruise market.

Terry was more equivocal, as was his nature with most things.

He searched the cruise company to ascertain if it had any connection with the Russian government, particularly with the Russian Department of Defence or the Russian Navy, since the embarkation point was Vladivostok, now a thriving commercial port but formerly the main navy facility at the extreme southern end of the west coast, a stone's throw from Manchuria. The Russian Navy was well established there still but there seemed no current operational link between the cruise company and the military.

However, Terry did not believe that something so unexpected in a highly competitive industry elsewhere should be ignored.

He knew the Russians had been successful in enhancing skills inherited from their USSR predecessors in concealment, deceit and reinvention of information, even though they seemed clumsy in other ways. Something so innocently unusual seemed inconsistent with the Russian way and was at least worthy of a second look.

In the back of his mind, Terry thought of the unthinkable—Russia and China forming an alliance against the US based on their mutual hatred of the West. *This,* he thought, *was not so unthinkable considering that Russia had sold to China conventional Kilo-class submarines and sophisticated jet fighters, such as the highly regarded SU-35.* He could not ignore the fact that both countries had conducted joint military exercises in the East China Sea and the Baltic, and both had flown strategic bombers over the East China Sea in recent times.

Their mutual hatred of the West coalesced their working together and far outweighed their traditional animosity one for the other.

His silent conclusion was unimaginable—the US would be hard pressed to fight two major powers at the one time, if conflict eventuated.

For the present, however, he had to concentrate on the Russian cruises, not the bigger picture.

He contacted an SSS colleague who held a similar view to Sir Jonathan's associate in Singapore and said the Service would be keeping a close eye on the ships when they berthed in Singapore. But he could not see a tangible problem. That both Russian ships were to visit Chinese ports and Taiwan was interesting, but nothing of a political nature could be deduced from this alone.

The ships were Okhotsk-1 and Okhotsk-2.

One puzzling aspect of both remained the apparent absence of any commercial Chinese involvement, although the cruise company advertised for passengers in several Chinese locations and the itineraries for both vessels involved extensive travel through the East and South China Seas. China's artificial islands were clearly not on the itineraries.

The company's marketing material was available publicly in only a few locations rather than broadly throughout the region. There was reference to scientists aboard who could engage passengers in a range of cultural and social experiences onboard and ashore. The usual cruise entertainment and lessons in Asian languages, dance and the arts were promoted. There was nothing out of the ordinary, or particularly informative, in the advertising material.

Terry's interest continued as both ships were to go to six ports initially but different ones later. Puzzling also was the embarkation port for passengers was not in Russia or China but in South Korea.

The ships would begin in Pusan, South Korea, travelling through the Sea of Japan. They would proceed to Shanghai on the east coast of China travelling through the East China Sea.

From there, they would go to Kaohsiung in Taiwan and on to Hong Kong cruising through the South China Sea.

The fifth port of call would be Ho Chi Minh City in Vietnam, also through the South China Sea.

The sixth port for both ships would visit Pontianak in Kalimantan, Borneo. Pontianak was not even the capital of Kalimantan but was promoted as 'something different' from other Asian ports.

To this point, the two vessels would travel in tandem but return by different routes. After Pontianak, one would visit Australia and the other PNG.

Afterwards, Okhotsk-2 was to head south-east to Australia's main port cities beginning with Darwin and then Perth, Adelaide, Melbourne, Sydney and Brisbane, virtually circumnavigating Australia. It was a simple enough itinerary but lengthy.

Okhotsk-1 also was to head south-east but not to Australia. It was to visit PNG instead calling at Port Moresby first followed by Lae, Madang and Wewak in the Sepik area, virtually circumnavigating PNG. This also was a simple enough itinerary but somewhat shorter in time and distance.

After Okhotsk-2 had circumnavigated Australia and Okhotsk-1 had circumnavigated PNG, their return legs would be via Ho Chi Minh City using the same ports as their forward journey.

There was no reference to the vessels returning in tandem. Despite calling at the same ports, the likely asymmetric return legs seemed to be due to the difference times and distances of each vessel.

No reference was made to Vladivostok.

Terry, Angelina, Sir Jonathan and Col Weingraf held a conference call and took notice of the comments of SSS and Sir Jonathan's associate. Terry's doubt about something unknown strengthened.

Sir Jonathan mentioned that his Singapore associate informed him both ships were old lavishly refitted 50,000-ton nuclear protected vessels very much like the old US 'liberty ships'. These US vessels were used until the end of the 1970s for 99-day Asian trips from the West Coast of the US.

They offered the best in US luxury cruising. The trips appealed primarily to wealthy American families who wanted to provide their elderly family members the best in their final holidays and to avoid American death duties.

Sir Jonathan explained deaths in international waters were not dutiable in the US. Passengers who returned from one trip would simply enjoy another. This

153

was a popular and more pleasurable and eventually, cheaper ending for the wealthy at the time.

Terry voiced a couple of observations. Firstly, there was no earlier Russian comparison to the US use of old war ships, even though utilising relatively cheap, disposable ships for luxury cruising was an idea worthy of considering economically for any country, refurbishment costs permitting.

Secondly, the Russian adventure into this market using Vladivostok as a base but not a point of passenger embarkation or disembarkation seemed odd. At best, he said, the whole thing looked like a big commercial mistake in the making. The alternative was that it had little to do with tourism.

All agreed it worthwhile to look more closely at the ports of call, the scientists and cargoes, while they had the time to do so.

Col Weingraf asked the Australian-United States global surveillance station, Pine Gap in the Northern Territory, to focus on the operator's communications with Vladivostok. The report that came back stated no signals of any significance were recorded between Vladivostok and Moscow but interesting signals were intercepted between Vladivostok and an as-yet-unknown party in Pontianak about the loading of cargo.

Pine Gap's opinion was that the cargo was likely to be illegal, possibly smuggled goods or even military equipment of some kind. This was uncertain and based on few options. People-smuggling, spy-smuggling and drug-smuggling were unlikely because of the complexity of such activities being arranged in such a remote Indonesian port. Nothing of an official nature seemed likely either.

The politics at the time and the language of the messages were such as to discount Indonesian Government collaboration with Russia. The history of Indonesia's civil fight against communism supported this conclusion.

More needed to be known.

Attention was focused on Okhotsk-2 as one or more Australian ports could be involved if this vessel was the intended carrier of illegal cargo.

It was less likely to involve Okhotsk-1 as PNG parties were unlikely to be able to organise and pay for smuggled goods, especially military equipment.

Lucinda was to book a return trip from Pusan on Okhotsk-2 and stay on during the Australian sector, if necessary.

Her tasks were to observe cargo movements, identify cargoes at odds with normal provisions, note changes of professional crew, see if lectures and information sessions conducted by any official guests for passengers were in any way political, and find out a little more about Pontianak's significance to anything.

In case the team's assumptions were wrong and Okhotsk-1 was to be the carrier, Angelina was to join Okhotsk-1 in Hong Kong and remain throughout its Papua New Guinea ports of call. She planned to disembark in Hong Kong on the return leg. Her tasks were similar.

Terry would spend time at the Australian Embassy in Jakarta and the high commission in Port Moresby. Col Weingraf would visit Perth, Sydney and Alice Springs (Pine Gap).

It was a large deployment of agents based on no hard evidence. Furthermore, the ICCC and ASIS had no reliable contacts in Pontianak who could confirm their assumptions or even provide useful background information about cargoes, especially of a military kind. In the ICCC's favour was that there seemed a break in tasks and key team members were available, at least for the present.

There was time to develop a contact in Pontianak or nearby in Kalimantan but seeking assistance from the Indonesian Government was not an option.

Both sisters began their respective journeys.

As soon as Lucinda joined Okhotsk-2 in Pusan, she tried to find out if any special guests had joined the vessel in Vladivostok. She could find no such guests unless they were embedded as crew.

The two Russian scientists joined her vessel, one a bio-chemist and the other a meteorologist. They had scheduled a series of lectures for passengers involving changes in biology as a consequence of advances in medicinal chemistry in Russian research laboratories and climate change, respectively.

Two lectures were delivered on the voyage from Pusan to Shanghai, neither consequential.

While in Shanghai, a visiting gymnastic troupe entertained passengers and held group singing sessions of a patriotic nature. Group singing involving tourists had become common practice in several Asian centres, particularly in Ho Chi Min City and other Vietnamese cities where guides frequently encouraged foreign tourist groups to participate in singing highly melodious patriotic songs in Vietnamese, many visitors knowing little about the lyrics.

Kaohsiung and Hong Kong were the next ports. An on-shore meeting was arranged with Angelina, Lucinda and Terry in Kaohsiung when the two ships berthed near each other.

This would be a relatively safe city between the two Chinese ports of Shanghai and Hong Kong and unlikely to be of particular interest to Russian government people. To date Angelina's enquiries had uncovered nothing and had yet to join Okhotsk-1 in Hong Kong.

However, Lucinda's fortunes seemed to change well before Kaohsiung when an Indian crew member in charge of cargo handling engaged her in conversation en-route to Hong Kong. On learning she was Australian, he wanted to know about life in her home country. She did not know if it was a genuine enquiry, small talk or something else. Crew members were not expected to chat with passengers but, after such a bold enquiry, Lucinda felt comfortable telling him about various conditions for Australian residency. She recommended he enquire at any Australian legation in the cities they were to visit.

She decided to go a little further, and said: "I'm not in the immigration business, although you could tell me a little about your background, particularly your family, and why you are on this trip. It could help me explain to you aspects of life in Australia. I may be better able to give you some tips when speaking with an Australian official."

He replied that his selection as a crew member was a surprise as there were several more qualified non-Russian people on the hiring schedule. It was an even greater surprise when he was promoted to cargo handling supervisor shortly after leaving Pusan.

"Why do you think you got this promotion?" She asked.

He said: "I have no idea. It didn't carry any more money but it suited me so I was pleasantly surprised. Perhaps it was because I am not East Asian or South-east Asian and speak English reasonably well."

"Perhaps it was your work ethic," Lucinda said somewhat patronisingly. "Or perhaps you are new to the job, a stranger without friends and connections."

She added hurriedly: "If you don't know much about what goes on, you can't gossip…and you can't give away secrets."

"Maybe," he said somewhat confused about her logic.

He explained: "You may be right. I don't talk a lot to the crew not involved in cargoes. The truth is, I was a policeman in Srinagar in the Kashmir region in earlier times but did not want to reveal this because all I wanted to do was to get out of India and particularly the Kashmir as there is considerable trouble with Chinese near the border and internally between the Sikhs and Hindus.

"My family is a long way away fortunately in Vishakhapatnam on the mid-east coast. Anything to do with policing and the Kashmir would have gone against my selection. I wanted to help out in the kitchen, on deck or anywhere else. I didn't even think about cargoes when interviewed. My interest was to make money, see Australia and think about the future for my family," he said.

Having been given a reasonable explanation and a virtual invitation to talk about cargo loadings, Lucinda continued hoping it would lead to securing his help, if needed.

She said: "Well, you probably will have an opportunity to see large cities in Australia. We can talk about particular cities later if you like."

"That would be very much appreciated. If I can help you in any way let me know," he said in a seemingly typical Indian bargaining fashion that was meaninglessly polite.

The following day, she met him again and took up his somewhat unintended offer in an oblique way. "I am curious," she said, "why these particular Russian cruises are going to Papua New Guinea and Australia separately but travelling to some Asian ports together. I am on Okhotsk-2 because I am returning to Australia and seeing some wonderful places on the way. Other passengers probably have all kinds of reasons for selecting these cruises.

"I wonder why anyone would want to visit Kalimantan for a couple of days. Why would Asian passengers want to visit Indonesian Borneo, other than for jungle trekking?" She quipped. "Onboard comforts suggest passengers are not interested in strenuous expeditions, and there will not be time in port anyway. It seems to me Pontianak would not be a final destination for anyone. It could be a waste of time for some."

Lucinda asked: "Perhaps some passengers will leave Okhotsk-2 in Pontianak. If so, why? Don't get me wrong," she continued. "I love all these ports but Borneo is better known for its orangutangs than its culture and scenic attractions. Anyway, most orangutangs are in the far north and in East Malaysia, as far as I know."

He admitted: "I don't think anyone will leave in Pontianak and I don't even know what Asian tourists want to see. I just want to look after cargoes and maybe get to Australia."

She prompted: "For me, I want to see different place, but not just a jungle city. Is it of interest to you?"

"No, not particularly but I think the captain is interested in Pontianak," he said.

"Why?" She said.

"I heard him discussing politics with an officer and suggesting the cruises would make people think of politics seriously. The conversation was not friendly. So, I think the cruises have something to do with politics," he guessed.

"But Pontianak has nothing to do with politics, and it is not even the capital of Indonesian Borneo," she said.

"I think it has something to do with provisions or consignments. I guess I will know all about it if cargo handling is involved. Whatever it is, it seems important to the captain," he added.

Lucinda was making headway and did not want to rush. They agreed to meet again and chat about this.

Lucinda thought immediately of *Diueliz*. Perhaps terrorist recruiters would join the Okhotsk-2 in Pontianak or drugs or weapons would be loaded for use in one of the many Australian ports of call. She could not see why *Diueliz* would use Okhotsk-1 to supply drugs to Papuans and New Guineans, attack installations or subvert the PNG government which did not need any help in destroying itself anyway. She was on the right ship.

She would report this to Terry and Angelina when they met in Kaohsiung. At the same time, she intended to report she could not find anything incriminating about the two scientists.

In a secluded Kaohsiung café, Angelina, Lucinda and Terry, who seemed to be everywhere, met to review what little they had learned most of which came from Pine Gap.

Their suspicions were strengthened by Terry who said: "I know it's difficult to find out much about the scientists when you are onboard. I have done a search in Canberra on the scientists who are scheduled to switch from ship to ship for their lectures. The chemist was of limited concern until now.

"The chemist had published a paper years earlier on the use of molecular explosions to destroy cancers, a topic that seemed to have little to do with the kinds of explosives of interest to us, but he had some hearsay links in the past with Kalimantan and Sulawesi. The pieces in any conspiracy may be coming together. What do you ladies think? Is this wishful thinking?" He asked.

Lucinda said: "As far as Okhotsk-2 is concerned, the Pontianak cargo and the captain are the key to everything, not the scientists.

"It seems we are talking about the supply of drugs or military supplies to subversives in one or more Australian cities. Darwin is the first Australian port and may be strategic from a military point of view but the demographics are not right. Perth, Adelaide and Brisbane are big but Sydney is probably better connected to Canberra and the most populous. Who knows! My guess is Sydney."

Addressing both sisters, Terry said: "You may be right, Lucinda, but let me say that when you are on the water and I am on land, you may be in a boat without a paddle and I am grounded. I cannot help you much other than in ports. You need more intelligence on everything before you berth in Pontianak—the skipper, the cargo, the guest lecturers and anyone in charge at the port. And you must be able to look after yourselves, even though you have had basic training," he said.

He then handed to each an automatic pistol and a box of bullets. He gave each also a bundle of US$1,000 in small notes and five packets each containing half a kilogram of high-grade heroin to be used to bribe anyone in return for information about illicit cargoes or to get out of trouble.

Terry and Col Weingraf planned to cause both ships to be searched in Ho Chi Minh City which was the only port before Pontianak ahead of Australia and PNG. The sisters' stash of heroin had to be well concealed. Remember, they will use dogs to search for drugs. Nothing is likely to be found if Pontianak is the pick-up point of this mysterious cargo.

He explained: "This is part of a negative strategy to put off-guard those planning illegal activities after Ho Chi Minh. Having been searched in Ho Chi Minh City and having nothing found, the criminals should consider themselves relatively safe to do whatever they plan on doing in Pontianak, even though they may be puzzled about the unexpected search."

He said: "Hong Kong is the port before Ho Chi Minh City but the Chinese authorities in Hong Kong could not be trusted to conduct a convincing search. In addition, it is unknown if there is an arrangement between the PRC and Russia as much of the cruising is in the South China Sea and many of the passengers are Chinese."

During their meeting in the Kaohsiung café, Terry received a call from his ASIS contact in Jakarta asking if he still needed further information about Pontianak to which Terry replied that he did.

The ASIS contact suggested further enquiries be made about Pontianak through Parepare, a small port town on the mid-west coast of Sulawesi, quite a distance from Kalimantan.

The reason was that Indonesia tolerated a small permanent community of Russians there, a remnant of Cold War days when USSR military personnel were permitted to holiday in Parepare, generally unknown to the rest of the world. It was then a remote, pristine seaside township of no interest to domestic and international tourists.

Terry's contact informed him that care needed to be taken in making enquiries directly, as if Terry did not know this. The advice was merely to reaffirm the need for caution, not that there was any personal danger in asking around. Suspicious enquiry would result in no one saying anything about anything anytime. Terry was reminded that he had to grease the palms of Indonesians he wanted to talk to if he was to get anywhere in Parepare. Several possible contacts were named but not guaranteed to be useful or even truthful.

"Still," he told Terry, "even if they are untruthful, this might be useful if you can see through lies, misinformation or efforts to get more rewards for saying something."

There was still time for Terry to investigate before the ships visited Pontianak. Several contacts seemed cooperative after receiving the necessary compensation. He knew there were other pleasantries expected as well. Nevertheless, the process was tedious, went against his grain and generally involved referral after referral. This was part of the so-called 'rubber time' nature of Indonesian intelligence. He played their game, although it did little to lower his blood pressure.

One of Terry's contacts was in Taraja in Central Sulawesi, a region of the Bugis people, an ethnic group of indigenous mountain people. They were known to hold annual ceremonies honouring the dead and after-spirits, resulting in death rituals *ad infinitum*. Some deceased folk were mummified in a traditional way, dressed in every-day clothes and given a place at the dining tables of families.

Some were buried in cliff caves in front of which their effigies, called *tau*, were exposed for everyone to see but in difficult locations to access. In earlier times, deceased infants were placed in the tops of tall palm trees. The use of cliffs and palm trees for the dead was, in part, to protect them from intruders interested in any valuables that accompanied the bodies.

Another characteristic of Taraja, which was said to be settled from China some 2,500 years ago, was that some practiced animist rituals. Some also believed sexuality and gender existed in the spectrum, a belief that gave the Bugis people a reputation for transgender inclinations that attracted tourists to other parts of South-east Asia where small Bugis communities lived and were exploited.

Terry met his Tarajan contact in a village house adorned with buffalo heads denoting community seniority. He was told that even today there were Russians in Parepare and Balikpapan, a small and untidy oil-supply town on the west coast of Kalimantan and about 250 kilometres across the Makassar Straits. The Russians seemed to have a regular supply route between the two.

His next contact was a little more remote. He was the chief of Indonesia's National Coordinating Agency for Surveys and Mapping (BAKOSURTANAL) which was based in Jakarta. It had branches in several locations, including Central Sulawesi and the capital of Kalimantan, Banjarmasin, not far from Pontianak.

On instructions from BAKOSURTINAL's chief, the Kalimantan branch manager was forthcoming and as helpful to Terry as he could be. Although mapping and border inspections in Kalimantan were generally focused on East Malaysian Sabah and Sulawesi, he expressed concerns about Russian interest in the border areas that did not appear related to tourism.

The Russians tried to be inconspicuous in Parepare but they were, as he put it, 'blundering, particularly when full of vodka and chocolate'.

"In Parepare and places like Pontianak, they can get away with anything. I think our national police and army should take a closer look at what goes on there. Our responsibilities are more to do with border control and compliance, not policing. I sometimes wish I was a policeman for a day," he said.

Now Terry was fast running out of time. There were two ports before Pontianak. He called Col Weingraf to report he was not getting anywhere on politics and criminality in Pontianak.

The colonel said he looked forward to Okhotsk-1 and 2 being searched in Ho Chi Minh.

This had been arranged without involvement. To avoid ICCC or some other outside group's involvement, a relatively unprotected low-level alert was issued internally by the Australian Embassy in Hanoi to its Asian legations suggesting drugs may be offloaded from both vessels in Hoi Chi Minh City. No information was provided directly to the Vietnam Government or any other government since this was an internal routine alert. Everyone knew no information needed to be sent as the Vietnamese intelligence services would pick up the alert.

Hong Kong also would have intercepted the alert but was certain to take no action; Col Weingraf knew the Hong Kong authorities preferred the Vietnamese deal with their own problems, rather than attract more international media attention to China's Hong Kong.

There was also the ICCC's unsubstantiated concern that there could be collusion between the PRC and Russia. If the PRC was involved in supplying illegal cargoes, unsuccessful searches of the vessels in Vietnam might give them confidence that there was nothing further to inhibit them. If there was no Russian-PRC collusion and the suspicious cargo in Pontianak was the doing of others, they also might feel comfortable to go ahead. The search was a long-shot signal that the vessels would not be searched further and the transfer of illegal cargoes could go ahead safely.

In Ho Chi Minh City, the ships were arrested and escorted to docks away from the main cruise ship berths. They were searched from top to bottom over a 12-hour period. Nothing was found and the ships were freed to continue.

Angelina and Lucinda were on their respective ships travelling in tandem to Pontianak.

It was not certain if one or both vessels would carry the questionable cargo. The prospects of foiling the Russians before Okhotsk-2 approached Australia and Okhotsk-1 approached PNG depended on catching one or both ships loading the cargo in Pontianak or arresting one or both in international or foreign territorial waters afterwards.

Again, Col Weingraf and Terry conferred remotely with Sir Jonathan to see if there were legal constraints in arresting the ships in Pontianak or immediately after.

Sir Jonathan's take on such prospects was predicated. He warned that arresting any ships outside one's territorial waters was problematic, not because of a justifiable cause for action but because of distrust of some national authorities which could hinder satisfactory completion of arrests.

"The exceptions for summary action are piracy, murder or an act of war," he quipped.

Sir Jonathan added: "There seems only one way open to us legally. The UN Convention of the Law of the Sea (LOSC) does provide for an arrest of a ship outside our territorial waters if an offence is suspected to be committed in our territorial waters. This possibly applies to Okhotsk-2 if the Indian crew member's account to Lucinda about the captain's political comments are true. Even if the comments are true, they are, as yet, irrelevant as they admit nothing illegal. They amount only to a vague threat.

"This means that, if Okhotsk-2 is suspected, based on reasonable evidence, of offloading prohibited cargo in a particular Australian port, we may be able to serve an arrest warrant on the ship in international waters. An arrest would be much more likely to succeed, however, if we were to wait until the ship was well within our territorial waters, preferably when it was being guided into a port by an Australian pilot. You may see this as leaving things a little late."

Terry asked: "OK, that's fine. What about Okhotsk-1?"

Sir Jonathan replied: "Again, an open waters arrest is possible but would be much easier if an arrest was made in PNG territorial waters. Some of those waters are very close to our waters, especially in and around Port Moresby. You will need PNG authorisation and that may require evidence.

"If there is evidence that the offload is to be in PNG, we would have to leave matters to the PNG authorities and this may not be desirable. If so, however, you and the PNG authorities will have to guess correctly where the cargo is to be offloaded. The PNG authorities may not be comfortable arresting a ship that is carrying an illegal cargo but has no intention of offloading it in PNG.

"To be honest, I am comfortable with legal games, not these guessing games. And, in any event, you need to know for certain that the cargo in either Okhotsk-1 or Okhotsk-2, or both, are illegal, so we are really talking theoretically at this point."

"Still talking theoretically, my money for Okhotsk-1 would be on Port Moresby or Wewak, not Madang or Lae which are intermediate towns with less strategic significance, further away from the capital and not centres of interest to international media. Wewak may have some attraction to those supplying weapons because it is closer to the border with Indonesian New Guinea."

Playing around with the pros and cons of Wewak, Terry mused: "It's still a fair way from the PNG-Indonesian border but the river systems may provide transport to the area where there is constant fighting by the locals for independence from Indonesia. Also harbour authorities would not be as effective as in Port Moresby and the Sepik council would welcome a large tourist ship like Okhotsk-1.

"Against this is the fact that independence fighters have little funds to buy weapons or anything else. But, if the primary reason for the supply of weapons is simply to cause regional disruption and attract international media, the Russians may not worry too much about the price."

He added: "I believe Port Moresby is the most attractive. This is not to say the port authorities are highly efficient but communications between Canberra and Port Moresby are good. Port Moresby is close but if an arrest is made a little further west in the Gulf region, one could almost walk across Torres Strait to Australia's Cape York Peninsula."

Terry confessed: "I find all our prospects for arresting the two ships confusing and uncertain. The targets could be Perth, Adelaide, Melbourne, Sydney or Darwin for Okhotsk-2, or Wewak, Madang, Lae or Port Moresby for Okhotsk-1, and even some port on the return leg. We could board the ships, take them over and become pirates of the Pacific. Like our BAKOSURTANAL mate, who would like to be a policeman for a day, I would love to be a pirate for a day," he joked.

"Before you do anything about arresting ships," Sir Jonathan said, "you should know that most LOSC provisions relate to *in rem* claims. They are to do with salvage, crew wages and damage. They also concern mortgages, ownership, registration, piracy, and even 'transporting slaves' and illegal broadcasts from war ships; all very interesting but irrelevant, so arrest warrants should not imply *in rem* claims or even interest LOSC authorities a great deal.

"I don't think claims come into it but it is worth knowing that the country in which a ship is registered determines what laws apply. Imagine the rubbish that would result if the law of Libya applied to an Australian claim.

"Another interesting point is that cruise ships are not required to report crime data to any official governing institution. Enforcement falls on the flag State the ship is sailing under, as crazy as that seems," he said.

It was agreed firm decisions about open water arrests could not be made. Solutions depended on intelligence from Angelina and Lucinda. Actions may have to be taken on suspicion, not evidence.

Terry added: "And justice may have to be applied summarily. We may have to make the law or take the law into our own hands. After all, that happens in Indonesia every day one way or another."

Time was of now of the essence. Lucinda contacted the Indian cargo handler again. This time she put it to him directly: "I have been giving your situation some thought. I may very well be able to help you and your family settle in Australia."

"I would like it greatly," he said restraining his enthusiasm. "Even though I have never seen Australia. I have read about the main cities and would love to live in Sydney, if possible."

"There are many hurdles to overcome," Lucinda said, "but I know how to tackle them and I have friends in government who might be sympathetic if they see some value to them. By this I mean if they see some value to the country. Understand?"

"Don't understand. I have little of value. I can only promise and work hard," he replied.

She said: "We can go a long way towards achieving your wishes if you show loyalty. You could do something for me that shows loyalty.

"I want to know what cargoes are being loaded in Pontianak on both ships, not just what the invoices and manifests state, but details of consignments, especially any unusual consignments. I'm not interested in food, fuel and regular provisions. Unusual ones interest me such as non-marine equipment, machinery, chemicals and the like. I really don't know myself what they might be, just anything you think out of the ordinary. Can you do this?" She asked.

This was a make-or-break question. Nothing had been achieved to date in identifying cargoes. She would not want him to walk away without immediate agreement or agreement within a minute or two of being asked.

If he refused, she could throw suspicion on him by secretly misinforming the captain about his background but this would backfire. It surely would result in him being silenced but she would have to abort her efforts to find out about the cargoes and would probably have to disappear herself. Kalimantan was not an ideal place to go missing.

The possible consequences of his not helping were very serious. If he balked at the suggestion, she would have to decide if he was genuinely confused or thinking about collaborating with the captain.

Now that he knew what she wanted and smart enough to know the seriousness of her question, she could give him no leeway. She commented: "Now there are no 'ifs and buts' involved."

Any unfortunate outcome would not be personal; it would be based on loyalty to the ICCC, national interest and her own safety.

All this went through her mind. She only had a second or two while he digested her request but it felt like ages. It did not change her resolve; it scared her that his decision possibly carried life and death consequences.

Her anxiety was relieved when he agreed and questioned what he could do. "But I cannot open all the cargoes," he said.

"As soon as we berth in Pontianak," she said, "you could get a copy of the cargo manifests and more importantly evidence of the sources of unusual goods. I need these well before loading begins."

He agreed to try.

Both ships berthed next to each other in the early evening. Lucinda's newly committed compatriot accessed the cargo warehouse which was clearly an Indonesian army store. He sighted documentation but could not remove the papers. They were attached to the cargoes. He recorded aspects of the documentation in a notebook and showed these to Lucinda. Okhotsk-2's notations in Indonesian stated that identical cargoes were to be supplied to Okhotsk-1.

Two particular consignments for each ship were signed off by the manager of the Indonesian regional TNI (army) storage facility in Pontianak. Each comprised a crate that would need a fork-lift to move and a timber box able to be lifted by two persons.

This was almost as good as having all the documents. Both ships were to carry military equipment of some kind. What was needed now was to visit the TNI warehouse and view the contents of one crate and one box without disturbing the contents or being seen.

The Indian contact told Lucinda: "I think it best if I do this myself. OK?"

Lucinda agreed.

In the early hours of the morning while Lucinda was on deck, presumably admiring the star-lit sky, he returned with eyes wide open. "The crate contains rifles. I don't know how many but there are a lot. The box has a number of plastic covered packages," he said.

He was surprised the warehouse was virtually unguarded indicating no one expected an intruder. The crates and boxes had roughly scrawled markings partially covering original labels, some indicating the contents or packaging or both had originated in the US.

Lucinda gave him about $500 for taking the risk and instructed him to carry on as normal. It would be desirable for him to stay on deck the following day and night, if that was normal.

Lucinda then called Angelina and sent a coded message to Col Weingraf and Terry. She signed off in both Angelina's name and her own.

The message read:

(Translated) **To Colonel Weingraf. The enemy is planning an imminent attack at uncertain ports. We need Terry to assist. Lucinda and Angelina.**

In code: Junior. Diueliz. Consilium appugnare. Sarziz. Dunsehia. Anceps. Durua TW. Aieganz 45.

In full: Junior (Colonel Weingraf, personal code). Diueliz (the enemy, in Lingua Ignota). Consilium appugnare (planning an attack, in Latin). Sarziz (action imminent, in Lingua Ignota). Dunsehia (at ports, in Lingua Ignota). Anceps (dangerously uncertain, in Latin). Durua TW (need Terry, in Lingua Ignota). Aieganz 45 (Lucinda, Angelina, personal codes).

Terry arrived in Pontianak by light plane at night. Presumably the cargoes were still in the warehouse. In particular, he had to know what the boxes contained. Not knowing what to expect, he had with him a small kit of miscellaneous equipment used by field officers in conflict conditions.

Again, Lucinda's compatriot helped. During the inspection, Terry discovered the boxes contained explosives. He decided to arm those assigned to Okhotsk-1, destined for PNG. He used a remotely activated detonator attached to a dedicated mobile phone.

Since Okhotsk-2 was destined for Australia, Terry thought it better to deal with this ship later in or near Australian waters.

Afterwards, he met with Angelina and Lucinda separately on their ships to advise them of a plan of action.

The scenario now was to disable Okhotsk-1 using the explosives in PNG territorial waters. This would happen when the ship was running up the PNG coast off Daru, just before the Fly River delta, some 420 kilometres across the Gulf of Papua from Port Moresby as the crow flies. Hopefully, the entire ship would not be destroyed quickly and loss of life would be minimal.

The plan included Angelina to be taken from the ship safely in a shallow draft speedboat. She had to be off her ship and well away when she detonated the explosives.

Okhotsk-2 would be arrested somewhere off Exmouth, about 1,200 kilometres from Perth and well inside Australian territorial waters, if it had not unloaded in Darwin by then. Lucinda would be part of the sting and should be safe.

Since both ships carried the same cargo and apparently had similar tasks, the team's scenario depended on Okhotsk-2 not assisting Okhotsk-1, if indeed Okhotsk-2 was not far away when she became aware of the explosion on Okhotsk-1.

It was expected Okhotsk-2 would ignore any call for assistance and high tail it to Australia lest both vessels found themselves in distress.

"Now it's my turn," Angelina said to herself as she reflected on Lucinda's close shave in the Philippines.

Her safety involved a fake pre-scripted message by Terry to Okhotsk-1, supposedly from the regional hospital in Daru, requesting Angelina be taken off the ship by speedboat near Daru for a flight to Port Moresby where a close relative was said to be seriously ill. She was briefed on this by Terry and had a credible story about her relative to present to the captain of Okhotsk-1, if necessary.

There was no 'Plan B', other than hoping life rafts could be deployed. Terry was direct, as usual, and said in a half-serious way: "Jumping overboard with or without a life buoy would not be a good idea. The shallows around the Daru Gulf country are known for large salt water crocs. At the hotel at Daru, I have seen the skin of what the hotel manager there claimed was the largest salty in the world. It was close to six metres."

Now all this depended on Angelina understanding clearly what was to happen. Terry had set a charge in the explosives box linked to a detonator and a dedicated mobile phone he gave to Angelina. He also handed her a small piece of plastic explosive he had taken from the box and a mobile timer.

He briefed Angelina: "There are *three* essentials you must know. You know all about what I am going to say, but I need to repeat it.

"Number *one* is this," he said pointing to her dedicated phone. "It has a protective cover marked clearly No. 1 and has only one button. Don't use the phone for anything except to detonate an explosion on the ship. It is not a phone. It's a pin linked to a bomb. It is set simply with a number. You don't have to make a call to set it off.

"Just press No. 1 when it is safe for you to do so. The main explosion should be instantaneous. I repeat, you have to be safely away when you do this. Right?"

"OK, that's clear enough. I'll set it off when I am clear of the ship," she said.

Terry explained further: "I'm not an expert in this plastic stuff, and there are many plastics. I do not know how large the explosion will be, but it could be enormous."

"OK, that's clear. How far will the signal carry and will it go through the steel hull of the ship? It's an old warship and I assume very sturdy," she said.

He said: "Number *two* is exactly that—how far away you should be. The signal should be strong enough if it is set off within about 200 metres of the ship. I expect 200 metres is far enough away for you to be safe, although it may be a little rocky.

"Number *three point* is about the timer. It is designed to activate the small amount of plastic I gave you. The timer is just that—a timer set to detonate the plastic at the time you set. You must find a suitable place on the ship where you can place the plastic and timer, preferably somewhere near an emergency fire warning station.

"The plastic is malleable and the timer is small. You should be able to find a place where it will not be discovered easily. Set the time to detonate the explosive just before you climb down the gangplank to the speedboat.

"This explosion will be small but strong enough to set off all kinds of alarms. It will give the crew something to do instead of standing around watching you join the speedboat. Right?"

"OK, Number *three* is clear," she said.

He concluded: "So, the sequence of your actions is that you keep handy the phone that will set off the main explosion, place and set off the small-time bomb as you board the speedboat, and get clear of the ship before setting off the main explosion that will destroy the cargo and should disable and perhaps sink the ship."

With the assistance of Col Weingraf, arrangements were confirmed to rescue Angelina from Okhotsk-1 by speedboat from Daru and for the raid on Okhotsk-2 days later when it entered Australian waters, preferably off Exmouth, everything working as planned.

After the briefings, Terry now enjoyed himself creating mischief. At his direction, Angelina quickly prepared several anonymous e-mails intended to stir up trouble between the PRC and Russia. Written in Chinese and scanned on

Okhotsk-1 passenger stationary supplied by Angelina, they were addressed to Singaporean, Indonesian, Taiwanese and anti-PRC Chinese language newspapers in Australia anonymously supporting Russian criticism of the PRC's efforts to subvert Pacific Island States.

The e-mails suggested Russia would protect Pacific Island nations from PRC interference, subversion and even PLA attack. They indicated also that PRC agents in PNG were observed acting in a hostile manner. The notes were sent from an untraceable location two days ahead of Okhotsk-1 being off Daru.

Terry's hope was that later some recipients would link the e-mails to the subsequent explosion on Okhotsk-1.

As enjoyable as this was so far, he decided to go further. He prepared an English language message purportedly to be by the captain of Okhotsk-1 to the Russian Embassy in Canberra stating: "Comrades: Packs in good order en-route to Moresby and Sydney."

It was to be sent in the same way when Okhotsk-1 was near Daru, hopefully the day before the explosion, and was expected to be intercepted by various Asian intelligence services.

His shenanigans occurred.

When Okhotsk-1 was near Daru, Angelina sighted the speedboat approaching and acted quickly. She moved some of her belongings near the rope gangway. She set the time bomb, which was in a suitably concealed place nearby, for about the time she expected to be boarding of the speedboat. Meantime, many of the crew and passengers were watching the approaching boat.

She singled out her Indian colleague who was among most of the crew watching and told him in no uncertain terms to do as she instructed. When the gangway was in place, she shouted to her colleague to assist with her luggage requiring him to carry her bags to the speedboat. There was no objection from the officers. Everyone onboard expecting him to return.

All this activity took almost five minutes. The small explosion created chaos. Crew members rushed around with fire extinguishers and hoses while Angelina and the Indian took off, virtually un-noticed.

Some 200 metres clear, she activated the main explosion.

There was a massive underwater thud as Okhotsk-1 virtually lifted out of the water with the centre buckling uppermost. There were no explosions outside the vessel or fire on deck or through portholes. It was as though the vessel's backbone had been bent upwards and broken. It settled back in a semi-submerged position and was clearly destined for 'Davey Jones's locker' in a matter of minutes.

Lifeboats were launched quickly and many boarded. By this time, Angelina's speedboat was well away but still able to witness the sinking.

Angelina reached Daru an hour or so before the lifeboats, some of which went directly to shore a considerable distance from Daru.

She and her assistant then flew to Port Moresby and checked in at the Australian High Commission where she left the Indian colleague with Terry to see what could be done about a permanent visa for Australia.

Throughout all this, Okhotsk-2 was not to be seen until it was near Exmouth where it was arrested along with its officers by Australian Border Force. Before the ship reached Perth under arrest, the international media was running stories about a Russian terrorist plot.

After Col Weingraf congratulated Angelina and Terry on the wharf, he broke the news that there would be little time for rest and recreation.

"Now was the time to reset our attention to Da'ish, particularly its concentration on the Philippines," he said.

Chapter 15: Targets

Col Weingraf met in Perth with the sisters, Terry and Sir Jonathan and announced that Da'ish was emerging from a relatively quiet period into an active global entity. "It is becoming more interested in our area," he said. "We need to know what this re-energised Da'ish is like, and just how important our area is in its global ambitions," he said.

Col Weingraf introduced Dr Liam McKenzie, an expert in Da'ish structure and operations globally and a colleague of Terry. They had worked together in ASIS years ago. He asked to be called Maka.

He explained: "Traditionally, many of its cells were able to plan and act autonomously. There was no centralised direction. Even within the one territory, one cell may not know what another is up to.

"Fortunately, this management philosophy of global diversity and internal and external secrecy seems to be changing to a centralised management structure and more open communications internally. What it means is that the ICCC may be better able to define targets. Some are in the Philippines and Indonesia. We may be able to do things in the Philippines more effectively in the not-too-distant future," Maka suggested.

Theodora pointed out that the Philippines was a Christian country with a reputation for brutal punishment for corruption and drug running. Indonesia had the largest Muslim population in the world, more than the whole Middle East, something like eighty-seven per cent of a population of around 280 million.

"Why then does Da'ish target these countries, one traditionally strict Christian and the other mostly Muslim?" She asked, knowing full well the answer but wanting to hear it from a specialist.

Maka explained: "Da'ish is essentially political, although it promotes itself and excuses its actions as religious. It sees political advantage in the Philippines because of social unrest, high degree of corruption despite the laws and a chaotic political scene. Da'ish sees Indonesia's rather moderate Islam stance needs changing to a more fervent stance, and it has achieved this with the introduction of Sharia law in parts of Sulawesi and Sumatra.

"Its religious pretence is reflected in its name. Da'ish is the Arab acronym for Al-Dawlah Al-Islamiyah fe Al-Iraq wa Al-Sham (the Islamic State of Iraq and Syria or Sham), commonly called Islamic State, IS, ISIS or Khilafat by the West."

Changing the topic somewhat, he said Da'ish was careful not to upset the PRC because of the proximity of its regional headquarters in the Philippines to the South China Sea. The PRC dislikes the conflicts promoted by terrorists because it believes it can win any conflict, even with the US, without fighting.

"It also avoids the Mariana Islands and the Federated States of Micronesia (FSM). This is because of their ties with the US. In particular, it avoids Guam, which is a US port, and Palau, which is a republic but enjoyed UN Trust Territory status and administrative assistance from the US," Maka explained.

Theodora asked about Australia's position in all this.

Maka said: "Da'ish can undertake hard and soft actions in Australia planned and even controlled from the Philippines. Hard actions, like bombings and assassinations, are feasible in the Northern Territory whereas soft actions, like recruitment, are problematic. It is difficult to recruit Territorians. They are a hardy breed and ideology is too much a fuzzy thing. It just doesn't work. In other Australian States and the Australian Capital Territory though there is scope for recruitment, particularly of 'sleepers'."

He added that, unlike Da'ish, the PRC was interested in the soft approach. They already had many agricultural, resource and trading footholds throughout Australia and in the Northern Territory a company with links to the CCP held a 99-year lease over the Port of Darwin…which had prompted the US Marines Corps to establish their own port nearby and another planned near Daru in Papua New Guinea. The PRC is not fighting, but is winning.

"Many Australians believe Darwin is small and far enough away from the main cities. They don't know Darwin Harbour is five times the size of Sydney Harbour and deeper than San Francisco Bay.

"There is reason for concern. An Indo-Pacific Civil Maritime Law Enforcement Centre is underway in Darwin as we speak, a Space Centre is established in the Dhupuma Plateau near Nhulunbuy in Arnhem Land with 80 personnel from NASA and there is a significant increase in the annual US Marine Corps rotational force in Darwin.

"As well as this, you know Australia houses one of the world's three largest satellite surveillance centres at Pine Gap run jointly by Australia and the US. The other two are at Buckley Air Force Base, Denver, Colorado, and Menwith Hill, Harrogate, Yorkshire, both probably less accessible than Pine Gap."

Maka continued: "One of Pine Gap's current tasks is to keep an eye on the development of PRC militarised artificial islands in seas other than the South China Sea and the Sulu Sea. Already evidence is clear that planning is underway for artificial islands in the eastern part of the Celebes Sea."

Theodora said: "I have two queries. Firstly, knowing what you know about the Philippines, why don't we, I mean the ICCC, identify, target and destroy particular Da'ish interests there?

"Secondly, because of the PRC situation in the Indo-Pacific, can we selectively snipe PRC interests in Darwin without creating an international incident?"

The two-pronged approach appealed to Maka and Col Weingraf. Early attention had to be paid to the Philippines in view of the opportunity to exploit Da'ish's change of management style and the proximity of the Philippines to Darwin.

As a first step, a relocation of the sisters was thought useful.

Lucinda would take a break in Guam. Her time there would be for rest and recreation after her experience in the Solomon Island. Being in the region, however, she could be called on quickly, if necessary.

Terry and Theodora would take the lead in the Philippines. Their aim would be basic. It would be to identify specific Da'ish strongholds and forecast activities.

Maka took the opportunity to reiterate that Da'ish's success was due largely to its propensity for internal secrecy, international notoriety and independent management. It wanted its bombings to be publicised, its direction diversified and its cells virtually unaccountable to any central group. In the Philippines, however, it now preferred a hierarchical style.

He suggested that one of the sisters assisted by Terry could do more in the Philippines than the three sisters together in the one place, partly because of the sensitivity of Da'ish to strangers.

Terry would re-establish contact with his local ASIS contact in Manila. He would also travel to Guam and Palau for a short time.

Angelina and Col Weingraf would go to Darwin to update themselves on the Port of Darwin and the new US Marines Corps port facility nearby. Col Weingraf also would visit Pine Gap to brief colleagues on their plans as they developed.

Maka would visit the ICCC office in Sydney as would Lucinda before her visit to Guam. Both would be prepared to travel, if needed.

What was to happen in the Philippines and Darwin depended on their investigations and intelligence.

On arrival in the Philippines, Terry and Theodora went straight to the Australian Embassy. His ASIS counterpart there provided a large amount of documentation on Da'ish. "You will need a day or so to go through all this but I prefer you did this here, not in your hotel. You have a room here to use at any time," the contact said.

"When you have digested it, we should meet with a Philippines military contact of mine. Let's say the day after tomorrow at 1100 hours at Tagaytay. It's a holiday area on Lake Taal, about 50 kilometres from here. It'd not too difficult to find," he said.

The four met at Tagaytay. After they were introduced using Christian names only, the ASIS operative left. The Philippines military intelligence officer revealed several locations in which Da'ish was established. However, catching its leaders was virtually impossible without having someone on the inside, and there was no insider. "We cannot have local spooks here as there is mistrust everywhere. So, we act on solid evidence only and instructions. It's safe but slow.

"If anything," the contact said, "it has the drop on us because it has sympathisers in government, perhaps active insiders. These Da'ish insiders are not 'sympathisers' in the normal sense of the word. They are not necessarily believers either. Indeed, most of the Da'ish hierarchy here may not be real believers. Only those duped into joining are. The government sympathisers are simply corrupt officials and there is a lot of laundered money to go around.

"It's not all bad news though," he added. "We know an important Da'ish location is Lebak at the southern end of Mindanao. In the nearby jungle, there is a training camp. A secondary location is Zamboanga, about 300 kilometres across the Moro Gulf from Lebak. Zamboanga is about as far away from Manila as one can get. It is a tiny township. The only outsiders are near regional locals and occasional foreign honeymooners and backpackers.

"Surprisingly, these two locations offer us something of an advantage. If Da'ish wants to attack parliamentarians, senior military officers and community leaders, Manila is the most likely place. It also houses most of the foreign correspondent corps and local media, and Da'ish needs publicity of violent events. However, it is well away from Da'ish's main hideaways. If the attackers are not conscripted or sub-contracted, they have a long way to travel home after an attack in or near the capital.

"To try to protect these two locations, Da'ish also has a number of safe houses. At least one is likely to be in Davos which also is a long way from Manila. So, we have a reasonable chance to chase attackers down between Manila and Davos as well."

Theodora asked: "Do any leaders get caught in this way? I assume the leaders give the orders and the lieutenants do the work."

He said: "Correct, Theodora, our problem is that the leaders do not perform attacks. Only underlings are caught while escaping. If they are caught by us, they don't survive. They are not worth interrogating. If they are caught by locals and handed over to us, their fate is the same. Some are suicide bombers, so often all we have to do is clean up what's left. That's a satisfying job, so to speak."

He continued to explain: "Not all bombings are in the main centres. Nor are they intended to be publicizable; small scale bombings are mainly to intimidate small communities. While they are having some success with the big events—to their personnel cost admittedly—in rural areas they are having considerable success with improvised explosive devices (IEDs) in rural and other small devices."

"How much success?" Theodora asked.

He said: "Well, many villagers are injured regularly. Those who try to cut through the jungle to avoid these booby traps encounter other kinds of devices much like those used in Vietnam during the war there. We need something that defuses these IEDs without having to creep along tracks with metal detectors at little more than a couple of kilometres per hour."

Theodora suggested she may have an idea based on the use of drones in commercial environments at home. "They are used to spray disinfectant in unhealthy areas and to spread fertilisers and weed killers on crops. These are basic applications that have been used for a long time but it may be worth some experts putting their minds to modifying them to identify or even disable IEDs."

She added: "I recall one of our ICCC sessions some time ago covered this type of problem, mainly applied to fairly open areas where vehicles were targeted in conflict zones, but we did not find a solution better than conventional sweeps. One never knows though.

"My quantum computer colleagues in the US may be able to help, although I believe they are now concentrating on military developments, including highly economic aerial systems—loitering munitions and hand-held quadcopters—and, at the same time, designing anti-swarm drone systems. So, they are designing a wide range of offensive and defensive systems.

"I feel sure they could put their minds to something that converts an agricultural drone to something that identifies and destroys a basic rice and vegetable farm IED. With an input from a few of my engineering mathematicians in Australia, perhaps we can convert a theory to reality, presuming the military here has a reasonably sophisticated electronics capability," she said looking at her companion.

The military officer said: "We do have a large engineering facility here and it deals regularly with computers and the like. But I assume this kind of experimentation has been tried before."

"I don't know. I will get back to you as soon as I can, if you don't mind," Theodora told him.

"Of course; go for it," he replied.

She asked also how she might, as she put it, nose around Lebak. "I would like to get a feel for the place you think is a Da'ish base, without becoming a curiosity myself."

In a robust voice, Terry interrupted: "No."

The military officer agreed Lebak was dangerous but added that there were several ways to exit Lebak fairly quickly. "It could be possible to carefully look around Zamboanga instead," he said. "There is a sealed road all the way from there to Davos, and one can catch a ferry across Moro Gulf, even though this would take longer to get to Davos."

He paused for quite a long while and suggested: "What about you and Terry 'honeymooning' in Zamboanga?"

Glancing sideways at Terry, he asked: "How can you say 'No' to that, mate?"

Terry had been silenced.

Ignoring the suggestion, Theodora said: "We may be able to sort something out but first, I need to get back to Manila to refer the IED problem to my colleagues and give them time to respond."

Back in their hotel, Theodora messaged her contacts in the US and Australia about how to detect and destroy IEDs in a basic rural tropical environment.

The military officer called and made two suggestions while Theodora's contacts were working on the IED problem. One was that Terry and Theodora visit Zamboanga for a day to reconnoitre the vicinity and make their own minds up about the value and safety of spending time there together.

With a little hesitation, he suggested they book a honeymoon suite in a local hotel if they felt safe and comfortable about doing so.

The other suggestion was for Theodora and the officer to attend a cock-fight on the coming Friday night in a semi-secret venue around Zamboanga. It sometimes alternated around the town of Butoan, in the northern part of Mindanao. Both townships were near where a number of vegetable farmers had been injured by IEDs.

The officer reasoned that Da'ish was unlikely to be represented as its strategy for recruitment was religion not gaming, and the risk of being detected by those who had been harassed was far too great.

When Theodora met her military escort on the Friday, she quipped: "A honeymoon and a cock-fight. An easy choice!"

The two went to the fight in an old car arranged by Terry. The officer carried an old 38 millimetre revolver in his belt clearly visible. It was a weapon that could be purchased easily throughout the Philippines, and not a police or army issue. Patrons carried a variety of weapons. One or two even shouldered old-style sub-machine guns. The patrons were a mix of hard-working small business owners and labourers who had experienced hard times, and were hard men themselves in need of cash. They were not gentle family farmers but they were honest among themselves and did not tolerate lawlessness during fight nights.

Several seemingly without arms were in groups. Clearly, any money won on the cock-fights would not to be stolen without consequences. There were no threats. Aggression among patrons was not evident.

The cock-fight nights seemed untroubled routine events. The organisers seemed to be the fight referees. There were no back-room boys, cheating or scams. There were no disagreements with referees, although they did not have to decide on close calls since generally one bird was fatally injured in nearly every contest.

When they arrived, Theodora was immediately noticeable, and became even more so as she did the betting and won three times out of four, returning her more than 50,000 pasos, equivalent to around US$1,000 in total. Her companion advised her to cease betting in case she won too much.

When asked by a referee if she wanted to place another bet, she declined and remarked: "This is my first time here. I've won more than I ever expected and don't want to be going home with a lot of cash, even though my friend here would look after me. I must say I feel safer here than outside anyway."

With the audience noise and the cocks fluttering around in an atmosphere of blood and feathers with four fight pens going at the same time, the referee assured her: "You are safe. Most of these men are businessmen," he said, seemingly defending any gangster connotation this newcomer might have in her mind.

"I suppose most farmers don't have enough money for this," she queried, hoping he would comment on the problems of farming in the area.

He said: "Occasionally, we get farmers but you are right, they don't have money. They sometimes breed a bird or two and make some money that way. Infrequently one puts down some pasos and when he wins everyone is happy. If he owns a bird and it's not too badly injured, he goes home with his cock to fight another day. Otherwise, he and his family have a few good meals. But no, we don't see many farmers."

Theodora remarked: "Obviously, I don't know much but when coming here I was surprised to see quite a few people with injuries. I guess farmers can get injured more than businessmen around here," she said wanting to direct the conversation, without really having seen any injured people at all.

"Where did you see them?" He asked.

For a moment Theodora felt she had gone too far but the body language and tone of his question did not signal doubt. It seemed merely a conversational response.

She said: "I don't know. Just here and there. And I took little notice of the first couple, but there was a third and, if I remember correctly, a fourth injured person, all in the one trip."

He explained: "We have a problem in some areas where land mines are placed in farm roads and tracks by what we call invisible demons."

"Do the farmers or the authorities try to find out who does this and why? I assume the farmers do no one any harm," she said.

"No," he said, "there are more invisible demons in this area than other places, although I don't know what goes on in Luzon and central parts. You don't want to ask too many questions about this. It might not be good for your health."

Before they left, Theodora asked if she could come to next Friday's cock-fights and was given a nearby address as venues changed regularly, making it difficult for the police to raid them.

"Mind you," he said, "the police are not a problem, just one or two officers who want to make some money by threatening to put us in."

Back in the hotel, the officer, Terry and Theodora reviewed what they learned at the cock-fight. It was clear cock-fight patrons were not only aware of farmers' concerns but some seemed frightened themselves. There was a possibility that one or two locals who seemed scared could be willing to talk openly about who was responsible and why, but this required caution.

That probably would mean attending a couple more weekly cock-fights. Time was pressing and a couple of weeks may be too long to turn a cock-fight patron into a resource.

The following day, Theodora received a lengthy response about counter-IED measures from her US friends and sent a copy to Col Weingraf for possible reference to her relevant ICCC tutor on the subject and possibly to one of her engineering mathematicians.

Col Weingraf indicated the proposed solution had merit and suggested she ask her officer companion if the Philippines military would be interested in prototype development of a counter-IED design.

The design parameter was based on a muffled drone that carried a few light-weight miniature devices all driven by a motor linked to its propulsion motor.

One device was an altimeter that could be set to adjust in slow flight to maintain a specific distance from the ground up to 600 millimetres, even if the ground was uneven, wet, rocky or leafy.

Another device was a metal detector that could be set to scan an area of up to 800 millimetres in radius, enough to cover the walking area of many farm tracks. It would need to be so sensitive as to pick up a signal from a metal object buried up to 120 millimetres deep and could pinpoint the centre of the object.

A third device was a twin barrel paint-gun that could spray precisely an object's centre picked up by the metal detector. This paint-gun would carry two coloured dyes, one fluorescent for daylight vision and the other visible using special night vision glasses.

The paint spray device was not modelled on those used for spreading anti-septic liquid over unhealthy public zones or weed-killers over infected plantations. While the principle was similar, the added devices represented original concepts.

Everything had to come within set weight, propulsion, operational, production, maintenance, materials, tooling and cost parameters. Patents could be involved later. Production within the country was important because the device was specific to jungle tracks between farms and was not intended for mass-production.

Preliminary specifications and drawings of several likely devices were provided quickly from the US.

All that was needed was a sharp-shooter to take out any identified IEDs. A very light-weight 22 millimetre rifle would be sufficient. They were readily available in most main centres. Alternatively, a sling-shot or bow and arrow could be used but were risky because of accuracy.

The US designers reported to Theodora that they were close to drawing up plans for this enhanced version that could be prototype developed in the Philippines.

The Philippines military went to work on the US specifications. Some materials and components were supplied through the ICCC from selected private sector defence equipment suppliers in Australia, including one producing computer chips.

The purpose-built IED detector drone was on its way.

Theodora and Terry went to Zamboanga and booked their honeymoon suite in the Peacock Hotel, an old building on the waterfront.

The room featured the mandatory use-for-purpose furnishings—A full-length female nude statue revealing everything; a life-size Bacchanalian painting of black and white female figures of greatly enhanced proportions; a mirrored ceiling above the bed edged with a string of small flashing lights; a heart-shaped double bed; 'his' and 'hers' dressing gowns in appropriate colours; a dressing area more suited to a strip club change room; artificial flowers in several vases; and a range of cheap wines. No second bed, lounge or chair. It was a room for action not relaxation.

"How to turn a lady on," Theodora said when entering the room.

They slept together, separately.

They vowed to tell no one and promised to administer 'the harshest of punishments imaginable' to anyone who joked about their secret slumber. One thing common to both was that they would never forget their predicament, as hard as they might try to do so.

Theodora thought about the circumstance of willingly sleeping in the same bed with a man without one touching the other. Neither fell out of the bed the two nights they were there, as precarious their positions were around the edge of the bed.

It was all in a good cause and part of their investigation but, she said: "None of my studies or training prepared me for this."

During their two-days honeymooning, they observed what seemed to be an excessive amount of cargo being delivered to such an insignificant port as Zamboanga from ships originating in countries across the South China Sea, particularly Cambodia and Vietnam.

Their curiosity led them to a waterside warehouse which held goods received from Davos. They could find out little more without creating attention, other than some consignments carried US markings. "*Deju vu* of things Pontianak," Terry said to Theodora, even though Theodora was not part of the Okhotsk-1 exercise.

They returned and prepared to attend the up-coming Friday cock-fight. They wanted to find the referee who had been so willing to talk previously and ask discreetly two questions. One was about the likely US-marked goods in the Zamboanga warehouse. The other was about the farmers' routes booby trapped or subjected to 'invisible demons' in recent times.

During the second cock-fight, they were successful in getting partial answers to both questions. For some time, the cargo in the warehouse had puzzled locals who had seen crates with US military markings on them. This meant such cargoes were probably regular and therefore could be traced or, more interestingly, could not be traced.

The local routes used by farmers were detailed on a roughly drawn map. The referee said the scale of booby trapping was extensive and extended well up the country, even past Manila to the Luzon area. He could not help with these but suggested they were well known to the authorities in Manila.

In the next few days, the locations of the routes were defined with the help of the military officer, even though he made it clear his particular security responsibilities related to foreign not domestic enemies who were dealt with by the police and special units attached to the prime minister's office.

The officer said that the cargo in the Lamboanga warehouse had not been identified, even though it was not believed to be from a US establishment in Manila or the Philippines army. It could be a matter for the police, rather than the military to investigate. He suggested the crates could be fair game, as he put it, meaning they were either smuggled or purchased with fake identification and could be sold by whoever had possession and bought by whoever had cash.

He agreed to help Terry and Theodora find out a little more about the consignments. The three sneaked into the warehouse during the night. There were no guards and access was easy through a forced window. Clearly, the consignment owners did not think there was a risk.

In one of the crates were four GLCMs with US markings. As soon as they saw them, the officer exclaimed: "How on earth do the importers and port authorities think there is no need for guards. These are high value items."

There was so little protection of the consignment that the three had time to chat quietly about what they had found. It perplexed them. Clearly, the GLCMs would not have come from China. The PRC had its own type of cruise missiles anyway.

Presumably, they were for a domestic target or a PRC target somewhere but the range of GLCMs limited their use against likely PRC targets. They could not have come from Russia as their missiles with the same range were distinctly different, unless the missiles were part of some type of deceptive plan. This seemed highly unlikely. The Middle East was a possible source if the missiles were stolen from a US base there.

If exploded in the warehouse, there would be little point trying to source their origin as investigations would focus on the attackers rather than the remains of the missiles which would be widespread, much of them offshore.

Why such high-risk items were not properly secured seemed to suggest opportunistic possession but this was not thought realistic either. Da'ish was most likely to be the importers, possibly with Middle Eastern support. Why Da'ish would be so careless about their security was puzzling.

Perhaps Da'ish's present preoccupation with persuasion and recruitment before direct action was the reason for leaving the GLCMs on hold in the warehouse until an irresistible opportunity arose for their use. It was too risky to go further and trace the ownership through shipping manifests. In any case, the find itself could be used to damage Da'ish, or create an opportunity for the PRC to do so.

As soon as the officer took photos of the crate markings and missiles, the three left as quickly as possible. Prints were sent to the Chinese Embassy in Manila with a carefully scripted, non-traceable note in Chinese prepared by Theodora.

The note was purported to be from a unanimous Chinese supporter working against the Americans as a whistle-blower. The supporter accused Da'ish as the guilty party. It suggested Da'ish had anti-PRC and anti-US agendas in pursuit of its aim to convert the Philippines.

The misinformation fuse was set.

If the PRC acted as hoped, it would take care of the consignment whoever was to blame. It would be a generally win-win situation for the ICCC. No casualties would result. The PRC would not excuse or blame the US. If by some chance the US was accused, it would deny involvement. Da'ish would lose its missiles and distract itself from its task of distracting others.

The officer thought the missiles were probably intended to be used in the Philippines, Indonesia or even Australia in due course.

The following day, the entire warehouse was destroyed by an enormous explosion, much greater than seemed necessary to obliterate the cargo. It seemed over-kill intended as a warning.

Clearly, the PRC had accepted and acted on the whistle-blower's message. This indicated the ICCC's whistle-blower was taken to be credible and similar communications could be used again if the opportunity arose. It was likely a PLA officer had inspected the cargo secretly and verified the advice.

Theodora remained in the Philippines to witness the reaction and travel to Manila and a small township further north, Baguio, where farmers had been subjected to coercion and booby trap attacks. She also continued to receive assistance from the officer.

The advanced drones were put together in Manila and tested successfully. Before being employed, Theodora and her contact visited farmers in the south and around Baguio. She instructed a select group of farmers in how to operate them and explode the IEDs using rifles.

The few drones used for training were left with farmers who could instruct others. Soon after a number of drones were produced and made available in the south and north. The project was successful and farmers generally were more confident in living a relatively peaceful existence.

The officer predicted Da'ish's reaction. It replanted IEDs in the same places as those that had been exploded in expectation farmers would think the particular locations were safe. So, the officer advised farmers in these locations to regularly scan the tracks and roads. His advice was useful as several of Da'ish's new IEDs were identified and destroyed.

Terry went to Guam to meet Lucinda. Both planned to go to Palau afterwards.

He met with his Guam counterparts, mainly US Major Joe Clausen, and informed him of the ICCC's work in the Solomon Islands and more recently in the Philippines, including the discovery of cruise missiles.

He touched on Indonesia, and said: "Fortunately, problems for Da'ish are emerging in Indonesia because of religious change and new powers given to the army and police.

"This target nation seems on hold for Da'ish now that both the police and the army have similar domestic terms-of-reference making it riskier to stir up trouble in the main cities. Any anti-government protest or small explosions are more likely now to be met with overwhelming force.

"The history of the republic demonstrates force is in their DNA. The early Suharto days prove this when, according to your own statistics, Major, up to 250,000 citizens were murdered, many by their own neighbours, for being suspected of being communist sympathisers," Terry said.

Maj Clausen replied: "That's right. During this time, whistle-blowers and those who carried out the killings, mainly in and around Jakarta, were congratulated and given credits based on the number of noses, ears and penises they were able to present to their bosses representing kills. Heavy neighbourhood treachery!"

Changing the topic, Terry said: "There are problems at home right now but together with the US, we will deal with them as they develop. The long-term Chinese lease of Darwin Port is an unfortunate development of our own making. The establishment of your Marines Corp port not far from Darwin, the construction of a 5,000-tonne ship lift in Darwin under Project Galileo and other developments are encouraging but must be considered by the PRC as serious provocation. The same applies to our upgraded joint exercises in the territory."

"Yes, I am well aware of these things also," Maj Clausen said.

"I have met Lucinda and she has been busy looking over our port facilities and equipment. I think she is impressed," he said.

He went on to say casually: "While we are not on major international shipping lanes, Guam uses regularly a route between China and the US via Hawaii. Fortunately, we do not have to go through the South China Sea.

"Nevertheless, we do not accept that the PRC owns an international waterway and demands permission to enter. We will not only sail through and fly over but reserve the right to conduct military exercises with other countries, including Australia, in what are international waters. We already exchange verbal threats between planes and ships as we go through these parts. At some point, this may become intolerable.

"We are a long way out for Da'ish or any other aggressor to attempt anything here or in Palau or Yap, where we maintain regular shipping routes.

"So, how can we help you? It seems to me there is little you can do here," Maj Clausen said.

Terry explained: "I have three matters I would like to float with you. Firstly, I want to share some perplexing intelligence we are still developing. As strange as it seems, Da'ish has surveillance devices in the Philippines directed at the eastern part of the South China Sea and the Sulu Sea. We know China is interested in building its first artificial island outside the South China Sea in what it does not dispute are foreign waters now. It claims to have historical agreements to do so in the Sulu Sea.

"The devices have been used. Surveillance has been detected. It's real and all very confusing as there appears to be no serious reason for it. In addition, the Philippines and Indonesia are the custodians of large areas of these waters and would not have agreements with the PRC to build artificial islands anywhere, currently or historically. They have enough trouble with the South China Sea. Apart from this, both the Sulu Sea and the Celebes Basin are extremely deep.

"Any devices not condoned by the Philippines Government would have to be small, easily managed, low-cost and highly mobile. None—small or large— has been found. On top of this, military surveillance anywhere in the Asia-Pacific area is out of character and, until now, beyond the competence of Da'ish. Its military skills have always been more basic.

"Possible explanations are Da'ish is changing, its technical support is increasing, financial and equipment donors are digging deeper, and it wants to embarrass the PRC as much as it wants to attack the West. I just wonder why it has launched surveillance against the PRC. Perhaps it is intended to have the PRC blame the Philippines, but there is little for the Philippines to gain and much to lose from doing so. What do you think?" Terry asked.

Maj Clausen said: "I don't need to know about all these vague scenarios. If I am going to help you, give me something more tangible. What are the other matters you want to discuss?"

"The second matter follows on from this," Terry said.

"I wonder if we can be a bit circuitous. Can we conduct cost-efficient long-range surveillance ourselves aimed at getting the PRC to blame Da'ish for creating an itch that needs scratching?" Terry asked rhetorically.

Maj Clausen wanted some clarity: "When you say 'we', do you mean you and I? How do 'we' conduct surveillance from such a distance? We cannot do it through the military in Guam. That would create an international incident."

Terry suggested: "We could rig either one of your patrol boats, one of Palau's or a reasonably fast private fishing boat from either country with mobile surveillance equipment to target a developing or prospective artificial island area, perhaps around the Sulu Sea.

"If a patrol boat, perhaps it could be disguised. A fast private boat from Palau would seem preferable as Palau is closer to both the Sulu Sea and the Celebes Basin than Guam. And it is unlikely to be pursued once it re-enters Caroline Islands waters. We are talking about up to a 1,000 kilometre stretch but with long-range equipment, we would be talking about a quarter of this distance and any response from the PRC would take time. It's possible. You agree?"

Before Maj Clausen had a chance to reply, Terry continued: "Only one trip would be necessary. It would be in international waters in the Philippines Sea the whole time. Even if it ventured into Philippines territorial waters, there would be no trouble other than being ordered to desist. It is likely the Philippines Government would think it fishing illegally. The point is the PRC would certainly pick up surveillance signals."

He said a surveillance attempt had to be real. The design of the scan would have to clearly show significant parameters including depths, sea bed composition and so on. It would not be intended to identify a particular PRC artificial island site as we don't know of any for certain in any case.

"When high-tailing it home, we could deliver a fake message in Arabic supposedly to Da'ish indicating that surveillance had been successful and payment was expected immediately the data was handed over. The commercial nature of this task would add credibility to the task and would be in keeping with what goes on in these waters. We can supply an encrypted Da'ish address in Lamboanga for this message. The PRC would decipher it easily," Terry said.

Maj Clausen concluded that the exercise could be undertaken, although it was unusual such an effort was necessary for an outcome that produced very little.

Terry said: "Our surveillance has a purpose: To cause Da'ish trouble with the PRC.

"Thirdly," Terry continued. "This is not a request, just a follow-up comment. At the same time, our whistle-blower in the Philippines could communicate in Chinese with the Chinese Embassy in Manila again, indicating that he/she had picked up surveillance data from an undisclosed party on a mobile sea platform. This would confirm the signal the PRC surely had monitored. Before you ask, I should assure you that the PRC already has found our whistle-blower to be reliable.

"Thus, the PRC could believe Da'ish was not only using an on-shore Philippine surveillance station to monitor their Sulu Sea activities but also a small sea platform, even if the areas monitored were far short of the mark. Hopefully, this would be too annoying to allow Da'ish to continue. The PRC could do something about it, perhaps even eliminate Da'ish stations and personnel they knew about.

"I dare say the PRC would not think the US would go to so much bother or would use such a primitive and detectable off-shore system."

Maj Clausen said: "It's as complicated as I have ever heard of for an uncertain end, but I will look into it. We may be able to do something, hopefully something less convoluted."

Despite the doubt, an assessment resulted in the idea being agreed.

Next day, Lucinda arranged with a private company servicing part of the Guam to Palau shipping route to use a fast boat, without giving a great deal of information about the purpose. The boat identification was altered simply with adhesive tape so that it could not be traced visually through a Palau registry.

A surveillance unit was loaded and a volunteer crew from a hand-picked group of US Marines in civilian clothes performed the task over-night and part of the next day. The Chinese Embassy was informed by the whistle-blower as planned.

Nothing more had to be done. Not even a follow-up was needed. Further involvement of Palau was unnecessary. Maj Clausen was happy nothing went wrong but was left scratching his head about the non-military tactic by a team that included several female agents and did not achieve a tangible result.

Lucinda and Terry returned to Singapore to meet with Col Weingraf, Angelina, Theodora and Sir Jonathan who wanted to be involved with anything to do with Darwin Port and the new US Marines Corps port.

Chapter 16: Cauldron

It took no time for the group to experience the cauldron that is the Northern Territory.

Its multiple ingredients frothed away: Da'ish's new *modus operandi*, Chinese influence, US military attention, steamy weather and refreshingly informal, if not raunchy, community attitude to life in the Top End. A more effective recipe for discomfort and uncertainty could not have been planned.

The group booked into three Darwin hotels. The sisters were in one international hotel and Col Weingraf and Sir Jonathan in another. Terry preferred what he called a 'scruffy pub', in which he said he felt more at ease, and probably less conspicuous.

A meeting was arranged at a roadside inn near Humpty Doo, about 75 kilometres south-east of Darwin on the road to Jabiru, a uranium mining village, now mostly a tourist spot.

The inn was on a secondary tourist route within the world-famous Kakadu National Park. It comprised a dozen motel-type rooms, a large timber bar and restaurant, a sealed car park large enough for buses and trucks during the wet, and a small zoo housing a few pigs and a buffalo. There was also a small indoor-outdoor pond housing several juvenile fresh water crocodiles that stared at patrons at the bar.

Even though it had all the makings of a top tourist establishment in the area, it did not attract as many visitors as the facilities could handle. Still, it seemed to survive financially. It appeared well kept, serviced by a small but smartly uniformed staff, and offered robust country food and a variety of the proverbial on tap.

Col Weingraf introduced three co-opted members of the group swelling the party to nine. He introduced them as experts in NT affairs. He said they were willing to brief the group on sensitive matters, particularly those related to Da'ish or any other group interested in illegally exploiting the territory or causing trouble.

Two were advisers only and not expected to be involved physically in ICCC actions. They were William Boyce, a long-term resident anthropologist, to be called, at his request, 'Billy', and James Kavanagh, a resident counsellor with the NT Government and expert on border security and policing, to be known as 'Jim'.

The third was 'PL', an ASIO officer from the ACT and skilled in counter terrorism. He was a former adviser to ONA. He said his nickname initials represented Pacific Larger, his preferred beer, although not brewed in the NT. It was a long-standing PNG beer from the days when PNG brewing was done on a barge, before the first brewery was built on-shore, probably around the late 1940s, just after the Japanese were defeated in PNG's jungle warfare with Australia.

He presented as something of a friendly rogue, nothing like his Canberra colleagues, particularly in his language, but was disarmingly incisive when explaining the peculiarities of NT affairs.

Col Weingraf opened the meeting by stating: "The intention of Da'ish to enter Australia through the NT was because the Top End seemed to provide easier access then the other States or the ACT.

"After Da'ish recently witnessed the complete failure of the two Russian cruise ships, as well as having problems itself in the Philippines and being accused by the PRC of war-like actions, the Top End seemed a much less complicated target not only because of its remoteness and relaxed community disposition but because of an apparent *laissez-faire* attitude of the Territory Government.

"The territory also provides suitable backgrounds for terrorist actions, including discomfort between the US and the PRC locally, environmental issues involving uranium mining and several political blunders by the NT Government causing community dissatisfaction.

"Our interest in the territory is supported by intelligence from Pine Gap about Da'ish's intentions. This suggests the destruction of Darwin's port facilities and city infrastructure. The rationale for this needs discussion because the Port of Darwin is administered by a company with links to the PRC which would not want to see its port destroyed. Nor would we for that matter," Col Weingraf said.

He added: "Not all things are bad in Darwin. Consideration is being given to an Indo-Pacific Civil Maritime Law Enforcement Centre there, with likely terms of reference relating to terrorism, piracy, border control, organised crime and more.

"As well as this, a so-called 'space base' is proposed for the Top End to be called the Arnhem Land Space Centre from which rockets will be launched, in association with NASA, for scientific purposes. In addition, the RAAF's Triton maritime surveillance aircraft are to be based in the Top End. Construction of a 5,000-tonne ship lift will add significantly to the port's ability to service and repair ships, including damaged destroyers and frigates if and when repairs became necessary.

"But our concern is the Port of Darwin. Right now, it's successful commercially but is highly strategic and a significant defence weakness for Australia potentially. This is why we need some background from our experts before we look more closely at the intelligence and plan any strategy and counter measures," Col Weingraf concluded.

He explained: "The main difference in Da'ish's methodology in the territory is that it can be expected to revert to its old ways of autonomous actions, quite unlike its management behaviour elsewhere. It will probably behave unpredictably and spontaneously."

Addressing the group, Jim added: "The NT Government is well aware of the problem it created by awarding the 99-year lease of the port but is wary about introducing legislation that addresses the problem. To do so would remind the community, and indeed the nation, of its mistakes. Compensation probably would not matter a lot. It would be costly but would have the support of the nation. It's not a good option.

"I can say confidentially that this group you refer to as Da'ish has tried to influence the parliament already and we do not know how successful it has been. As for the PRC, parliamentarians and bureaucrats are aware they should not discuss foreign relations in case there are a well-placed PRC sympathisers listening in or a few corrupt officials willing to exploit hearsay. It's clear the problem is two-fold—the PRC and Da'ish. You may like to consider them together," Jim concluded.

PL spoke forcefully: "This cotton-pick'n port lease is for 99 years. It's there for a bloody long time. The granting of it has been described by Australian media as nothing less than parochial short-term thinking. That's a more polite way than

192

I would put it. It's a fucking disaster," he said while giving Jim a sideways glance.

"Apologies to present persons," he added. "But you agree with that, don't you, Jim?"

Jim nodded acknowledgement. "I'm a counsellor, not a Member of Parliament, but yes, I agree," he said sheepishly.

PL went on to say: "The port has serviced the cattle and mining industries for a long time and is now a major supply centre for Australian oil and gas projects. We cannot close it down or renege on the lease without international consequences. It's working well and they have done nothing wrong. Still, they are answerable to the PLA. They have got us by the short and curlies.

"We are comforted to know a new US Marines Corps port has been established in the Glyde Point area, about 40 kilometres north-west of Darwin. It can accommodate 2,500 US Marines and their equipment during rotations. It's clear this is a signal the US remains engaged in the Indo-Pacific, although there is much doubt about this in the media and even among professional observers. If this doubt is true, we have ourselves a can of worms militarily.

"Even so, there is a feeling in Beijing that the Marines Corps port in the territory is inconsequential in the broader scheme of things. The PRC's policy is one of winning world dominance without military engagement, at least not engagement with the US, even though the PRC's ambassadors in this part of the world make threatening sounds, and its media often show parades of hundreds of thousands of PLA troops goose-stepping ahead of some pretty heavy weaponry. We have seen this kind of thing before in Europe.

"And Pine Gap is hardly a secret. It really does get up the PLA's nose but the PRC tries to keep a lid on criticism. Even a popular Australian television series has been produced about it. It must remind the PLA annoyingly of its presence every minute of every day and reflect a degree of Western interest in the facility, even though the series is intended for Western couch potato viewers," PL said.

As he paused, Angelina asked Billy how the NT environment was a target for Da'ish.

Billy replied: "Everything is a target. In my particular area, the destruction of ancient Aboriginal art and what has been going on in and around Jabiru where uranium mining has been operating since 1980 worries me. Uranium mining in the territory began in 1953 in the Rum Jungle and South Alligator River fields near Kakadu National Park well before Jabiru's Ranger uranium mine began. And this is only some 250 kilometres from where we are now," he said.

A great deal of the next day was occupied in two-way briefings between the ICCC group and the three experts who agreed to be available for at least a week.

The briefings included an exchange of information about what Col Weingraf called the 'unexpected that can be expected' from Da'ish. Strangely, some 'unexpected' actions could be predictable 'with fingers crossed'. Others were hard to fathom.

After an intensive day yesterday, PL lightened the meeting. "One of the comforting aspects of the territory, or more correctly Darwin, is its entertainment…not the type you are thinking of, you dirty old man," he said looking at Terry.

"Have you heard of this?" PL asked, holding up a book. It was a compilation of front-page photo commentaries in the NT Times newspaper. They showed pictorially behaviour focusing humorously on drink, sex, nudity, crocodiles, driving, boating, and occasionally just rude stunts accompanied by entertaining captions and quotations.

One photo showed an injured groom at his wedding having been hit by a flying dildo. Another related to a man lighting a fire cracker held between his buttocks cheeks with a caption alluding to his consequent injury. Still another was about a lady-of-the-night leaving the territory in disgust because someone had stolen her sex toys.

After the entertainment, which took most by surprise, Col Weingraf and the others were keen to begin predicting likely mining, port, community, environmental and industry threats.

He said: "Any threat to the Ranger mine, one of three in the area, and the township of Jabiru is difficult to assess. Nonetheless, intelligence suggests both are targets. This has to be taken as a likely scenario. Let's accept that."

Angelina asked: "Why? Overall, they are not significant, especially since I understand decommissioning of the mine has begun and the township is virtually a tourist spot with several homes vacant. What is the strategic advantage to Da'ish or any other terrorist group of destroying one or both?"

Jim could not see a specific advantage in attacking the Ranger mine site or Jabiru other than to cause localised mayhem. If this was the aim, such actions must be secondary to something else.

He explained the complexity of Jabiru. It had a population of only 1,000 and was established originally for uranium mine workers. The Ranger mine was scheduled to stop by now and close in 2026. The leaseholders were rehabilitating the area but very slowly.

PL also tried to draw a conclusion as to why these might be targets. He said: "The federal government approves uranium mining. The Territory Government does not but prefers the township is saved. The federal opinion is based on Australia holding one third of the world's known uranium reserves and has two other mines, Olympic Dam and Beverley, both in South Australia.

"As well as this, the PRC and India plan to extend their nuclear power capacity. Australia could be a major supply source and, therefore, uranium a great revenue earner. There may be Commonwealth, NT Government and operator interests in not closing down Ranger entirely while appearing to allow closure to occur.

"Indonesia still has a plan that has been shelved for three decades of establishing 17 mini-nuclear power plants, most along the south coast of Java, fairly close to WA and the NT. Their likely source of uranium would be the NT. This sounds logical but the main problem is what country would process the material for power generation. Our only processing is for medical purposes.

"Indonesia might throw lots of money at a processing plant but history indicates it has a habit of screwing up high technology projects, particularly those related to security and defence.

"Years ago, a technology minister, who later became the Indonesian president, approved the purchase of advanced and expensive remote sensing equipment, only to realise the area in which it was intended to be used was generally covered in cloud rendering the particular type of equipment useless. Need I say more. I should say, however, modern remote sensors can see through cloud.

"Eliminating Ranger may send a message to markets that it's time to look elsewhere for supplies. All that has whiskers on it," PL said in his roguish way.

He paused and said: "There are many suppositions that can be made from this. Da'ish could place long-term value on eliminating one of the three sources of supply for other countries if it believes the Ranger mine will not close in 2026. It could spread disinformation about the mine closing. It could promote an argument between the NT Government and the Commonwealth, even stir up the on-going energy controversy or it could spread a rumour through anti-government media that the ADF is secretly lobbying the Commonwealth for nuclear powered submarines. But all this is highly speculative."

He went on to say: "The traditional Aboriginal owners want the multi-million dollar mine to remain but undeveloped. Already, they say, ancient Aboriginal art has been destroyed. Tourism is expected to cause no further destruction if properly managed. But Billy is the expert on this."

PL suggested that an attack on the mine could have something to do with the miners' leased houses in Jabiru. An attack on them could destabilise tourism.

"Fortuitously, the Ranger mine does not include Kakadu National Park but is very close. The park is one of two main NT tourism attractions for local and international visitors and any nearby attack could be significant. The other, of course, is Uluru. Both enjoy worldwide appeal to international tourists.

"Or it could have something to do with the production at the mine of a limited amount of heavy metal concentrates. In recent times, zircon concentrates and ilmenite have been mined there. These are highly valuable and not surrounded by controversy, not yet," PL said.

It was agreed that stealing supplies of these elements prior to destroying the mine might be a Da'ish plan but it could hardly be a primary reason. This was not Da'ish's current *raison d'etre.*

Despite the intelligence, the uncertainty about the possible attacks on the Ranger mine and Jabiru confounded the team. However, it had to accept the intelligence.

Theodora said protective measures had to be considered. She would take the lead, assisted primarily by Terry and PL, and the rest of the team, if necessary.

Theodora's first move was to suggest a search by Terry on the general manager of the mine and the property manager of the township.

The result was that both had no backgrounds of concern. They were locals who seemed primarily interested in doing their jobs properly. Both also drank at the same hotel as Terry.

Once the two were confirmed as probable honest workers, she hoped to get to know them over a beer at the hotel.

At the same time, PL wanted assurance that the local police could be relied on if the ICCC became involved in problems. He did a search of the NT Police management and received a Commonwealth response that indicated the assistant commissioner, Devanic Van De Hoffkirken, was an exceptionally efficient and trustworthy manager but a little 'prickly'. This was the reason for her posting to

Darwin where zero tolerance to back-chat was needed often for crowd control, misdemeanours and community protection.

The response also affirmed it probably was safe to introduce her to the team in due course. A post script suggested: "PL, don't get off-side; be nice."

PL bluffed his way into the corridor leading to the assistant commissioner's office at police headquarters. He knocked on her door without introduction. She was an imposing South African-born woman recognisable by her stature, accent, and apparent anti-nihilism disposition.

"Who the bloody hell are you?" She exclaimed as she opened the door. "You better leave before I toss you out myself."

PL countered: "Sorry for not getting someone to show me in. I'm a Commonwealth officer and have some information for you alone. You will be interested."

Then, in a direct manner he said: "Please listen."

"Identity?" She demanded.

PL showed her his card, the absence of any organisation virtually verifying him as a Commonwealth intelligence officer.

They went into her office where he told her he was an ASIO operative and asked for her confidential support in acquiring inside information and cooperation from the mine general manager and the Jabiru property manager to avoid or foil suspected criminal attacks on both facilities, and perhaps others in and around Darwin. He revealed his suspicions were based on Pine Gap intelligence.

She accepted his credentials.

He said: "I don't want manpower or facilities, just support by association with you among two apparently trustworthy locals of likely value to us. They do not know me and should not. They only need to agree with me."

As they continued, PL and the assistant commissioner got along well. Their professional connation supported their working together.

She asked him to call her Di. "I go by the name Di Kirk," she explained, "which is best for most non-official occasions, although our meeting should probably look official."

"I want to ask you for two things, Di," PL said. "Firstly, I would like you to accompany me to my pub tomorrow for a drink. It would be nice if that was all to it, but it's not."

After hesitating a second or two to see her reaction, he explained: "At the pub, a companion of mine will meet these two company people. Hopefully, at the right time, he will get them to assist him keep an eye on the mine and the village without others at head office and local line management knowing. It's a tall order for a first meeting over a beer with a stranger. He will say he has authority from the Commonwealth but not give any evidence.

"Your presence at the right time will allay any doubts they may have about my friend, although he will not be telling them about us, other than referring to us as a group of 'good guys' who may be in a position to protect the mine, the village and the residents. We firmly believe something criminal will occur and want to be in a position to ask them for further assistance a little later. At present, however, we have no specifics as to what this 'something' might be. But I'm certain something is in the wind.

"Of course, you will be in the loop all the time, officially or unofficially, as you wish. If they agree or decline, we will not change our task. If they decline, our surveillance will be covert and more difficult. It will not be unlawful. If they agree to hire us for a time as 'guards', it will assist us a great deal. Their company seniority suggests they can do this. If it works, we will be unseen most of the time," PL said.

Di said: "This is borderline stuff you know, but yes. I will come to the party. If they are somewhat hesitant or agreeable, I assume you will introduce me to them. If they disagree, I assume you will not introduce me to them. Is that so?"

"Yes. We will not compromise the NT Police or yourself if they prove to be disagreeable," he said.

She asked: "What is the second thing you want?"

"The second is to introduce you to our team," he said. "This will be important if we gain agreement from the two company officials but will not be predicated on their support. This is because, if things happen, the NT Police will be involved anyway. We may be able to help each other.

"The team includes three female agents with particularly high levels of technical and other skills, even linguistics and mathematics. Another is a high ranked military officer and there is a specialist in terrorist groups, including IS or, more correctly, Da'ish. There are two co-opted outside experts, an anthropologist and a senior NT Government counsellor. They have been cleared by Canberra and enthusiastic to help. If everything looks good at the pub, you will meet a couple of them there before meeting the others later," PL said.

She concluded: "I would be delighted to meet your band of visiting spooks whenever it suits you."

PL continued: "Without pre-empting our team meeting, I might foreshadow two other concerns we have with Da'ish here. Please do not get alarmed. When we know what's going on, we will know how to deal with it, and so will you.

"One concerns the leasing predicament of Darwin Port. The other is a threat to the safety of the US Marines Corp port development. There may be a third problem involving severe disruption of the NT Government and the community but this is as clear as a billabongs in Kakadu. If we can coordinate protective and counter measures, we will be more effective than handling one at a time.

"But first things first. Our pub meeting with the mine general manager and the Jabiru property manager, tomorrow after hours," PL asked indirectly.

Terry met the two managers at the pub. PL, Theodora and Di were seated at another table waiting for Terry to give the all-clear for Di to join them, followed by Theodora.

The distancing of the team members in the pub was to give Terry time, without others around, to move the conversation from drinking to the security of the mine and village, and to suggest he had the resources and, by association, the authority to keep an eye on the mine and the township at minimal cost.

After a couple of drinks, the property managers freely revealed they could do with some help as personnel numbers were down. There was nothing secret about this and Terry's approach seemed more like a job application.

Terry then put a serious proposition to help, the emphasis being on help rather than on a job. To this point, the conversation had been just pub talk as far as the two village managers were concerned. They could not take their new drinking companion at face value. At the very least, they needed corroboration of the capability of this stranger who could be talking nonsense or even planning a criminal act himself. The fact that management was not to know bothered both the mine general manager and the property manager.

Instead of walking away, both played along and were cautiously hopeful that what they were hearing was genuine. Terry sensed this and soon Di was called over and introduced to the two. This seemed to provide the corroboration needed. The pub talk had produced results.

When Terry raised the threat of attacks on the mine and the village, the atmosphere changed to serious sobriety and the beers stopped. Di witnessed the suggestion of a threat and left. Being there for this was sufficient. Her silence was taken as agreement that there may be a threat, the hiring of Terry and a colleague as pseudo-guards was a good idea and that the arrangement was to be kept confidential in the circumstances.

The mine general manager and the village property manager convincingly agreed. They were on side.

The same night, Terry and Theodora inspected the stores of the Ranger mine and the vacant Jabiru homes but found nothing that would suggest they had been or were to be used illegally.

They then accessed an inconspicuous village warehouse used mainly to store building materials and tools and discovered a large amount of trinitrotoluene (TNT), an old-fashioned explosive used in the mining and demolition industries. They also found fuse wire used for TNT and a charge box sometimes used to set off a wired connection to TNT. The storage of this material was careless but not criminal.

More significantly, however, they found several boxed of incompatible detonators suggesting there was another type of explosive in the warehouse. It did not take long for Terry to locate a box of malleable plastic-type blocks. It was C4, about a dozen 15-kilogram blocks.

Terry broke off a piece of the C4 and put it in his pocket with two detonators. He whispered to Theodora: "I could smell it; it's like almonds. Anyone with very little skill can use it but it is hard to access. You only need a detonator. Mining companies don't use C4. If this amount is used here, the whole village would go up. We are fortunate that the explosives are not armed. So, we have some time," he said.

Outside the warehouse, Theodora asked: "Can we set a trap by defusing the detonators and placing hidden cameras in the store so that we can monitor what goes on from our rooms in town or, preferably, from the home of the village manager or mine general manager. Maybe we can monitor the whole area from a manager's home.

"This means we will have to be nearby. The person who attempts to arm a bomb will want to be a fair way away when he expects it to go off so, I agree, we have time. The detonators won't work…will they, Terry?" She repeated herself: "They won't work, will they?"

Without an immediate answer, she said: "So, we should have plenty of time to identify, chase and catch the…" using the vernacular more likely from PL.

"If the Da'ish culprit is a mine employee, perhaps you can use your powers of persuasion to find out who hired him," Theodora suggested to Terry.

"That's a plan," Terry agreed. "We will fiddle with the electrodes in the charge box and replace some of the fuse wire with inert wire. This should deactivate the TNT, which I think is not intended to be used anyway, but we have to be sure. We have to rely on the C4 defused detonators. All this seems OK but it goes against the grain to leave a large amount of C4 unattended. It's not volatile on its own but its dangerous military grade stuff," Terry said.

As it happened, they gave the mine general manager and the village property manager the heads up. Cameras were installed in the warehouse. They were operated from the property manager's garage which was detached from the house and manned by the manager, Terry and PL on shifts.

More precautions had to be taken, according to Theodora. The village had to be evacuated without revealing the trap, just in case the cameras missed the arming of the explosives, the defusing work was unsuccessful or the culprit had arranged to activate the C4 and TNT remotely.

She and the property manager arranged to have all village residents prepared to vacate their houses at an undisclosed time on the pretext of a random but mandatory fire drill. The residents would be taken to a mine building a few kilometres away.

They would be provided with refreshments and their houses would be guarded against theft. As inconvenient as this could be, the timing of the exodus could not be pre-announced to give the fire drill credibility. The residents' transportation had to standby, presumably for several days.

Evacuation had to be as the arrest or arrests were made or a few minutes later. Timing was critical.

The trap required at least two of the team being on-site to restrain the culprit and communicate with Theodora who would manage the evacuation with the village manager.

Defusing was done by Terry assisted by Col Weingraf who had bomb disposal training years earlier.

The trap was set.

It all depended on the cameras detecting one or more individuals preparing the explosives.

Meanwhile, Angelina, Col Weingraf and Sir Jonathan concentrated on the PRC. They discussed Darwin Port's relationship with the CCP and the PLA with

Jim who had undertaken personal and corporate searches on the port superintendent. There were few skeletons in the cupboard as the leasing arrangement was awarded properly by the NT Government, neglected by the Commonwealth and well publicised in Australian media.

Still, something had to be done about this predicament, legally or otherwise, as long as what was done did not backfire. Angelina and Sir Jonathan, who now had become agreeably an unappointed member of the ICCC team, visited the Darwin Port superintendent on the pretence of familiarising themselves with the facilities and advocating a 'sister port' arrangement between two Australian ports—Adelaide and Darwin, and two major Chinese ports—Shenzhen and Ningbo. During an extensive visit, Angelina was able to record some communications data about the port.

The three agreed private messaging could be desirable in the very early planning of the 'sister ports' arrangement prior to it being presented to the PRC, the NT Government and the company's board. This was in case the arrangement could not be finalised in which case other interested parties would not be disappointed or embarrassed. When all agreed the idea in principle, the other parties would be asked formerly, in particular the four port authorities.

But for the first couple of days, the idea was private. As a result, Angelina was given the private text message address of the superintendent.

Angelina reported later to the ICCC group: "Now we have the data, there is room for getting the port company into real bother with its parent, and therefore, the CCP. We may even be able to re-excite national dislike of a major Australian port being leased to a company with links to the CCP. Perhaps the company's leasing arrangement could be reviewed by the NT Government with minimum compensation.

"There are a number of scenarios that can be developed to support this. Fake news about the port's interest in a 'sister ports' arrangement and a planned attack on the US Marines Corp facility could be part of all this in good time. It may be possible to emphasise the ports agreement as a PRC inspired move to further influence Australian transport and communications industries."

Col Weingraf said: "I'm with you here, particularly since the port lease has been promoted worldwide by the PRC as an innocent, trade related, infrastructure investment in Australia. For the port to function and to be seen to function as intended, it has to appear operationally detached from its parent and certainly anything to do with the PLA. What is suspected but not known publicly is that the port has a political agenda determined by Chinese Foreign Affairs and the Chinese International Development Cooperation Agency responsible to the PRC's State Council."

Angelina concluded that changing the port's commercial image would seriously upset the company's relationship with its masters.

She said: "Evidence of the company conspiring with Da'ish to attack the proposed US Marines Corps facility would be seen by Beijing as preposterous and acting against the interests of the CCP. I would not want to appear before a PRC court accused of this.

"Can we somehow use the sample of C4 pocketed by Terry during his warehouse search as evidence of collusion between Da'ish and the port?"

"Maybe so," Col Weingraf said. "It would be important also to let the US Marines Corps commander know what we are thinking, although there would be no real threat to its facility. Pine Gap should be advised well in advance."

It was time to selectively inform colleagues in a limited way of the never-to-be 'sister port' proposals.

The Adelaide Port authority was appraised of the plan by Sir Jonathan who enjoyed complete confidence of the authority and was on the board. Col Weingraf contacted DFAT informally.

It was time also to initiate ICCC's deception plans beginning with fake messages. One was a confidential message in Chinese from an entity in Sydney, set up as virtually untraceable, to the Darwin Port superintendent whose direct message address had been acquired by Angelina. The message reported on progress in arranging for a supply of 10 kilograms of C4 'for the US facility'.

The message thanked the superintendent for a partial cash prepayment for the consignment. It advised a small sample of C4 would be delivered the next day to the superintendent in Darwin addressed PERSONAL AND CONFIDENTIAL, as a sign of good faith. The full consignment would be delivered by a Da'ish colleague soon after the balance was received. The delay was necessary because Da'ish could not risk sending it by mail or air. It had to be sent by train inspections were easily avoided.

When sent, the message was expected to be picked up instantly by the PRC's Asia-Pacific surveillance system. The reference to Da'ish was expected to create a degree of confusion and even consternation in Beijing as any such involvement was completely unexpected.

Angelina also proposed an un-named person send an open message to the Darwin Port superintendent delaying temporarily the Adelaide-Darwin/Shenzhen-Ningbo 'sister ports' arrangement. The planned delay would be couched in highly polite and apologetic terms hinting it was because of a rumour of a problem between Darwin Port and the US Marines Corp facility. The message would say the rumour was obviously untrue and would pass in a week or so. It would emphasise the port authorities looked forward to the arrangement proceeding as soon as the rumour dissipated.

Action on this was to await the right opportunity to maximise its effect.

Sir Jonathan would not be identified with any of this, although his input was essential. This was to protect him later from any public knowledge of his involvement in the deception and to protect his Adelaide admiralty law business. His personal port contacts in Australia and elsewhere would not know anything about his association with the ICCC. Hopefully, nor would the PRC or its agencies.

Col Weingraf expected the message delaying the 'sister port' arrangement would support the credibility of the fake C4 message. He suspected the PLA would get rid of the port superintendent even if the threat to the US Marines facility seemed fanciful but hoped he would not be assassinated too soon. He could still be useful.

While briefing the US Marines Corp facility commander about the ICCC tactics and notifying Pine Gap, Col Weingraf asked if the number of guards around the site could be increased noticeably for a week and the number of drone flights over the site increased as well. This would be paid for by the ICCC which would be pleased to provide reliable civilian guards, if manpower was a problem at the time.

Col Weingraf said: "Of course, our attack scenario is fictitious but should be taken seriously by the PLA. It would show the Darwin Port superintendent was going well beyond his authority and potentially creating a dangerous diplomatic situation. In our opinion, would be no risk of this developing into anything more than a serious internal PRC incident.

"If this works, we could institute an international media campaign highlighting the infiltration of the PRC into Australia and the risk of a well-connected PRC port here. It could provide a reason for the NT Government to reconsider the port without the kind of penalty involved if it simply broke the lease.

"Looking at all this from the side-lines and not being involved may be of some comfort and amusement to you, Commander. If anything, the US would be seen as an innocent potential victim," Col Weingraf suggested.

While Angelina and Col Weingraf were weaving their web around Darwin Port, they were also assisting Lucinda and Billy who were looking at the possible damage to the environment by Da'ish and infiltration of PRC interests in the NT parliament.

Preliminary work involved them meeting with selected parliamentarians proposed by Jim who thought it best to be at arm's length publicly from the ICCC team. Meetings also were held with Aboriginal groups, including several elders. Billy attended these and led the discussions about protection of Kakadu, Jabiru and surrounding sacred sites. These were the only actions that could be taken before the village matter was resolved.

Angelina explained: "It would be ideal if the Jabiru, Darwin Port, US Marines Corps facility and government matters were coordinated but it depends on our having a lot of luck. We have been here just over a week and a lot has been done. We are still on the front foot but there are matters we cannot control.

"I know synchronising our activities depends largely on Da'ish's move on Jabiru. We have been holding back which means we are being dictated to by Da'ish, even though my prediction is that Da'ish will act very soon. What's your guess?" She asked Col Weingraf.

He suggested hastening the Jabiru attack by leaking information now about the delay of the Australian-Chinese 'sister port' relationship and increasing surveillance of the US Marines Corp facility. "The fuss of all these preliminaries could focus attention away from Jabiru and Ranger and may be seen as an opportunity for Da'ish to act," he said.

This was agreed now was the time to act on these matters, and hope it would prompt Da'ish to act on Jabiru.

Terry and PL were to stay overnight in the warehouse while these other actions were being taken. They were to neutralise anyone trying to activate the C4, even though deactivation of the proposed explosion had been undertaken.

Terry said: "We did this kind of thing in the Philippines and it worked well. Why not here? There should be less risk?"

As luck would have it, however, an intruder was caught in the Jabiru warehouse on the first night. He appeared to be a senior Da'ish officer. Terry and

PL wanted to 'look after' him but were advised against doing so by Col Weingraf.

The exodus of Jabiru residents went like clockwork and the explosives were removed safely.

The following day, PL and two senior NT Police officers selected by Di Kirk escorted the extradited prisoner to Canberra for processing and interrogation as a terrorist. Just before they left the airport, PL muttered to Di Kirk: "Thanks for the help. Incidentally, when we arrested this grub, we could have saved you the trouble of escorting him to Canberra. He saved himself by not resisting."

"Pity that," she replied.

The sisters and Col Weingraf then began putting the icing on the cake by briefing the foreign correspondents and news agencies in town. The sisters shared the job of sending internet messages to the main Asian, Western Europe, British and North American media groups, as well as Australian and New Zealand outlets.

No one saw the port superintendent again. Silence from the PRC was prophetic.

PL suggested he take a holiday in Darwin where he hoped to meet up with Di.

Chapter 17: Circumvention

The three sisters revisited Beth and Judith in Adelaide to relax for a short time before joining Col Weingraf in Sydney, where they hoped to learn of any further consequences of their work in the Northern Territory.

They also met Lee who had learned of their Adelaide visit. Invigorated by his overseas work with the sisters, he had done a little homework on the PRC's subversive activities globally and its changing attitude towards Da'ish from facilitator to antagonist.

This pre-empted the ICCC's next assignment which was to change the regional focus of their projects to one of a broader regional scope.

As Lee saw it, while terrorist organisations assisted the PRC occasionally in creating the groundwork for Chinese propaganda, they no longer fitted comfortably with its grand objective of creeping world dominance.

The excitement of spying for the 'good guys' had gotten into Lee's blood, even though he had partially returned to a sedate routine of language tuition. Instead of locking himself in a closet, as he referred to full-time teaching when trying to entice Theodora to become an international simultaneous interpreter for the UN, he independently expanded his circle of contacts to include university researchers and academics expert in PRC policies and processes. He felt this kept him in some kind of touch with informed opinion on PRC expansionism, even though he had no direction or reward for doing so.

He hoped this continuing side interest protected his ICCC memories drifting into a world of exaggeration, even unreality, a situation that could happen if his collaboration with his early accomplices ceased completely. His subconscious concern about this lessened with the return of the three sisters and Col Weingraf to Adelaide.

Lee told Theodora he and one of his most informed colleagues, a Dr Lei Kung, were sure the PRC had intensified its recruitment work using higher education institutions and intellectual groups.

The age-old method of gaining support had progressed from combining corruption, coercion and blackmail inherited from the former Soviets and enhanced subsequently with no less cruelty under Mao, to one today of enticement based on a process of gaining understanding and winning intellectual opinion. This process involved adroit evaluation of individual leaders in academia likely to listen to alternative argument and well-informed opponents of the Western status quo.

Lee explained: "The intended outcome is the same but the integrity and pace of support from those who are won over are greater. The premise is that they are the 'good guys' after many years being punished economically, territorially, socially and even racially as being inferior. How hypercritical is that?" He asked.

Lee continued: "I have learned a lot from Dr Kung in recent times. We are sure the old tactics still exist but this new emphasis is very interesting. What it means to you and your sisters, I do not know, but it surely is worth investigating much more than I have been able to do."

Theodora asked Lee to give her a written outline of what he had learned and his sources. She said she would pass this on to the ICCC when they next met in Sydney.

She also asked Col Weingraf if Dr Kung could join them in Sydney.

This was agreed and all met at the ICCC offices where Theodora handed over the report prepared by Lee. Dr Kung was warmly welcomed.

Col Weingraf remarked to Theodora: "Well, you and Lee have done a lot of work in your couple of days together in Adelaide."

In whispered tones, she corrected him: "No. This has nothing to do with me. Lee and Dr Kung have done all this themselves. We seem to have given Lee a new lease of life about the world and what should and could be done. He's really our sleeper, without our knowing it until now."

Addressing Lee, Col Weingraf said: "You have touched on a matter that has been worrying our foreign policy analysts and homeland strategists, and the planners in most democratic countries.

"We have always known the PRC as the No. 1 enemy but have not confronted it directly because of the enormity of such a task. Nor have we been particularly involved in PRC recruitment techniques. Our immediate challenges have centred on disrupting Da'ish in the Indo-Pacific region, and hopefully embarrassing the PRC in the process."

On being invited to comment further, Dr Kung explained: "The change by the PRC to more finely targeted recruitment gives the impression it is slowing down other more obvious programs. It's not. What seems very good news to the casual Western observer is very bad news for the serious China-watcher. It's clearly insidious. It's well planned. The PRC has no lack of clever minds or resources.

"What is happening now is managed by the International Liaison Office (ILO)—the acronym is unfortunate as it is common to a legitimate UN labour organisation—and the United Front Work Department (UFWD) assisted by behavioural specialists in the PLA. The ILO works with a more visible group known as the Professional Advancement Unit (PAU).

"This group selectively targets Western and Eastern ministers, bureaucrats, politicians, diplomats, senior embassy, high commission and presidential staff and government advisers. These are generally sources from Australia and New Zealand, the United States, South Africa, Singapore, Malaysia, the Philippines, and several Pacific Island nations, and possibly other countries of which we are unaware. I suspect some Scandinavian and European countries are targeted.

"They do not focus on foreigners who openly express sympathy for the communist cause or distain for democratic causes. They want people who are not easy to win over. They are more reliable in due course. In trade, for instance, the PRC is looking for Asian, Western and even, African trade commissioners or foreign trade advisers. It is only after commitment that plans for trade restrictions, tariffs and other hostile moves are implemented with the assistance of their new recruits," Dr Kung said.

Angelina suggested that this would take time. "To convert someone who shows no sign of conversion must be difficult.

"Another time-consuming element of all this is that the type of official they want would have to be researched to the nth degree before being approached. Before any familiarisation, the recruiter who arranges any contact would have to know nearly everything about the target. After a time, he or she presumably would have to be in a position to guess the right time to put a proposition. Sounds even more difficult!"

"That is right Angelina," Dr Kung said, "but converting one hard-to-convince official out of one thousand researched would be more valuable than one prospect out of one hundred easier-to-convince officials."

"So, where do we start?" Col Weingraf asked.

Angelina partially answered the query: "Assuming we leave military categories out, we need to know the PAU's other occupational priorities. It may need pharmaceutical scientists, for instance.

"We also have to know what incentives would be offered, assuming that like-mindedness is achieved. I don't mean corrupt payments. Genuine converts would have to be compensated appropriately. After all, senior officials probably would come from rewarding environments. Something nearly equivalent would be necessary in terms of the scope of work, recognition, status, accommodation, security, remuneration and assets. In some cases, even schooling may be necessary.

"It also means the public environment in the PRC may have to be seen by a prospective convert to be changing or be able to be changed for the better. Fixing a problem or rejuvenating a sector may be fine but a firm convert would not want to work in a failing economy with a disadvantaged population. Prosperity is difficult to falsify. I assume there would have to be evidence of some advances in social engagement within the general populace. The cost of living would have to be seen to improve in some areas.

"I suppose not everything has to be falsified. Shanghai is a thriving place with strong tourism support, and some of the top designer names are represented in Beijing," she said.

"Look at me," Angelina said, "I am advising the PAU in defining its executive-spy search criteria. To answer your question about where to start, Col Weingraf, if I were the PAU, I would work on combining the skills the country needed most with the occupational comfort that could be afforded highly skilled converts. Nationality, age, race, religion and even ideology would not matter a great deal. This sounds simplistic, but it would be my starting point," Angelina said.

She added: "I assume our purpose is to infiltrate the PAU recruitment program using volunteer ICCC applicants who are expert in priority areas."

Lee and Dr Kung agreed to put some definition into a likely program for this.

Together they also would identify secondary incentives that would appeal to candidates and relate these to occupational needs. This could indicate employment locations. Then it would be useful to evaluate 'unlikely' candidates who might be successfully recruited.

Dr Kung admitted: "I assume finding the right people to help the ICCC infiltrate the PAU in this way may be more a matter of guesswork than research, unless you know already of willing volunteers matching likely priority areas. But the PAU has no less a problem. Its selection of the right recruits cannot be certain. After exhaustive research and surveillance, it seems unlikely the PAU will hit the mark first time.

"Can I suggest we examine also the possibility of conducting surveillance on any local PAU spies we suspect conducting surveillance. In the beginning, they are unlikely to be diplomats or PRC officials. The best recruiters would probably be specialist influencers, not officials. How such things can be done is your business. I do not pretend to know," Dr Kung said less than convincingly.

After a short break, Dr Kung continued: "I would identify major events the ICCC believes would be useful to the PAU for recruitment purposes. Then I would select a manageable number of relevant target groups to keep an eye on. This might be done initially by attendance at social events, such as lectures, seminars, cocktail functions and certain social events, industry and national celebrations and even press conferences.

"It might be possible to confirm PAU recruiters and link them to attendees of likely interest—key-note speakers, hosts, guests-of-honour and attendees given special recognition or attention. At the same time, I would look at major conferences in the PRC and elsewhere and relate the topics to the expertise in Australia and the countries the ICCC has a particular interest in. At least this could match events and people. This is something Lee and I can do, if you wish," Dr Kung said.

Col Weingraf said the advice was most useful and logical but it was 'a little nebulous'.

He confirmed the countries of initial interest to the ICCC included Australia and New Zealand, unless an opportunity arose elsewhere that could not be ignored. He realised that recruiting from first-world countries would be more difficult for the PAU than recruiting from developing countries because of the difference in facilities expected by leading experts, although there was no shortage of skilled people in third-world countries.

Dr Kung agreed. He suggested: "The ICCC could conduct research into non-work-related incentives offered to those who had accepted PAU offers already. This may not be as difficult as it seems. They even may be promoted in Chinese newspapers within China. I am personally aware that small farms, houses and luxury cars have been offered in the past. Such incentives have been offered to people who have declined offers. They may be accessible."

At the conclusion of the meeting, Lee warned jokingly that Dr Kung's advice had to be taken seriously 'or else', a comment that puzzled everyone.

"In human form," he said, "Kung is the same family name as the Han Dynasty's God of Thunder who had a close working relationship with Tien Mu, the Mother of Lightning. According to legend, he would sound the names of disagreeable targets with thunder and she would destroy them with lightning. I'm pleased the good doctor is on our side."

Over the next few days, Lee and Dr Kung found several events matching departmental changes, some unexpectedly broad in their stated scope. None had any reference to recruitment of foreigners.

These were covered briefly in a preliminary report to the ICCC.

It was noticeable that the venues for these events did not match the areas and cities in which earlier ICCC projects had been conducted—the Philippines, the Northern Territory and Papua New Guinea, and even international waterways.

The PAU venues ranged from Hong Kong, Macau and Shanghai to Singapore and New Zealand.

Of these, the PAU conventions and other events that seemed to match the capabilities of the ICCC and its friends involved:

- New scientific establishments within the Ministry of Science and Technology (MST) that planned a wide range of regional seminars including advanced IT developments, such as quantum computing and oceanography;
- a newly established China Banking Insurance Regulatory Commission (BIRC) together with the long-established People's Bank of China (PBOC) that scheduled a series of exclusive seminars on private sector day-trading, wealth management and property and marine insurance;
- the Division of International Organisations (DIO) within the Department of International Cooperation and Exchanges that planned a range of seminars, including some conducted by linguistic experts aimed at internationally recognised simultaneous translation and interpretation services; and
- a totally new PAU bureau without a title that offered foreign regionally based academics and business leaders with diplomatic backgrounds a series of discussion groups aimed at international dispute resolution.

One unusual PAU interest dealt with social services, particularly retirement village developments, family relocation and a range of aged care benefits. Another concerned medical and dental services with emphasis on aged related macular degeneration, mental health, rehabilitation and management of private clinics. These two and others in agriculture and mining were managed by relevant departmental committees chaired by PAU representatives. The event topics seemed to mirror social and economic priority areas of other countries, including most first-world democratic nations.

Most sessions or seminars promoted the involvement of international experts.

All dealt with matters of specific PRC's interest in making the nation more appealing to global experts not only by demonstrating social benefits to all citizens and lifting long-standing restrictions but by improving services taken for granted in the West.

The events were intended to appear inconsistent with the Western view of the PRC's version of communism. Many Western commentators saw them as not entirely representing genuine reforms but not simply window-dressing either. They had nothing to do with the armed forces. They sought recognition locally and internationally as accepting socially responsible. The PAU was well aware this naturally appealed to Westerners.

As a whole, the PRC would have welcomed any economic and scientific developments resulting from foreign conference attendees expressing an interest in investment and exchanges, but being a political instrument, the PAU program was clear to serious Western researchers and analysts as a clever means of recruiting experts and ultimately spies.

On receipt of the preliminary report, Angelina commented to Col Weingraf: "Now which categories stand out as representing global leaders from Australian and New Zealand? How do we get an invitation from the PAU to include Australian or New Zealand experts? Now is the time for some brainstorming."

Finally, the ICCC came up with several possible expert volunteers in whom the PAU might be interested.

In a conference call with Lee and Dr Kung and the ICCC, several important procedural points were listed.

Dr Kung said an essential point for any ICCC participant should be to begin by being a listener only, then move to being a reluctant coadjutant well before expressing any kind of interest in administration or processes.

He said: "It is likely a handpicked selection of foreigners who accepted invitations to attend an event would be offered a free familiarisation package involving a guided tour of the PRC, probably for not less than two weeks. This would be several weeks before the event.

"If an ICCC candidate was among those offered a free package, he or she should be careful about expressing views on almost anything. If a comment was sought about the reform process in the PRC or an industry associated with a particular seminar or session, the answer should be politely guarded. Certainly, no outright criticism of the participant's home government was likely by the guide and no criticism of one's home country or host country should be made by the participant. It's a touchy-feely situation."

Col Weingraf emphasised to the likely ICCC volunteers that the early objectives of any applicant were to have their interest in a particular event known, to be registered as an attendee and hopefully to be invited on a guided tour but without any expectation of this happening. Such an invitation would signal acceptance to participate, not just to attend. The objectives during an event were to perform modestly and unobtrusively, and to leave behind the impression that he or she could be interested in furthering an association with relevant PAU events.

Eventually, on being asked to join the PRC, successful participants should be well aware the PAU's expectation of those who accepted would be to relocate permanently. Successful infiltrators would be under PRC laws, including national security and commercial provisions, and should be seen to have no difficulty with finger-printing, photo and eye identification, written declarations and other security processes.

Col Weingraf repeated that the reality was any relocation by an agent would be temporary, depending on circumstances. The hope was that any useful intelligence enabling counter-action to be planned would be obtained within six to nine months. Anything longer could be excessively stressful and too long to maintain the masquerade.

If leaving seemed difficult or was necessary earlier, an exit plan would come into effect, including a program to avoid any home-based media speculation of double agents and the like. Personal protection would be provided for a time also.

A secondary aim, he said, would be to involve Da'ish in ways that would cause PRC pain.

The first event of ICCC interest was a conference on international tourism. It was also the first event in the PAU's international events program.

Entitled 'The future of International Air and Sea Travel', the event was a two-day conference comprising several sessions in different locations on the obligations and responsibilities of carriers, national priorities to develop new destinations and setting targets for economic development benefits.

The opening session was in Hong Kong. Others were in Shanghai and Singapore where speakers' partners and non-participant invitees were offered site-seeing tours while sessions were in progress. The entire exercise was as flamboyant as most national tourism promotional functions were that attracted tourist agents and wholesalers.

It was hosted by the Ministry of Tourism supported by the PAU and attended by representatives of the International Air Transport Association (IATA), the International Hotel and Restaurant Association, the Pacific Area Travel Association and the International Tourism Association of Professionals.

ICCC's interest was how future destinations contributed to national development and, incidentally, if any were associated with PRC's artificial islands. Everyone knew the new South China Sea islands were military bases and that tourism was not an integral part of their establishment. Even so, one of the islands had been promoted in China to non-defence force citizens as an attractive location to raise families.

Col Weingraf said: "A puzzling question is whether new islands elsewhere may be promoted falsely as domestic tourist destinations firstly and foreign tourist destinations later. If so, what would be the reason since the military significance of existing new islands was well known internationally and surely new islands would be regarded similarly? In particular any emphasis on funding destinations on Pacific Ocean islands would be of interest," he said.

The ICCC's man, who registered an interest in attending, was a former Cathay Pacific captain who gained a reputation after leaving the airline industry as an adviser on cultural and government exchange programs. He knew several ICCC board members. He was a trusted and reliable person, well aware of the risks involved had he been invited to participate and eventually to relocate in the PRC.

Unfortunately, he was not selected as a participant but could have attended as an interested industry viewer. The ICCC's first attempt to gain access to a PAU event had not worked as hoped. This failure to infiltrate through a seemingly easy route was disappointing as only three other events seemed to offer opportunities for ICCC to present.

The next one was a two-day seminar a week later in Hong Kong entitled 'Regional Understanding, Cooperation and Effective Communications' hosted by DIO and overviewed by the Ministry of Education.

It seemed to the ICCC aimed cleverly at professional journalists and media organisations about which the political views of nearly all were known. The apparent aim seemed to be to find a journalist attached to a right-wing or even an anti-China media group who might be inclined to switch opinions and allegiance.

"If this is so," Col Weingraf said, "it is a big ask but the DIO would have some clever researchers working on this. Failure could be disastrous but success would be significant. This is all part of the PAU belief that the best recruits come from the most difficult sources."

Main topics concerned the relationship of private and public sector media groups, the responsibilities of national information officers and their duties for objectivity and accuracy, the distinction between public relations and perception management and media training for crisis managers. The topics would be seen generally as unexpected for a country known in most parts of the world for limiting free speech and controlling media organisations, but their selection could open the door for responding to criticism in an appealing way rather than in a defensive manner.

ICCC's main interest was to learn more about and document the PRC's propaganda mechanism. In particular, the centre was interested in how to accurately predict responses to international criticism and the point at which threatening responses would cease either because of success in achieving an image outcome or under pressure of criticism escalating beyond accepted limits. This could have relevance to future activities in the South China Sea.

The centre's prospective participant was a person who had foreign newspaper reporting experience, several years managing public relations companies in Asian countries, speech writing at senior government levels and occasional lecturing on a range of topics from articulation and presentation to foreign media interrogation and news agency management.

This also failed, although the prospective participant would attend both days of the seminar. He was not approached and was not offered a visit to the PRC.

This was ICCC's second failure.

The whole ICCC idea seemed headed for failure after a considerable amount of research and surveillance.

The remaining two opportunities were the ICCC's last chances.

One opportunity was offered to Conrad Wong, the ICCC's primary Singapore contact and defence adviser to the Singapore High Commission in Canberra. He was an expert in concealing his identity and had help from US, Japanese, Australian and Singaporean specialists in identity fraud.

Theodora would not forget him. She had met him with Lee at a Japanese musical recital at the Japanese Embassy in Canberra where he surprised her by asking her opinion of the desirability or otherwise of combining diplomatic and trade policies when discussing relationships with the PRC. She also had invited him to a cocktail party at Beth's and Judith's Adelaide home. Both events were well before the three sisters joined the ICCC as a team.

The other opportunity was offered to Robert Rogers, an international accounting expert who had been in the background until now.

Both functions were to begin simultaneously in Macau but at different venues. Later, subsequent sessions of the conference Rogers was to attend would be moved to New Zealand.

The topics for each of the events were considerably more complex and sensitive.

Wong was invited to present at a two-day conference promoted as 'International Relationship Building', hosted by the Ministry of Foreign Affairs and the Ministry of Justice. It was set down for Macau and later Hong Kong.

He was invited as one of several key-note speakers and wanted to be assisted by Lucinda who was accepted, albeit begrudgingly, because of her constitutional law qualifications and knowledge of a number of Pacific Islands. Clearly, Wong was the target for grooming by the PAU, even before the conference begun, although no approach was made to him.

Topics for this conference were aligning jurisprudence, diplomatic accreditation and recognition, historical issues defining sovereignty and international dispute resolution. Each of these four topics was covered by a key-note speaker followed by a panel question-and-answer session. Wong was the speaker on dispute resolution and mitigation, as well as the chair of a panel on the same subject.

The other main speakers were from the PRC, Singapore and the Netherlands. The senior one was the director-general of the Dutch Department of Justice. He also held an official Interpol position in The Hague, and was associated with the Dutch government's secret service which operated without formal designation. At the outset, Wong was surprised the PAU chose the Dutchman.

As the director-general was concluding his address in a converted Macau casino and the other participants, including Wong and Lucinda, were waiting in another part of the building, a bomb exploded near the dais.

It killed the speaker and several PRC staff members and attendees seated in half a dozen front rows of the venue.

The police had difficulty in taking control, securing the area, cordoning off groups of nearby people and arranging for ambulances. The enduring Macau *laissez faire,* inherited from the earlier Portuguese administration remained evident in nearly all parts of local government. Combined with the pervasive social informality of the casino precinct, the police and emergency services had difficulty in dealing with the occasion. In the presence of so many foreign participants of both seminars, the PRC could not apply the kind of heavy-handed resolution to the event had it occurred on the mainland.

Speakers and panellists were sent to Hong Kong where they were instructed to remain until preliminary investigations had concluded.

Wong and Lucinda did not communicate with the ICCC or the Australian legation for fear of messages being intercepted, but they were safe for the present. Wong did not know if he remained a person the PAU was interested in recruiting.

Col Weingraf, Angelina and Theodora had time to contrive a plan to throw a cat among the pigeons; to have the PRC blame Da'ish for the bombing, although no claim had been made publicly.

They were mindful the main target seemed to be the Dutch Interpol representative, a valuable contributor to the PAU conference, if only because of his presence.

The three formulated and sent a message in Arabic purportedly from a Da'ish group in Lamboanga to the Dutch Embassy in the Philippines, stating that the bombing was in retaliation for collusion between the Netherlands and other unbelievers in destroying a Da'ish warehouse in Lamboanga.

The three knew the Netherlands had no part in the destruction of the warehouse but the accusation suited the circumstances and offered an opportunity to encourage the PRC to take action against Da'ish.

The message was such as to be untraceable but easily intercepted by PRC intelligence. It deliberately ignored any reference to the PRC indicating other attacks might follow. The distain of the PRC in the Da'ish revenge on the Netherlands was evident in the message and intended to insult the PRC. As weird as the Da'ish message would seem, the ICCC believed it would be taken seriously.

The Da'ish message seemed to un-nerve the PRC Ministry of Foreign Affairs and the Ministry of Justice which waived any investigation of Wong and Lucinda and invited Wong to relocate, an invitation he accepted. Clearly, the PAU felt it had not made a mistake with him.

Rogers was not investigated either and remained a participant in his event, the 'South Pacific-East Asia Finance Conference' now re-scheduled a little earlier for New Zealand.

The ICCC were in with one invitee and hopefully another in the making.

At this stage, the PAU felt it necessary to hold preliminary discussions with Rogers about his interest in the PRC, even though its persuasion process had to be cut short risking his rejection of the idea of visiting the PRC and living in China. PAU discussions concluded with Rogers seeming agreeable to relocate.

The ICCC had balanced its failures. It now had two prospective agents with likely privileged access to the PAU. Of course, it had no idea how many other foreign experts from other countries were persuaded to work for and reside in China as a result to other conferences the ICCC did not attempt to join.

The 'The South Pacific-East Asia Finance Conference' was held in Auckland and followed conventional ministerial conference lines, such as those held regularly in Davos, Switzerland.

There were several major topics such as taxation arrangements and regional base options for international accounting and legal firms but the ones in which Rogers had global experience and on which he spoke were more specific. They included hostile and friendly takeovers, mergers, manipulation and protection of boards, multi-national joint venture agreements, the safety and privacy of off-shore funds and stock exchange compliance.

Angelina was accepted as Roger's 'council assisting' but her expertise was not well aligned with his. In any case, the PAU was more interested in Rogers, as it was in Wong instead of Lucinda.

After the event, a PAU representative and Rogers met in a coffee shop in an outer suburb of Auckland to discuss relocation arrangements.

While having coffee, both were assassinated in broad daylight. It was a highly professional and simple assassination by a single passer-by shooting both with a silenced pistol and moving away quickly on a motorbike, momentarily un-noticed.

The ICCC took the opportunity to frame an Arabic message to the Ministry of Foreign Affairs in the PRC copied to the New Zealand Government, again purportedly from Da'ish claiming the assassinations were to teach the governments and populations of unbelievers.

Angelina also drafted a bizarre message to be sent a day or so after the incident. It did not claim responsibility but fascinated Col Weingraf, partly because it was to come from a part of the world as far away as it could from New Zealand. Her suggestion was that Terry contact a reliable person in Kazakhstan to arrange a message in Chinese and Uyghur, the language of the Xinjiang Uyghur so-called autonomous region of the suppressed Uyghur people in the north-west of the PRC, to be sent to the PAU in Beijing insultingly praising the assassination of its PAU official in New Zealand.

A post-script to this message was a promise of support to any groups interested in punishing the PRC for its ethnic cleansing of the Uyghur people because they were Moslem. It included a reminder to the PAU that the Uyghurs were the dominant group in Central Asia until the Manchu conquest in the 18th century. Now they were seeking refuge in nearby countries, including Kazakhstan and elsewhere.

The idea was accepted by Col Weingraf.

The Chinese part of the message was penned by Angelina. After discussing the idea with his counterpart in the Australian Embassy in Turkey, Terry was referred to a reliable individual in Alma-Ata on the southern border of Kazakhstan who filled in the Uyghur language part of the message, and was in a position to transmit the message while ensuring no evidence of the source remained.

"This is another one of those 'suck it and see' tactics," Angelina remarked.

Col Weingraf responded: "You sisters seem to be highly proficient with these strange messages."

He added: "Perhaps Wong will be successful in providing intelligence from now on. He will have his work cut out collecting intelligence and getting anything back to us without visiting the Singapore Embassy in Beijing more than he would be expected to do.

"A breaking point will be when he is required to renounce his Singapore citizenship. If this happens, it may indicate the PAU has doubts about his loyalty because him having easy access to Singapore would be an advantage to the PAU. This will be the time to repatriate him."

He concluded: "Put bluntly, the ICCC lost a candidate and the PRC think it gained a recruit and nearly succeeded in gaining a second. Out of a list of ten functions we knew of—finance, diplomacy, travel, education, communications, health, education, agriculture, mining and retirement housing—we could offer candidates for four only—travel, diplomacy, finance and communications—and only one succeeded and we lost one agent. Not a great outcome," Col Weingraf said.

Angelina said: "I know. This is a bitter-sweet result but I must say, Wong is the one of our team most likely to ultimately succeed because of his security background. This does not detract from Rogers in any way as his credentials were spot on for his conference and the PAU interest in him was demonstrated. We all regret his passing greatly," she said.

Wong undertook his all-expenses paid trip to many parts of the PRC, including areas in the far west and north of the country, even though the PAU did not think it necessary as his recruitment had been confirmed. Nonetheless, it helped Wong settle in and his minders develop even greater confidence in his commitment.

In time, Wong amassed considerable intelligence, largely in global expansion plans and economic and defence capacity. He tried to retain this mentally rather than rely on messages or documents that could be unsafe.

At the request of Singapore for a bi-national exchange on economic cooperation with the PRC, a visit by Wong as part of the PRC team was agreed. This was his opportunity to regurgitate an eye-watering amount of PRC policy detail to his SSS colleagues and ultimately the ICCC, much of which could provide the framework for future major joint ICCC-Singapore projects.

Wong was home for good, safe, successful and looking forward to working again with the Singapore Government and hopeful about joining Angelina, Theodora and Lucinda in any future tasks.

Chapter 18: Planning

It was not long before something unusual came up. Except for the task just ended, one not without the tragic loss of Robert Rogers, the task was from generally managed attacks on specific targets in limited locations to assessment of the People's Republic of China Navy's (PRCN) submarine movements.

In signalling this approach, Col Weingraf introduced to a limited meeting of the ICCC Professor Dean Metcalf as an expert in submarine warfare and some other more 'benign aspects of marine research', as he put it.

Prof Metcalf began by indicating there would be no direct aggression against *Diueliz* or the like, an assertion that pleased the sisters because of the likely absence of violence. He warned those present also that his comments could appear instructional, for which he apologised.

His theme was based on the need for a different style of task management while maintaining secrecy. This was because the target was an arm of the PRC military itself.

He explained: "Because of the technical sophistication and capacity of nuclear submarines, the end game is to circumvent the PRC, or indeed the US, inadvertently or otherwise triggering an event that could lead to international conflict. This is a higher risk game than those against *Diueliz* or Da'ish.

"Our current intent is not to destroy anything," he said. "If a PRCN—or more correctly, the People's Liberation Army Navy (PLAN), as awkward is this title is—nuclear submarine was to seriously threaten a US warship in international waters, this would be something for the US military to resolve, or perhaps the ADF if it happened near Australia, not for us.

"Such a resolution would have to be based on my understanding that the PRCN—as I will call it—is the largest navy in the world with 355 major ships and 250 ballistic missiles, more than the rest of the world combined. It will have up to 700 deliverable nuclear warheads by 2027. It has several nuclear submarines. The US probably has 60 so-called 'attack' submarines.

"We know about their likely capacities. Our interest is not so much in these but rather in the movement and detection of PRCN submarines in the Indo-Pacific."

Theodora interrupted: "So, how can we do this?"

Prof Metcalf replied: "It involves our consideration of deep-sea drones, autonomous underwater vehicles (AUV), remote underwater vehicles (RUV) and smart submarine sensors. Obviously, we cannot use these undetected within the South China Sea or the East China Sea. AUVs mostly require mother-ship support. Trying to hide these vehicles is impossible. I am going to suggest a possible plan to utilise these assets close to these seas without suspicion.

"First, let me give you some background," he said. "The PRCN recently salvaged a light Philippine cargo ship that sank in an area known generally as the Challenger Deep between Guam and Yap. It is virtually in the Philippine Sea and in a highly strategic location for the PRCN. It is an area the PRCN is interested in so as to protect the South China Sea from foreign ship incursion.

"It secured the salvage rights because it offered to recover the ship free. Other countries offered their services for a fee. It would have been a very expensive exercise for any country as the location was on the edge of the Mariana Trench, which is more than 11,000 metres deep. Any mistake in the recovery process would have meant the ship slipping into the trench and could never be found.

"The point of the exercise was to lay PRCN submarine sensors in the area. We assume this was done. The exercise also confirmed the sophistication of the PRCN's AUV and heavy lift technology," he said.

Theodora interrupted: "Does the US have sensors there also? After all, it is quite close to Guam."

"Yes, I am sure we do, but mainly on the eastern side of the Mariana Trench and nearer the shoreline. We can detect submarines heading towards Guam, Palau and Yap," Prof Metcalf said, using the plural to purposefully identify himself as American, even though he had an Australian accent.

Angelina joined in: "I assume our task will be to assist you in laying sensors. As far as I know, Australia has no sensor manufacturing facility either within the RAN or our defence equipment industry, not like our private facility for producing hyperbaric chambers which are sought by many navies, including the US.

"If this is our task," she said assuming a positive answer, "I guess you are not interested in laying sensors in the Lombok Strait, the Malacca Strait, the

Makassar Strait or along other main Asian shipping routes as they would be full of sensors already, not just from the US and PRCN. And areas west of Thailand, Myanmar and in the Bay of Bengal are out of our jurisdiction. So, where do we place our sensors?" She asked, purposefully using the first person plural identifying her sisters and the ICCC in whatever he had in mind.

"You are generally, but not entirely, right," Prof Metcalf said. "Our primary task will be to find unexpected locations for our submarine sensors, as strange as that sounds. Our secondary task will be to find any PRCN sensors in these unexpected locations.

"We will be only partially successful if we find PRCN sensors in our preferred spots because it means these routes will be covered already. If we do not find any PRCN sensors in areas, we want to lay our sensors we suppose these are safer, at least for the present. It's very much a hide-and-seek process and a complicated one at that.

"Hopefully, the PRCN will not be looking for our sensors as there is no sensor technology that allows sensors to detect sensors. The only way we will find any of their sensors visually is by accident while laying our own," he said while grimacing at his wordy explanation.

Angelina asked: "How good are our sensors? Are they better than the PRCN's?"

Prof Metcalf said: "I think we are better but I'm not certain. No-one uses Lithium-Ion or Sulphur batteries these days. Some of our sensors utilise the piezo-effect of vibrations given off by certain natural substances by transferring pressure waves into electricity to create a charge that enables ongoing operation."

"In other words," Angelina said, "they operate with no energy. How's that?"

"That's right," he said. "The US developed this technology using the world's leading naval laboratory, the US Naval Sea Systems Command (NAVSEA). It has developed another exciting project using extremely low radio frequencies but details are secret.

"We use also magnetic anomaly detectors that show very small disturbances in the Earth's magnetic field caused by the metallic hulls of submarines. However, the PRCN is said to have a submarine demagnetisation facility at its southern Longpo Naval Base designed to demagnetise the hulls of its Jin-class submarines," Prof Metcalf explained.

Angelina persisted: "Are we able to demagnetise our submarines?"

"I cannot say," he replied.

Changing the topic, he said: "As for our submarine sensors, we generally use both vibration and magnetic detection types. Both types have been miniaturised. They are circular, able to function whatever way they fall on the sea floor and weigh about 20 kilograms each. I expect we need 30 for what I have in mind."

"Fine," Angelina said. "What about these AUVs, RUVs and drones?"

Prof Metcalf said: "I was getting around to them. They are particularly useful because of their manoeuvrability, precision control and adaptability to submarine warfare conditions. They represent some of the highest maritime technology for small craft. Their sonar screening capability, together with excellent acoustic communications and electronic manipulator arms, make them indispensable in dealing with arduous search, rescue, recovery and salvage situations.

"They can be used also for reconnaissance, surveillance and mine detection. We need to think carefully about how we will use any one of them."

"Why? Is there an inherent problem with them?" Angelina asked.

He replied: "The problem is visibility. I should say invisibility in using them to lay sensors. The most sophisticated AUVs require surface vessel control and ships are visible regardless of how far away they may be.

"The task I invite the ICCC to participate in with me is to lay submarine sensors in dangerous places and identify any PRCN sensors we come across using a visible mother-ship to control a small AUV. All of us know where US and PRCN submarine sensors are likely to be right now—in all the major commercial shipping lanes. That's a given. We want to know what we don't know and we don't want the PRCN to know what we know. Sounds a bit Irish, but it is what it is," he said, prompting Col Weingraf and the sisters to suggest solutions.

Angelina took the bait. "Sounds a little like a job for Houdini. Let's look at it this way. If we cannot operate without being seen, let's not worry about being seen. To do this safely, we need to appear to be seen entirely innocent. We need an acceptable excuse about our purpose for doing what we are doing in the locations we are doing it. That's about as crooked an Irish explanation as yours, Professor."

He replied: "This is precisely the strategy we must use. We may not need to start from scratch either. I can help a lot but the ICCC will have to do some heavy lifting of the risks involved. The PRCN will not be expecting us to be laying sensors or looking for sensors if our reasons for travelling all around the seas contribute to the preservation of nature through scientific research. I will explain soon."

At this point, the group had a coffee break but before Prof Metcalf had a chance to take his first sip, Col Weingraf contributed to this Irish conversation. He philosophised: "If we do nothing, nothing is likely to happen, at least not for now. If we do something, the prospect of something disastrous happening by accident, on purpose or by third-party mischief, may not happen."

Theodora then joined in: "Who wants nuclear submarine warfare. Were that to occur all sides could be annihilated."

Concluding the break, Angelina acted as the ICCC's spokesperson. With Col Weingraf's silent consent, she said: "Of course, we will support you in any way we can…especially if there are no fisticuffs involved."

Prof Metcalf said: "Thank you. I should explain that the 'benign areas of my research' referred to so vaguely by Col Weingraf in his introduction, are relevant. Areas of my research provide opportunities to use a very small AUV controlled by a surface vessel in ways that should cause little concern to others, including the PRCN. When we are near the South China Sea, the East China Sea and other sensitive areas, we should appear innocent, transparent and apolitical, albeit conspicuous, in pursuit of globally accepted scientific goals.

"Scientific research will be our cover. It would not go against us if we were regarded silently by some as conservation weirdos with funds to lavish on expensive exercises to promote ourselves as world-class researchers, as well as seeking a worthy ecological cause. If our activity is unremarkable to the general public, other than perhaps for its eccentricity, we may minimise attention to ourselves.

"We must not appear to be resource or profit driven, particularly in fisheries or mining both areas in which the PRCN may wish to participate. If we become a nuisance, we will simply pull up anchor and go away…for a while," he said.

Angelina said: "Sounds precarious but reasonable."

Prof Metcalf said: "To be successful, we will have to rely on cooperation from certain neighbouring countries and institutions."

"That's fine," Angelina interjected.

He added: "But our on-shore supporters, except for Guam, must not know our real purpose."

Angelina raised her eyebrows and muttered: "You mean we have to deceive our supporters?"

"Well, yes," he said. "Security will be paramount and so we cannot trust our neighbours. If they suspect us and there are leaks, as there would be particularly in the Philippines—I understand from Col Weingraf you are well aware of this, Angelina and Theodora—we would be shot out of the water. Even speculation that we may be surveying their fisheries for an unknown party would cause big trouble. It is vital everyone is convinced we are genuine in using specific scientific research to sustain healthy marine environments for all."

The group retired to a wine bar near the ICCC headquarters hoping to relax for an hour or so. Despite Col Weingraf, Prof Metcalf, Angelina and Lucinda looking forward to a little sedate chit-chat, Theodora could not help herself asking questions: "The underwater drones and AUVs are very interesting but what about the submarines? Do we need to know about them."

Prof Metcalf obliged: "We will not come across a submarine, at least I hope not. As for numbers, the PRCN says it has three nuclear powered submarines while the US has 36, but the PRCN number is a propaganda-based underestimate. We know the PRCN has more than a dozen conventionally powered submarines being converted to nuclear power very rapidly.

"It might not be too far off the mark to say that the US and the PRC have equal numbers, all with medium to long range missile capability. These are not inconsistent with the numbers I have mentioned already.

"I would prefer to talk about our proposed marine research but, as you seem to be like a dog with a bone, Theodora, if you will excuse me for saying so, I will give you some further details. The PRCN is concentrating on Jin-class submarines, known generally as Type 094. Most are based at Yulin Naval Base on Hainan Island, in the northern part of the South China Sea and partly in disputed Vietnamese waters. Some are in their demagnetising facility at Longpo Naval Base.

"This type of submarine is said to be equipped with 12 new type missiles known as Jl-2s. The claim is that these have an extraordinary range of 7,500 kilometres, enough to reach US western Pacific waters. The PRCN also claim to have developed a Ji-3 missile that can reach the US mainland from the South China Sea. Perhaps they do or, more likely, their spin doctors say they do," he said.

He continued: "The submarine is vital but the weapon of choice in the new era is the missile. The outcome of any future war will depend entirely on missiles, in my opinion. The problem is their availability. Even North Korea and Pakistan probably have medium-range nuclear missiles and a wide range of other missiles are traded all over the world, particularly by Iran and other Middle Eastern countries and by some Eastern European countries assisted by Russia. I hope that answers your questions," he said.

But it did not stop there. Lucinda, who had been silent until now, had got the bone in her mouth also. She said: "What you have said sounds ominous but I assume the US is developing new missiles and missile defence systems and its submarines are still the best in the world.

"I must say," she said, "our earlier discussions at the ICCC painted a bleak picture of US military developments largely because of ideological polarisation and weariness of extended overseas conflicts of questionable value and doubtful conclusions leading to budget restrictions and policy indecision. The last thing I want to do is denigrate our strongest and loyal ally but real statistics and wise observations are important. Where, for instance, do submarine statistics come from?"

He replied: "Firstly, I can say the US is scrambling with amazing speed to review its nuclear doctrine, deterrence signalling and force structure. Secondly, some of the statistics and comments are from some of the sources already indicated by Col Weingraf. Some are from experts attached to the Lowy Institute, a highly reliable institution supported by some of the West's leading experts in their fields."

Three other matters Prof Metcalf referred to were: Supersonic missiles and 'hyperglide vehicles' capable of travelling at one mile per second (Mark 5); the value of the Quad alliance (Australia, the US, Japan and India) in applying a 'deterrence by denial' approach to the PRC; and the PRC's new infrastructure projects on its artificial South China Sea islands in preparation for higher military capabilities, including the installation of sophisticated 'sound surveillance systems' (SOS). These systems are networks of hydroponic arrays to detect submarines and surface vessels.

Col Weingraf interrupted: "That's enough for today. Let Prof Metcalf finish his drink. I'll have another. Your shout, Theodora."

The following day, Theodora's incorrigibility came to the fore again. She asked Prof Metcalf: "Let me ask you about something less pugilistic. What about the fish we are going to research?"

"Pugilistic!" He exclaimed. "It's interesting you relate submarines and missiles to boxing matches and marine research to fishing adventures. We will be researching plankton. How about that!" He said with a grin.

Lost for words, all Theodora could say was: "Plankton!"

Prof Metcalf said: "Because plankton research is important globally and researching it is doable, relatively easy, significant, open-ended and an ideal cover for our work. It is doable because I am qualified to do the work and some of the Asian waters of interest to us are plankton rich. It is open-ended because we can select a species among many that scientists around the world acknowledge requires further documentation. As strange as it seems, this generally single-cell critter can be as complex as most man-made objects.

"Our selection of plankton as our research project is based on the accepted fact that plankton is fundamental to the entire aquatic food chain globally and not a human resource in itself. Some of our research will be near the South China Sea and the East China Sea, but I expect the PRCN will regard us as irrelevant scientists on a doomed mission. I believe the PRC's scientific community will think attempting such research without them impossible.

"This is because there is history of unfortunate collaborative marine research between Australia and China. Australia's Commonwealth Scientific and Industrial Research Organisation (CSIRO) and China's Qingdan National Laboratory for Maritime Science and Technology conducted research together into ocean currents and temperature years ago but this collapsed for political reasons. The CSIRO also undertook work on plankton communities around the Daya Bay area of the South China Sea some time ago, the success of which is unknown, probably of little value.

"These types of collaborative projects would not be agreed today by either Chinese or Australian scientists," Prof Metcalf said.

Before describing the proposed plankton project, he said: "Documenting this type of research can be as complex as most sciences, including medicine and astrology."

"As complex as quantum physics and pure mathematics," Theodora said.

"Touché, I realise the three of you are experts in these kinds of topics. Sorry for being so simplistic," he said.

Explaining his point, Prof Metcalf added: "Collecting specimens is simple. Documenting them scientifically is not. We have to look at many aspects of the life cycle of specific species. Studies include biomass and density of homogeneous layers, physiological and morphological differences in location, effects of ultraviolet rays on distribution and survival, genetic variations and even the effects of monsoonal rains directly and from land runoff on salinity, oxygenation and anthropogenic pollution of plankton food sources. And much more.

"Another phase of our work will involve life forms in and around hydrothermal vents which act like geysers heated by magna. These create warm water environments that nurture all kinds of life, much of which look like advanced forms of multi-cell plankton. This suits us because there are many vents along the main fault lines near the South China Sea, perhaps near where there are PRCN sensors or where our sensors may be most useful," Prof Metcalf said.

All agreed that three main matters needed examination before planning could be finalised. They boiled it down to *how, where and who.*

The *how* begins with acquiring a vessel and selecting equipment, particularly an AUV, RUV or underwater drone.

The *where* involves mapping locations to lay sensors under the cover of research.

The *who* is about the ICCC. Who is to be involved. Job descriptions had to be set and the crew had to have credible reasons for being part of the team in the event of the ship being intercepted and those onboard interrogated.

He said: "As for where we operate, certain areas can be eliminated. We should openly avoid Singapore waters because of the density of shipping and the many commercial interests monitoring ship arrivals and departures. Although, a Western ally, even housing a secret arms depot in a small ship-building facility, Singapore is mindful of the veiled warning by the PRC which has repeatedly reminded the republic in diplomatic language that 'you are small, we are big'.

"Nevertheless, Singapore's proximity to exit and entry points of the South China Sea makes the vicinity tempting for us but requiring a degree of stealth."

Theodora said: "And I suppose with all that traffic, the density of plankton is low."

Prof Metcalf said: "That's right. I will have more to say about Singapore in a minute. In the meantime, the Malacca Strait is inappropriate for the same reason, heavy traffic. The Taiwan Strait between Taiwan and the PRC is out for obvious reasons. The Korea Strait connecting the Sea of Japan with the East China Sea narrows to about 200 metres at one point, which is too constricted. It is surely full of PRCN sensors anyway. If we went too far without PRC approval, we may not get out."

Theodora added: "We may even be invited in and not get out."

"Where then?" Prof Metcalf asked himself aloud.

"We will start with *how*. We will begin in a safe haven, Palau, where we will acquire a boat, a type of research trawler," he said. "Then we will plan and proceed to three target areas.

"Two are highly unlikely sensor locations," he said, emphasising the word 'unlikely'. "Let me explain. It is unlikely the PRCN would think we would be interested in these particular locations, other than for plankton research. Hopefully, they are uninterested in these locations.

"Intelligence indicates the PRCN has not visited two of these areas recently. However, the PRCN will look for such exit points if US-PRC relations worsen because the PRCN will know many major exit points will be covered by US sensors. One of these two target areas is in the Luzon Strait between Taiwan and the Philippines, separating the South China Sea and the Pacific Ocean.

"It presents difficulties because it is wide, open and deep but I think we can get close to the South China Sea innocently and inconspicuously, if we hug some of the islands just north of the Philippines called the Babuyan Islands. Our aim is to cover with sensors an unexpected exit route for PRCN submarines to enter Pacific Ocean waters," Prof Metcalf said.

"And to collect plankton. Right?" Theodora said, lightening a little the professor's description of the area.

Gracefully ignoring her interjection, he continued: "Another target area is in the vicinity of Palawan, a long narrow stretch of land between Panay in the Philippines and the northern-most point of East Malaysia in Borneo. It separates the Sulu Sea and the South China Sea. Our interest is to lay sensors south of Palawan in the Balabac Strait near the tiny seaside town of Kudat.

"I should say the location is shallow and rich in plankton. Like the Babuyau Islands in the Luzon Strait, this too presents difficulties. The waters around Palawan are narrow and there are several islands that are virtually unknown except to the Eastern Malaysian fishing community.

"Palawan south is a highly unlikely area for submarines, but may be attempted by the PRCN if it regards the northern parts around Palawan too risky. So, our job will be to cover this unexpected southern exit.

"It is worth noting, Palawan is near the PRC's artificial islands in the South China Sea and the nearby waters are contested by Brunei, Vietnam, the Philippines, Taiwan and Malaysia, as well as the PRC. We may be able to hide among the various different national fishing boats in the area, if we need to hide at all. The downside of this may be that we are regarded as taking an interest in the traditional fishing grounds of several nations. We need to be careful and demonstrate we are not a commercial threat to small fishing communities.

"Studies and intelligence suggest the PRCN would use the northern Palawan exit from the South China Sea through the Calamian Group, not the southern area we are interested in. This is reassuring. From the north or even the south, PRCN submarines could travel south through the Sulu Sea to the Celebes Sea and into the Makassar Strait from where they could go through the Bali Strait and into the Indian Ocean very close to Australia. This is a worry.

"I assume the US has laid sensors in the northern waters around the Calamian Group. I will double check with my US colleagues as soon as I can but we cannot cover Palawan north and south."

Prof Metcalf added: "Even if PRCN submarines get past the US and our sensors secretly, they may be detected later by US sensors exiting the Makassar Strait after passing the narrow sector between Kalimantan and Sulawesi. I prefer to exclude the Makassar Strait as a possible target area for us. As mentioned, it's too busy and wide.

"This brings me to our next move," he said. "It requires a little deception and stealth but is no less tricky. This is the exception to my partial exclusion of the Makassar Strait. In fact, we hope to use it partially. Our identification will be certain, although hopefully we will be seen as a plankton research vessel. Even if our presence puzzles the PRCN, we may be able to answer any query by exiting the strait in the wrong direction," he said.

"How is that?" Theodora asked.

Prof Metcalf said: "At the end of our southern trip through the strait, we will steer south-east, not west to Singapore and the South China Sea as any respectable tracker would expect."

"And why would we do this? It's out of the way," Theodora queried.

"Precisely. It appears the wrong way," he said. "The reason is to lay sensors—and collect plankton samples—in the Flores Sea near Raba between the Indonesian islands of Sumbawa and Flores.

"This is another unlikely route to Australia for PRCN submarines as it is fairly shallow but is only 1,000 kilometres in open water from the Western Australian coast. I am informed there has been no sign of PRCN activity in this area known as the Sumba Strait. By having sensors in this strait, we close the door to the PRCN which may want to try this route if tensions between Australia and the PRC get to breaking point. At this point, we will have laid the last of our sensors," he said.

Theodora said: "We will be a long way from the South China Sea. We will have a boat load of plankton samples but no more sensors. And we will be a long way from Palau as well. Will this be the conclusion of our research project and what about the hydrothermal vent and warm water research?"

He said: "This is only part of our third target location. Now we steer north-west and run along the Indonesian coast in the Java Sea to the Sunda Strait between Java and Sumatra. In current conditions, PRCN submarines are likely to use the Bali Strait to enter the Indian Ocean. If they do, they will be only 900 kilometres from the West Australian coast.

"Were they to use the Sunda Strait, they would find themselves about 300 kilometres from Christmas Island which is some 1,500 kilometres from the nearest part of Australia, a remote area in the north of Western Australia. While Australian territory, Christmas Island has no military significance. Presently, it seems the Bali Strait is the most likely route for PRCN submarines to enter the Indian Ocean and, thus, Australia.

"We need to search for PRCN sensors in the Sunda Strait and hope we find none.

"It gets particularly interesting scientifically from here," he said. "We have no incriminating equipment onboard. We have high quality plankton documentation and we now try our hand at researching sea vent environments."

"Of course," Theodora said. "Krakatoa is near the Sunda Strait which has a history of world shattering volcanic activity and probably a number of underwater vents. Right?"

He said: "That is right. The Krakatoa group of small islands has erupted many times and remains active. Records show that in 1883, it erupted, killing more than 30,000 people. In recent times, it erupted in 2009, 2011, 2012 and 2018. A recent one was at 1.14pm on 11 April 2021."

"I know it well," Theodora said. "My sisters and I were holidaying at Pulaumerak on the Java side of the strait in March of 2021, and Krakatoa looked and sounded menacing then. Maybe the PRCN will be the least of our worries."

He said: "Therefore, to answer your earlier questions, Theodora, we are targeting the Sunda Strait to look for PRCN submarine sensors, and of course, to demonstrate that our trip is for genuine scientific research purposes if we are questioned."

Chapter 19: Interceptions

Prof Metcalf and Col Weingraf made arrangements to lease a US Guam trawler moored in Palau. The professor already had selected the research equipment needed and the type of sensors to be deployed.

In previous days, Prof Metcalf had spoken with two Singapore colleagues, one a senior marine scientist from the Maritime Studies Centre at the University of Singapore and the other a scientist experienced in tidal and blue water navigation from the Nanyang Technical University, who agreed to assist in tidying up research documentation. He also agreed to falsify the registration and provenance of the vessel and to re-register and moor it in a safe marina in Singapore at the conclusion of the project. He expressed an interest in joining the research team.

"In particular," Prof Metcalf said, "we have to take particular care in fitting out the vessel to be renamed 'Poco-A-Poco', meaning 'little-by-little' in Italian. It's a typical nonsense name, perhaps more likely to be used by semi-professional seamen rather than regular seagoers who tend to use unimaginative place or personal names.

"I have selected an AUV tethered to Poco-A-Poco, instead of a remotely operated RUV. Customary AUVs carry cameras and articulated arms for cutting and grabbing in naval environments. To make it less like a naval AUV, the arms are being modified to carry fairly primitive pumping devices for collecting plankton in shallow water and glass bottles for collecting samples where plankton is distributed differently in vertical and horizontal layers in slightly deeper water.

"A more complex netting apparatus is being attached to flow metres for use where currents make using pumps or bottles difficult. A davit clearly holding the AUV will be aft of the cabin. So, we will have bottles, pumps, nets, an obvious AUV, and everything else needed to make our plankton research highly visible and easily accessible.

"Of course, a fully operational laboratory is being installed. It will have a computerised drawing unit dedicated to profiling plankton species and clearly unsuitable for military purposes. It will contain all the usual equipment, such as microscopes, chemicals for analysis, pipettes, petri dishes, test tubes and so on. Printed statements of our environmental objectives, test procedures and the global value of plankton will be displayed in the laboratory indicating the biogeochemical cycling and climate variation associated with plankton," he said.

Theodora commented light-heartedly: "We are going to a lot of trouble to drop a few sensors."

"That's right, Theodora, but there are few other options," he replied.

Taking up Theodora's comment further, Prof Metcalf said: "An essential aspect of fitting out Poco-A-Poco will be hiding the sensors. Areas that seem part of the hull will be created so that inspectors will find nothing by looking in the usual compartments or in boxes of equipment or provisions. The sensors must be easily and quickly accessible to us but not visible to others. This is being achieved with a panelling technique commonly used by architects to disguise under-floor doorways in timber houses but, to my knowledge, not used to create false internal hull spaces in boats.

"As we will have around 30 sensors, each weighing 30 kilograms, they must be stowed in a balanced way so that they do not cause a lean as some are being used."

Theodora asked: "Ultimately, what is this project's contribution to US-PRC conflict avoidance keeping in mind our expertise to date has been to confuse terrorist groups and create disagreements with the PRC by using misinformation and deception? While we have been at arm's length to the consequences of our work, except for a couple of explosions, we have had reasonable expectations of some success but we will have no idea at all of the success of our sensor laying exercise."

Prof Metcalf replied: "You are right again. Our project is but a small contribution to monitoring hostile PRCN submarines exiting the South China Sea and the East China Sea. We can only imagine the favourable consequences over time of our work but it takes little imagination to know the unfavourable consequences instantly of our being caught.

"As we all know, this is the nature of building clandestine protection from a significant potential enemy. So, let's think about what we can do without being caught out. To maximise our contribution, we have to rely on the placement of our sensors and their capacity to do their job over time.

"I have to say our sensors are highly effective but they are not the most advanced. The more sophisticated ones are 'direct' detection devices which work on how a hull of a submarine absorbs specific laser light creating an image or a spot on a screen. This type generally involves arrays, so it is extensive. We cannot do this kind of thing with a plankton trawler.

"In the broader scheme of things," he said, "we must rely on US technology matching, if not bettering, PRCN technology. As we know, the level of the PRCN's technology may be indicated by its claim to have a submarine demagnification facility at its Jin-class submarine base. The Chinese also claim to have a 'superconductive magnetic anomaly direction array' capable of showing tiny disturbances in the Earth's magnetic field caused by metallic submarine hulls. The next development may be non-metallic hulls that screen metallic equipment inside," he said.

"And another question, please," Theodora asked. "Apart from the technologies involved, how long will the project take and who will be going?"

He replied: "I estimate it to take about 20 days in non-monsoon conditions, give or take a couple of days. This is based on time spent around the Babuyan Islands in the Luzon Strait, around the southern islands group in the Balabac Strait in the Philippines, around the Flores Sea area near Raba in Indonesian waters, in the Krakatoa area of Indonesia's Sunda Strait and finally travelling to the sanctuary of Singapore."

Together Prof Metcalf and Col Weingraf said the vessel was large enough to carry a crew up to ten. They decided on six.

Prof Metcalf would be the research leader. The captain would be from the US Guam base and have all the authority of a seagoing captain. He would be accompanied by a naval-navigator/engineer also from the Guam base. The scientist from the Nanyang Technical University in Singapore would assist the research leader and be available to offer assistance to the navigator/engineer.

The other places would be taken up by Theodora and Terry who would offer assistance in communications and security, respectively. They would be able to converse with communities they were likely to encounter in Malaysian and Indonesian dialects, as well as Filipino and Portuguese. They would not be out of their depth with New Guinean and Papuan Pidgin if the research took them unexpectedly into the Timor Sea or the Arafura Sea.

Angelina and Lucinda would stay in Singapore while Col Weingraf would spend his time in Sydney, Canberra, Darwin and Pine Gap.

The crew planned to arrive in Palau to agree the refit of Poco-A-Poco as soon as the sensors arrived from the US via Guam and the laboratory items arrived from Singapore.

Necessary documentation was completed early and special exemptions were granted for the crew and the vessel to spend time in Singapore, Philippine, Papua New Guinea and Indonesian waters on a highly flexible basis. Acknowledgment of the project from the ASEAN Secretariat was limited to six of the 10 members but was sufficient to endorse the plankton work in the waters of member countries.

The four rejections were from Vietnam, Laos, Myanmar and Cambodia. Validation of the research project was acquired also from the Australian branch of the International Marine Research Organisation in Townsville.

Everything seemed in order.

In early March, as soon as the monsoon season ended, the captain set a course from Palau to the first target area, the Babuyan Group of islands in the Luzon Strait, a direct route across the Pacific Ocean of about 1,800 kilometres.

He described to the crew the island group which comprised five main islands—Babuyan, Camiguin, Calayan, Fuga and Dalupiri—and cautioned against piracy in the Celebes Sea and the Sulu Sea which probably would be entered in subsequent legs of the trip.

He advised: "There should be no such threat in the Luzon Strait. Nonetheless, we should not be complacent about piracy. Not so long ago, piracy in South-east Asian waters was greater than in the West Indian Ocean and West African coastal areas. There is little difference between being shot with an automatic assault weapon from being carved up with a fishing knife," the captain remarked.

Theodora echoed the captain's comments: "The long history of piracy in this area goes back to the days of the Spanish but contemporary piracy seems to be mainly in the Malacca Strait between Malaysia and Indonesia and the Makassar Strait in Indonesia where we will be heading. I have heard also that some piracy occurs in the southern part of the South China Sea, as surprising as that may be."

The captain agreed.

Theodora quietly expressed a wish she had consulted earlier with Sir Jonathon and his firm's Singapore admiralty law associate but she was confident of the captain's knowledge of the region. She could not seek advice now anyway because any messages would be intercepted by the PRCN.

The captain elaborated: "The reasons for piracy in South-east Asian waters today are corruption of officials, weak maritime law enforcement, and rivalries between states and municipalities mainly about territorial claims. But, as I said, it does not matter why one is attacked. It's a matter of avoidance and, if this is not possible, it's how we handle the threat that matters," he said.

As they neared the Babuyan Group, Prof Metcalf detailed the logic of the target area. "The northern-most island in the Luzon Strait, Babuyan Island, is interesting. On the one hand, north of the island is not of interest as it is open water to Taiwan. As such, the entire northern area is a major entry and exit passage to the South China Sea and must be covered well by US, PRCN and perhaps even Taiwanese submarine sensors. On the other hand, south of Babuyan Island may be concealed enough for us.

"We will stay clear of Calayan also because it is the only port in the Babuyan Group and we don't want to be too obvious on our first research stop. It is more than likely there will be PRCN *cockatoos* there reporting on unusual ship movements in the open waters of the Luzon Strait."

"We will focus on the southern-most islands of the Babuyan Group," the captain said.

Prof Metcalf commented that there were no large plankton communities there but surface conditions, currents and depths were suitable for plankton. "Should we be questioned," he said, "a reasonable excuse for being there would be to find out why plankton is not present in the density that conditions seem to provide. A statement of this goal will be documented and posted in the laboratory. It should be enough for a non-specialist enquirer.

"There seem to be channels that are deep enough for submarines. What do you think, Captain?" Prof Metcalf asked.

"We have to look at particular areas you like, Professor, but there are channels that submarines could use, even large submarines," the captain replied.

Together, they identified three locations in the Babuyan Group.

One was south of the largest southern-most island of Camiguin. This offered a relatively wide stretch but sensors could cover most of the area a submarine could use if it was urgently exiting the South China Sea by this unlikely route.

Another was near Fuga, also south, off the tiny island of Barit. The third location was between Fuga and Dalupiri, near the very small island of Mabag.

These two locations would be more difficult for a submarine to navigate but would seem highly attractive options as emergency exit points, if necessary.

Poco-A-Poco circumnavigated Camiguin and Fuga. It criss-crossed the area between Fuga and Dalupiri over 9 days laying 12 sensors and finding no PRCN sensors.

The first leg was uninterrupted and successful.

During preparations for the run-down of the Palawan coast, a Palawan municipal launch, which had strayed north, engaged the Poco-A-Poco.

It was a dilapidated 30-metre craft, a little like a converted fishing boat, but it carried municipal and national colours. The skipper said he wanted to 'have a look around' and seemed friendly enough. He was welcomed aboard by the captain and was completely satisfied with what he saw, so much so that the interception seemed an opportunity for the skipper to have a chat about sea conditions. He was even happier when the captain opened a bottle of single malt whisky.

The Poco-A-Poco proceeded down the Philippine coast, through the Bohol Sea and into the Sulu Sea.

On its way heading to the Balabac Strait, which led to the South China Sea and near many disputed islands and the PRC's militarised artificial islands, it passed too close to what looked like a guarded refugee camp.

Poco-A-Poco was flagged down and an official Filipino boarding party was dispatched from the camp. It became clear that the camp was manned by armed soldiers. The captain whispered to Prof Metcalf: "A single malt whisky is not going to do the trick."

An officer boarded the research vessel with three armed soldiers. After a short-hand courtesy, the officer demanded: "I want your delivery. Where is it?"

Before the captain could say anything, the officer exclaimed: "If you don't hand over the stash, you will end up over there." Pointing to the camp, he said: "Make it easy on everyone. Hand it over, otherwise we will have to find it and that means some heavy punishment when you get over there."

The captain was lost for words. He knew the officer was talking about drugs. Terry positioned himself in case there was a hand-to-hand confrontation—the captain and he against the official and three armed soldiers.

Instead of saying anything, the captain shrugged his shoulders.

The officer said: "If that's the way you want it, we will find it." The soldiers then proceeded to look through the boat. No drugs were found.

"If you are not delivering anything," the officer said, "you are picking up someone. If you reveal who you are helping escape and who in the camp staff is complicit, we may even let you go."

Again, the captain said they were not there to pick up anyone or deliver anything. They were merely curious. "We came too close, obviously."

After a time, Prof Metcalf explained the research purpose of the trip citing the World Heritage reputation of Balabac Strait and its importance as a Maritime Biodiversity Conservation Area that was world renowned for its water characteristics and its extraordinary range of crustaceans, some newly discovered.

The disinterested officer turned to the captain and said the camp was for serious drug offenders with international connections. "We deal with them here and anyone who takes an unwelcome interest in the camp. Be on your way. Don't come back," he demanded.

He and his boarding party left without another word.

Relieved at the outcome, Poco-A-Poco headed further offshore directly towards the Balabac Strait at the southern point of Palawan where they hurriedly laid 12 sensors, 6 on each side of a small island off Bangg, in one and a half days. Despite the haste, the coverage seemed satisfactory because of the narrowness of the channels. No PRCN sensors were detected. There was no time for plankton research even though the area was known to be plankton rich.

Having spent 11 days and laying 24 sensors, they steamed out of the Sulu Sea into the Celebes Sea and the Makassar Strait. They wasted no time. On the way, they did not consider plankton research and the southern end of the strait was not suitable for sensors.

Near the closest point in the strait between Kalimantan and Sulawesi, the captain picked up a blimp on the radar. It remained constant for a time indicating Poco-A-Poco was being tracked.

The source of the tracking caught up to within horizon sight but the type of craft remained indefinite. The captain assessed it was a medium sized pirate ship probably waiting for an opportunity to attack. He knew the best time for an attack was at night, particularly when the moon was obscured.

He said: "They are probably well armed and may have a crew larger than us."

Prof Metcalf said: "In the circumstances, we would do well to make it appear we are well armed and supported by others. If we can do this, we may make it appear we would not avoid a conflict, or may even invite a conflict. Again, if successful, they may think attacking us could be a trap. We may need to call their bluff because there would be no contest if they decide to attack. What do you think?"

All agreed. Changing Poco-A-Poco's profile got underway while each vessel could not distinguish the other.

Two false antennas were raised, each much larger than the type a vessel like Poco-A-Poco would carry. They were combined with one of the plankton nets raised to appear to indicate wind speed and direction. The impression intended was that the research vessel had support, possible air support.

It was unlikely the pirate ship possessed sophisticated communications equipment. In case it did, however, an unprotected message addressed to the 'port police' in the capital of Kalimantan, Bajarmasin, was sent suggesting the likely capture of pirates within the next two days. The address was real but not that of the 'port police' or any authority. It was selected at random from a directory and carried a no-response block. What the recipient did or did not do with it did not matter.

A third precaution was to release fake floating mines. This depended on the tide at night. As the tide was outgoing on the first night, the captain moved closer to the Kalimantan shoreline, anchored early and threw overboard six empty fuel drums tethered to the boat. Each carried a small inoperative antenna. The six floated in a semicircle on the seaward side and were allowed to float about 120 metres from Poco-A-Poco.

They looked every bit remotely operated floating mines inviting an intruder to get within explosion range.

If the pirates were not scared off on this first night, the alternative plan was to stand off the shoreline more the following night late and reverse the procedure. This would have been necessary because of the change of tide but would have left the open water side vulnerable.

In the morning, there was no sign of the pirate boat, either visually or on radar. The tactic had worked.

The captain explained: "This method has worked for small salvage vessels against raiding canoes in close coastal waters in Malaysia and even near Singapore. Perhaps our would-be pirates were more open-water criminals."

All acknowledged that as soon as they entered the Java Sea, the PRCN and the Indonesian authorities would be aware of them. The PRCN would expect them to turn towards Sumatra and might take less notice of them if they turned the other way towards Flores.

Prof Metcalf said: "This third part of our journey is significant because there are several options for PRCN submarines to enter the Timor Sea and Australian waters. 6 sensors, the last of them, will be laid in two areas around Raba and Rutung."

As they headed towards Flores, named after the Portuguese word for flowers and renowned for its scenic beauty, Theodora mentioned: "I look forward to a long, warm bath ashore. And some of my companions could do with a good scrub-down as well—apologies to you, Professor."

After laying the 4 sensors on the east and west side of the narrow channel between Flores and Sumbawa, they proceeded to Ende, the capital of Flores, where Suharto, later to become the Indonesian president, was exiled by the Portuguese in the 1930s.

No PRCN sensors were seen on either side of the channel.

Ende was only 2 kilometres from the main port, Palubuhan Ipi, where Poco-A-Poco was moored, and some 110 kilometres from the channel.

The captain booked 2 bungalows for 2 nights at an Ende hotel complex called Wisma Flores, a sprawling hill-side establishment of 30 well-appointed bungalows. Each was equipped with a piece of bamboo suspended from a veranda. Occupants would ask for service by beating the bamboo. Theodora wondered how a servant could recognise one out of 30 slightly different bamboo sounds.

The captain volunteered to spend the first night on the boat with the navigator/engineer and swap with two others for the second night.

The environment was surprisingly serene even though the community comprised serious Muslim and Christian practitioners. There was no current or past ideological conflict evident, although on the nearby island of Sumba, a history of animist practice could be seen in areas featuring ancient tombstones and roughly hewn, and clearly well used, stone monuments to past human sacrifices.

The 2-day stop-over was welcomed by all. With the crew refreshed, the refuelled boat left for Rutung on the other side of Flores. The remaining two sensors were laid there.

On the way through the channel again, they concentrated on their research using all three techniques—the net, bottles and pump. A large amount of plankton and some seaweed samples were taken, documented and stored.

The next part of the journey was through the Flores Sea and into the Java Sea to the Sunda Strait between Sumatra and Java bypassing the Bali Strait. In the Sunda Strait, the research changed to inspecting and identifying minute life-forms in the warm waters around the hydrothermal vents.

The boat surely was tracked by the PRCN and Indonesian authorities but there was no incriminating material onboard and the research work was evident for anyone interested to see, including the use of the AUV which was used throughout the trip ostensibly to identify and record the density of research samples but really to search for PRCN sensors.

This took 2 days before Poco-A-Poco headed directly for Singapore, a trip that was uneventful, to the relief of all.

The project had been completed without causing an international incident or getting into trouble. It took 26 days. 30 US sensors were laid in three locations and no PRCN sensors were found in any of them.

The boat was moored in a safe marina and work commenced on its restoration. The Nanyang Technical University scientist began tidying up the research. Some of the findings were attributed to the university.

At the Australian High Commission, the team got together to review the kid-gloves project and have a rest which was short lived when Col Weingraf said: "I'm very sorry, guys. We have a problem in the central Pacific. A PRC military base may be in the making."

ENDS

Epilogue

Apollo's forecasts of the future and his priestess, Cassandra's, equally true predictions cursed by Apollo to ensure no one believed her, were as confounding as the calm and storms the three sisters encountered in recent times and as uncertain as any future tasks.

Selected Abbreviations

ACT Australian Capital Territory
ADF Australian Defence Force
AFP Australian Federal Police
AIEGANZ The team
ANSA Australian National Security Agency
ANU Australian National University
APAF Asia-Pacific Aqua Fit Pty Ltd
ASD Australian Signals Directorate
ASEAN Association of South-East Asian Nations
ASIS Australian Secret Intelligence Service
AUV Autonomous Underwater Vehicle
BAKOSURTANAL National Coordinating Agency for Surveys and Mapping—
Indonesia
BIRC Banking Insurance Regulatory Commission—China
BOKATOR A Cambodian martial art
CBIRC Chinese Banking Insurance Regulatory Commission
CCTV Closed Circuit Television
CCP Chinese Communist Party
CSIRO Commonwealth Scientific & Industrial Research Organisation
CSIS Centre for Strategies and International Studies
CSIT Centre for Strategic Intercom Technologies—Singapore
CSOC Cyber Security Operations Centre
C4 A military grade 'plastic' explosive
DA'ISH Al-Dawlah Al-Islamiyah fe Al-Iraq wa Al-Sham (Islamic State of Iraq
and Syria or Sham)
DFAT Department of Foreign Affairs and Trade—Australia
DIUELIZ The enemy (code, impersonal)
DIO Department of International Cooperation and Exchanges—China

FSM Federated States of Micronesia
GLCM Ground-Launch Cruise Missile
GSU Greater Southern University
HF Heritage Foundation—US
HSBPS Homeland Security and Border Protection Service
IACI International Association of Conference Interpreters
IAPTI International Association of Professional Translators and Interpreters
IASDC International Aid, Supply and Defence Conference—Singapore
ICCC International Conduct and Control Centre
IED Improvised Explosive Device
IHRS International Hotel and Restaurant Association
ILO International Liaison Office—China
INTERPOL International Police
IRA Irish Republican Army
IRBM Intermediate-Range Ballistic Missile
IS or ISIS So-called Islamic State (see Da'ish)
JID Joint Intelligence Directorate—Singapore
LINGUA IGNOTA A secret language
LOSC UN Convention of the Law of the Sea
MINDEF Ministry of Defence—Singapore
MIS Ministry of Science and Technology—China
MRBM Medium-Range Ballistic Missile
MSD Military Defence Department—Singapore
NSW New South Wales
NAVSEA Naval Sea Systems Command—US
NT Northern Territory
OSA Official Secrets Act
OSD Office of the Secretary of Defence—US
PAU Professional Advancement Unit—China
PBOC People's Bank of China
PIF Pacific Islands Forum
PLA People's Liberation Army—China
PLC Program Logic Controller
PNG Papua New Guinea
PRC Peoples Republic of China
PRCN Peoples Republic of China Navy

RAN Royal Australian Navy

RUV Remote Underwater Vehicle

SA South Australia

SAS HQ Special Air Services Regiment HQ—Australia

SEA-ME-WE South East Asia/Middle East/Western Europe, fibre optic marine cable system

SHARIA LAW Islamic Law

SOS Sound Surveillance System—China

SRBM Short-Range Ballistic Missile

SSS Singapore Secret Service

STUXNET A Programming Language

TNT Trinitrotoluene (a common explosive)

UN United Nations

UNESCAP UN Economic and Social Commission for Asia and the Pacific

UNESCO UN Educational, Scientific and Cultural Organisation

UNODGI UN Office of the Director-General of Interpretation

USSC United States Studies Centre—Australia

UYGHUR Ethnic community—N/W China

UYGHUR Language of the above community

The Author's Previous Book:
Ends by Any Means

Comments:

The author wishes to express his thanks to four friends who made comments on his first book, *Ends by Any Means*. The comments follow:

"The world is a nasty place and don't we know it after reading Ian Ingleby's book *Ends by Any Means*. The author knows his stuff and you won't be able to put it down." —Neil Marks, cricketer, raconteur, and author of six published books about sports and Australia.

"The author's extensive experience working in South-east Asia makes this book (his first one, *Ends by Any Means*) an interesting and entertaining thriller that takes you on an exciting journey into the world of political intrigue, murder and corruption...to sum up a good read."—(now the late) Antony Kidman, PhD, clinical psychologist, author.

"The author has used his full armoury of Asian regional experience to develop an engaging and thrilling story of international intrigue. An enjoyable read." —David Connolly AM, former Australian High Commissioner and diplomat in Asia, the Middle East and Africa and former Member of Parliament.

"The author's extensive experience in South-east Asia and the Pacific has enabled him to prepare the backbone and marrow of an intriguing painstakingly researched fictional thriller with a macabre finale worthy of the darkest film noir." —Air Vice Marshall Bruce Short AM, RFD (Retd).

Background

Ends By Any Means was the author's first book. It was published in Melbourne in 2013 but not distributed deliberately. The current manuscript is his second.

Unlikely Destinies is a work of fiction dedicated to my wife, Helen, and my three daughters, Kristin, Donna and Lynn, all of whom have travelled internationally with me over the years. Particular assistance by Lynn in formulating the manuscript is appreciated.

Assistance in gathering material on some security matters by Kara, one of my granddaughters, lawyer and cyber security expert, is acknowledged with thanks.

Credits

Some statistics of USA and PRC military inventories mentioned in this book (Chapter 8 and elsewhere) are sourced from a researched report by the United States Studies Centre at the University of Sydney, Australia, entitled 'Averting Crisis: American Strategy, Military Spending and Collective Defence in the Indo-Pacific' by Ashley Townshend and Brendan Thomas-No one with Matilda Steward, August 2019.

Some other references are credited in the text or are from publicly available sources. None is classified.